Gallico, Paul
The hand of Mary Constable.

DATE DUE			
June 18	Jan 30	MAY 8 1973	SEP 2 5 1975
June 22	Feb 19	AUG 1 1 1970	FEB 2 3 1976
July 2	MAR 2 5 1965	JUN 1 1	MAR 2 5 1978
Aug 5	APR 2 3 1965	JAN 1 8 7	JUL 03 '78
Aug. 1	MAY 2 1 1965	JUN 1 1	AUG 30 78
Aug.	JUL 1 4	MAY 1 7	JUL 1 9 78
Sept 8	APR 1 4 19	SEP 4 1974	AUG 1 6 79
Sept. 30	APR 3 0 1966	SEP 2 5 19	AUG 2 8 1980
Oct. 8	SEP 2 7 19	SEP 2 5 19	SEP 9 1980
Oct. 21	MAR 1 3 1967	JUL 1 4 1975	9 198
Nov 23	DEC 2 6 1967	AUG 6 1975	DEC 2 7 1983
GAYLORD M-2	SEP 9 1968		PRINTED IN U.S.A.

MYNDERSE PUBLIC
LIBRARY

Seneca Falls, N.Y.

JUN 1 1 1964

THE HAND OF MARY CONSTABLE

THE HAND OF
MARY CONSTABLE

by Paul Gallico

1964
DOUBLEDAY & COMPANY, INC.
GARDEN CITY, NEW YORK

*All of the characters in this book
are fictitious, and any resemblance
to actual persons, living or dead,
is purely coincidental.*

TO
TONY HAVELOCK ALLAN

CONTENTS

CHAPTER I

R.S.V.P.

The sheet of paper clutched in the hand of a backward-twisting arm was being jiggled in front of the face of Alexander Hero, investigator for the Society of Psychical Research of Great Britain, and roused him from the doze into which he had fallen. The air in the BOAC jet airliner had that stale smell of narrow confines too long occupied by human beings engaged in eating, drinking, and sleeping.

The paper had now acquired an impatient rustle. Hero snatched at it guiltily, and the arm disappeared. It was another of those curt but informative messages from the captain advising passengers of altitude, air and ground speed, whereabouts as of the moment, and estimated time of arrival.

Outside the porthole window it was still too dark to see Newfoundland and St. John below as advertised, but the red-hot glow of the port jets had begun to fade; for although they were racing the sun westward there was but one more time zone through which to pass, and dawn could not be much longer retarded. The time of arrival in New York was eight o'clock in the morning.

Hero stirred, produced a handkerchief and wiped some of the sleeping-in-his-clothes sweat from his neck and face, readjusted his seat from reclining to sitting up. Then, with a careful and tentative tongue-tip he probed the temporary filling in the lower-left rear molar which Mr. Reardon, his London dentist, had been trying so assiduously to save. So far so good. But it was like having an unexploded bomb in his mouth.

"I don't think she'll blow up," Mr. Reardon had said, "but if she does, you've got Dr. Hofstetter's address in New York. He's a good man. I've written to him."

Instinctively Hero reached under the seat between his legs to touch his brief case, inside which was the address of the American dentist, his succour in case of trouble, treating it almost as a kind of talisman. He had had one or two experiences of wrenching agony and a sleepless night from the thing and wanted no more. Then, for the seventh time on this trip, he shifted the brief case to his lap, unsnapped the catch, produced and reread the letter which had led him to leave behind in London an unfinished laboratory experiment, the proofs of his book, *Evidence in the Occult*, a study and compilation of the collapse of human intelligence and reliability when giving evidence concerning supernatural phenomena, and, of course, the treatment for his ailing tooth.

The letter was from Dr. Frank Ferguson, president of the American branch of the Society for Psychical Research, but it was written on the letter head of the Department of Ancient Oriental Manuscripts of the New York Public Library on Fifth Avenue and Forty-second Street, of which Ferguson was the chief curator. Hero also knew that had he wished to do so, Dr. Ferguson might have availed himself of yet a third official address, that of the Department of Oriental Languages at Columbia University where he was consultant and lecturer.

And each time he read it, the letter, with its stilted style, recreated the portrait in his mind of the courtly, old-fashioned, yet wickedly brilliant septuagenarian who had written it. But if the prose was filled with old-fashioned circumlocution there was no mistaking the anxiety and urgency verging upon panic that came through the fine, Spenserian handwritten lines.

The letter read:

My dear Hero,

May I recall myself to you as being an ardent admirer of your work and techniques, as well as having been the recipient of your generous hospitality upon the occasion of my last visit to London, at which time you were so kind as to illuminate our field with a number of impressive demonstrations.

I have been thinking of these during the past weeks and wonder whether we could persuade you to come over and give us the benefit of your knowledge and experience.

There has been an occurrence, or rather let me say a number of occurrences, the implications of which are so far reaching and of a nature so potentially dangerous, that they have engaged our Government at its highest level, and which, unless checked, I suspect would also seriously impinge upon yours. Added to which, I must say, is a personal involvement which is most distressing. I assure you that it would not be possible to over-estimate the seriousness of the situation.

I feel quite ridiculous at being compelled to write to you thus enigmatically, but you must believe me that I _am_ so compelled, and trust your intelligence to accept my word regarding a most unfortunate and astonishing series of manifestations which I am not permitted even to confide to paper.

In short, my dear fellow, we need your help. We need it _badly_.

I would not dream of asking you to put yourself out by coming here had we not ourselves exhausted every means within our scope to find a solution, leaving us no other remedy but to appeal to your particular talents. Unfortunately time is likewise of the essence. We are impaled upon the horns of a nasty dilemma. We cannot wait. We cannot afford to fail.

And so, dear boy, if you can see your way to postpone for a brief period the important work upon which I know you must be engaged and fly over to consult with us, you would be placing us greatly in your debt, one we would find it difficult to repay. Needless to say, your expenses and anything you might care to name in the way of a fee, are guaranteed as a matter of course. A cabled reply would greatly relieve us all.

Yours very sincerely,

_Sd_. FRANK FERGUSON

P.S. It is in your private rather than your official capacity that
we are inviting you. F.F.

The stressing of the words "am" and "badly" in the letter
somehow to Hero, almost more than anything else, struck the
keynote of gravity, for Dr. Ferguson was of an era and culture
that would rather have died than commit such a literary breach
as underlining for emphasis.

Hero remembered him from a visit he had paid to London
several years before as a tall, soft-spoken, cultured old gentleman,
addicted to slightly Edwardian clothes and a gold pince-nez attached to a black ribbon which he rarely donned, since the eye-
sight in the pair of very keen blue eyes seemed to be perfect, but
used chiefly for gesticulation and effect. His speech was almost
English, since he had been Harvard-educated. Behind a certain
amount of cultivated academic vagueness there lurked a most intense and vital interest in everything outside his own fields, from
British politics to football pools, modern art, food, wines, racing,
and the latest sex kitten of the cinema. He was young in mind
and enthusiastic as a sixteen-year-old and as quietly conservative
as any member of Buck's, to which, incidentally, he belonged as a
distinguished foreign member.

He had been elected president of the American Society of
Psychical Research, Hero knew, not because he was or ever had
been an ardent spiritualist but because his cool, impeccable, and
unswervingly honest judgment was needed to settle the civil war
between the believers and the sceptics which had broken out in
their ranks some years back during a momentary resurgence of
spiritualism. Since his incumbency a decade or so ago, he had led
them along the path of experimental exploration of thought
transference and extrasensory perception.

He had paid several visits to Hero's private laboratory at the
rear of his house at 88a, Eaton Mews North, behind Eaton
Square, and had studied with unconcealed fascination apparatus
developed by Hero for the measurement and testing of claims
put forward by mediums. He had also been wholly in agreement

with Hero upon the futility of trying to set traps for ghosts, since by the very nature of what a ghost ought to be these must prove useless. At the same time he had greatly admired the subtlety of some of the different kinds of snares Hero had devised to trap humans who, for one reason or another, mostly venal, had been tempted to play spook.

Hero remembered Ferguson saying to him, "My dear boy, how very fortunate you are over here to be having so much fun. Alas, that kind of thing has almost died out with us. An occasional hysterical maiden or youth in some farm community unable to deal with the onset of puberty takes to poltergeist tricks to attract some attention, or the odd pseudo-clairvoyant who falls into the error of fortunetelling and eventually is carted off by the police, and that seems to be about all. We are rarely called upon to investigate any serious claims."

But now, it seemed from the distressed letter of the distinguished old gentleman, they had. And what is more, something appeared to have fallen into their laps with which they were not able to cope.

The BOAC air hostess, threading her way down the aisle of the aircraft to her galley with the last of the finished breakfast trays, paused involuntarily for an instant to look down upon the passenger musing over a handwritten letter, for she wondered who he was. She thought he was smashing. She knew he was tall, for he had had to bend low so as not to strike his head when easing himself into his seat. What she found herself susceptible to was his mouth, which appeared to be sensual yet humorous above an extraordinarily firm and stubborn chin, which proclaimed him a man. She would have liked to have put her fingers through the cockscomb of light brown hair gathered over his brow.

Her partner, carrying another tray, nudged her in the back and said, "Go on, Elsa!" The hostess sighed and passed on. Why was it always the fat, disgusting ones who made the passes?

Unaware of the fluttering he had set up, wholly engrossed by the mysteries both in and between the lines of the missive, Hero's trained, analytical mind, which was a filing cabinet of extraordinary information and skills as well, was once more reviewing what might possibly lie behind this anguished summons.

Alexander Hero (the name was a contraction from the old French Huguenot, Heureux) had a unique profession. In addition to his work as chief investigator for the British Society of Psychical Research, he had established a practice as an independent private detective of the occult, or ghost-breaker, an occupation which called for a thorough grounding in normal and abnormal psychology, physics, chemistry, biology, photography, magic, sleight-of-hand, as well as laboratory procedure. A seeker after the truth in the obscure and often dangerous regions of the paranormal, he was required to keep an open mind, to be an accurate judge of human nature, free from superstition, unswayed by bigotry of any kind, including the scientific. He was as eager for genuine proof of a life in the hereafter as he was active in destroying the charlatans of spiritualism who preyed upon the misfortunes of the bereaved and ignorant.

Reflecting upon the letter from Dr. Ferguson, he was wondering which part of his training was to be called upon and whether he would prove adequate.

Hero put the pages down and let his mind lead him where it would. He thought that if the letter had been composed specifically to tease and exploit his curiosity it could not have been better written; yet its very lack of sophistication, so unlike the man he remembered, indicated the general absence of design. Dr. Frank Ferguson was a man close to panic and had permitted it to show.

And what could he have meant by "unfortunate and astonishing series of manifestations" which could not be discussed or mentioned in a private letter? Something in Hero's particular field calculated to astonish a man of Ferguson's attainments and experience must be extraordinary indeed. A breakthrough? Something genuinely paranormal? That long awaited and greatly sought for inexplicable manifestation which indicated the possibility of a contact with the "other side"? But if somehow a genuine breakthrough had been achieved, the Americans would have

already announced it instead of calling upon a British investigator in his private capacity, for help.

Then why unfortunate? And what could be the implications
engaging the American Government, and possibly the British as
well, at its highest level which were likewise personally distressing to an astute and Chesterfieldian old scholar?

And what were the highest levels? How far was up? The
President? The Cabinet? The Prime Minister? Did it involve
scandal, exposure of some kind, or had someone by accident unlocked some terrible secret, with those at the top the first to be
notified?

The world in recent years had grown a good deal more sceptical about life in the hereafter, both in the religious as well as the
occult sense. Yet, underlying every man's complacency was still
to be found that residue of terror that one day proof might establish survival of some heretofore hidden forces more powerful
even than the overweening ego of man. Was this then what was
troubling those at the highest level?

Hero tried a new tack. What was it that one did not wish to
confide to a personal and private letter and in that case as well
certainly not to a transatlantic telephone call, which might have
conveyed even more urgency? There was not much yield from
that source, the answer was simply—anything that one did not
wish anyone else to see or know about. Even a letter marked
"Personal and Private," as this one was, might be opened by a
secretary or some unauthorised person or persons.

Only one thing was certain; the letter said "Help! Come
quickly!"

Although the time had not been opportune for Hero, he had
not hesitated to cable his acquiescence to Dr. Ferguson, particularly after he had shown the letter to his stepsister, Meg, the
Lady Margaret Callandar, who, after reading it, had said instantly, "You've got to go, Sandro. This man is in deep trouble."
He had the curious impression then that she wished she had not
said it but did not know why, since he was still blind to the fact
that she had been in love with him for a long time. She had

clung to him for an instant cautioning him, "Oh, Sandro, Sandro! Do be careful! It said dangerous."

Hero had postponed several lectures, cut short the laboratory experiment designed to expose a particularly nasty specimen of spiritualist hoaxer, and consulted his dentist, who had then done some emergency and temporary work with misgivings and advised him to call upon Dr. Hofstetter almost immediately upon arrival in New York.

The intercom system of the airliner came to life, and the soft voice of one of the hostesses announced, "We are now beginning our descent and will land at Kennedy Airport in New York within twenty minutes. Please fasten your seat-belts, straighten your chairs, and refrain from smoking."

With the sunrise, the big BOAC jet came pouring out of the east to fly down the white, surf-fringed beaches of Long Island and pick up in the morning haze the glorious towers of Manhattan, a million windows reflecting the fire of the orange sun. It was Alexander Hero's first view of that New World which the descendants of one branch of his ancestors had built. And as so many before him, who for the first time looked upon this eighth wonder of the world, he was staggered by a beauty and impressiveness he had never imagined.

It also gave him a feeling not quite of fear or apprehension but rather of awe. Before entering the approach path to Kennedy the pilot flew over the city, lining up with the silver of a river to give his passengers the treat of the great metropolis bathed in morning light. Looking down upon this forest of tall buildings, spires, and towers, Hero thought that it was too grandiose even for the hand of man—and for that matter for ghosts and bogies too. It suddenly appeared to him ridiculous even to consider the spirits of the dead or occult manifestations in connection with the stunning poem in stone beneath the wings of the plane. As he looked down upon the spider-webbing of the bridges spanning the river and massive buildings occupying so much space in the sky, he wondered about the people below and how the giants who could rear such edifices should suddenly turn into fretful human beings, worried, irritated, frightened by some little thing they thought they did not understand. No, it was definitely not a setting in which one would expect a ghost to flourish. The aircraft banked and turned east once more, towards a vast plain of less impressive city blocks beyond which lay the sea and the glide path to the airport. Hero craned around for one more breath-taking, eye-filling glimpse of the magic of Manhattan.

Thereafter it was all anticlimactic. There was no one at the airport to meet him, and the entrance into America could hardly be called commensurate with the majestic view of a few minutes before. The immigration official was a big, jowly man with suspicious eyes, clad in a uniform something like that of a prison turnkey. He examined Hero's passport and Hero himself with disfavour and took his time over it. He asked, "What business you in?" and when Hero replied, "Investigator for the Society of Psychical Research," he said, "Psychical, eh? What are you, one of them headshrinkers? Boy, ain't we got enough of them over here already?" He shook his head over the folly of admitting another but stamped Hero's passport and handed it to him.

The Customs inspection was less grim. Hero had been led to expect that they would go not only through his bags but his clothes as well. Instead, a cheerful young inspector made only a perfunctory pass at his opened suitcase and, coming upon a small, black tube, asked, "What's that?"

"Sniperscope," Hero replied, "your chaps used them in Korea. As a matter of fact, that one was made in America."

"What's it for?"

"To see in the dark."

"Well, I'll be darned!" said the Customs man, and waved him through. "Enjoy your stay here."

Hero now regretted that he had not brought with him more than a few essential pieces of equipment in his bag, but then, Dr. Ferguson's letter had given him no hint of the problem. He would either have had to transport practically his entire laboratory or the minimum which he had packed.

Wheeling his luggage to the taxi rank in a kind of stainless-steel pushcart, he kept listening for his name to be called over the public address system but heard nothing, nor did anyone official or unofficial accost him. And so he took a next-in-line yellow cab, glittering, bejewelled with chrome and coloured lights like a rajah's palanquin.

In reply to the driver's query, "Where to, Mac?" Hero consulted the brief cablegram he had received from Dr. Ferguson, advising him of accommodations reserved.

"The Hotel Tuscany."

"'Ats on East Thirty-ninth. Okey-doke."

The cab pulled away and flowed into the main stream rushing down the wide boulevard, curiously lined, Hero thought, with lampposts of stained timber looking like gallows. Rising up from the horizon beyond the arrow-straight pathway, Hero could see the island of towers that was Manhattan. He had heard something of the chattiness of New York taxi drivers, but this one was a silent specimen except, as they approached the fantastic complex of bridges, cloverleafs, and freeways of the Triborough Bridge, he inquired, "You're a Limey, ain't you?"

"Yes."

"Ever been here before?"

"No."

"Then brace yourself, brother. This is some town."

Hero felt he might have something there.

At the Tuscany, he was welcomed to a fabulous suite, the feature of which appeared to be the most enormous television set he had ever seen, capable of receiving colour pictures and in addition a patent, mechanical, reclining chair, a pantry with a refrigerator and a telephone extension strategically situated in the bathroom. A card informed him that maids, valets, and waiters were equipped with walkie-talkie receivers for instant contact. The bellboy who accompanied him closed the windows, drew the curtains and turned on the lights, and asked whether Hero wished the TV set activated, as though that were what he had flown three thousand miles to see.

By then it was ten o'clock in the morning. Hero said, "No, thank you," and opened the note addressed to him which had been handed to him at the desk.

It was again on Dr. Ferguson's Public Library stationery and was brief and to the point: "We shall be waiting for you here at my office. Come over when you are settled in. F.F."

Hero wanted a bath, but suddenly felt so overwhelmed and surrounded by things American that he took a shower instead and found himself enjoying the violent attack of the water after his cramped and stuffy journey. He shaved, changed his clothes, and had himself transported to the library.

CHAPTER II

Operation Foxglove

Dr. Ferguson's office was an eyry almost under the eaves of the roof of the huge white building at Fifth Avenue and Forty-second Street. The windows looked out upon the Avenue itself and its endless river of traffic, green buses, yellow cabs, and shining cars, whose hum rose muted from below. There was a small board room leading out from Dr. Ferguson's private office, to which a uniformed attendant had guided him. Dr. Ferguson met him in the doorway, exactly as Hero had remembered him—quiet, gentle, urbane, dressed in comfortable country tweeds and holding his pince-nez attached to a black ribbon around his neck. He greeted Hero as though the latter had just arrived for a luncheon or cocktail party.

"My dear fellow, how very good of you to come. Inexcusable not to meet you at the airport. Do accept our apologies." A circular wave of the pince-nez took in Hero as well as the men Hero could discern over his shoulder, sitting at a long table, one in military uniform, the other two civilians. "Let me present you."

As he was ushered into the room the three men arose to greet him. His instant impression was that the getting to their feet was grudging and the atmosphere was one of unease, suspicion, and even hostility. They looked like people who were there not because they wished to be.

Dr. Ferguson said, "May I present General Walter Augstadt, Mr. Saul Wiener, and Mr. John Ferris. General Augstadt is in charge of a special project. Mr. Wiener is the Regional Director of the Federal Bureau of Investigation for the metropolitan area, and Mr. Ferris is an FBI expert specialising in fingerprints." Then, turning to the three, Ferguson continued, "Gentlemen, may I present Mr. Alexander Hero, who has been so very kind as to come all the way from London to assist us."

The man introduced as Wiener said, with very little show of interest, "Did you have a good flight, Mr. Hero?" The general, who had a fist like a ham, tried to crush Hero's fingers when they shook hands, and the third, a young man, merely nodded an acknowledgement.

Dr. Ferguson was still apologetic as he showed Hero to a chair at his left and seated himself at the head of the table. "Both Mr. Wiener and I agreed it might be better if no attention were attracted by your arrival through your being met." He settled himself and examined the covers of a pile of filing folders.

Hero, who was still somewhat fuzzy from the trip and the speed with which he had been plunged into this extraordinary civilisation, pulled himself together and concentrated upon learning what he could from these varied and antagonistic men, with whom he was about to be thrown into contact.

The older of the two civilians, the man introduced as Wiener, Regional Director of the FBI, looked exactly as Hero would have expected an American Indian in the days of the Five Nations to have looked, bar the colour. For he had a crown of glistening black hair that grew almost like a scalp lock, a thin hatchet face, and a great beak of a nose dividing a pair of brilliant, inquisitive dark eyes that were giving Hero a thorough going over. From the name he was probably Jewish, yet Hero felt strongly certain telltale anthropological indications such as the high cheekbones, the placing of the eyes, and the general expression that said "Indian," and he wondered whether he would ever be able to have his guess verified.

The general was a contrast. He was huge and a bustler, with enormous shoulders and a great, square head set upon them with not very much neck between. An American would at once have assigned him to the fullback position of any football team and would have been right, for in his youth the general had bullied and bustled and crashed his way to a record number of touchdowns, first for Minnesota and then for the Military Academy at West Point. The set of his jaw marked him as a doer, the kind of man who, when yardage was needed, would snarl, "Give me the ball and get out of my way!" Subtlety would not be his strong point. However, if direct action was wanted, Hero concluded, one would like to have General Augstadt at one's side.

Quickly, too, Hero had the feeling of the young man introduced as Ferris. His interest would be his speciality, but whatever the situation that faced them he was not emotionally involved, and since he was young and probably ambitious, he would take his cue from his superiors.

It was Saul Wiener, occupying a chair at Dr. Ferguson's right, who impressed Hero the most, and there was a sardonic quality to the lively intelligence marking his expression, an intelligence that was probably not in the habit of presenting very high marks to his fellow humans.

Yet, from the very first, Hero was drawn to him. For whereas he judged that Augstadt was disgruntled and Ferris wary, Wiener too was dissatisfied but at the same time amused, and even though the smile was slightly smug and cynical, it had also a quality of wryness which gave it a certain charm. He felt that the man could also be warm and kind if he wished and wondered whether in him he would find friend or foe. If the latter, he would be formidable. At the moment Wiener was simply giving no evidence. He sat, his hands stuffed into his pockets, his chair tipped slightly backwards, studying not only Hero but also the big, military man opposite, and for an instant, as his dark eyes rested upon the enormous patch of fruit salad spread over the left breast of the general's uniform, the line of the cynical smile appeared to deepen. Hero thought that Wiener's mind was like a prize fighter coming out of his corner at the bell, balanced on the balls of his feet.

Dr. Ferguson had finished arranging and riffling through all his folders. He brushed both sides of his neat white moustache with the back of a forefinger into even greater neatness, put on his pince-nez, took them off again, hunched himself into a more relaxed attitude in his armchair and said, "Well, gentlemen, I suppose then we may proceed to business. Let us begin by asking Mr. Hero whether the name Samuel Hale Constable means anything to him?" He motioned towards Hero with his eyeglasses and added, "Professor Constable, to give him his full title."

Hero reflected a moment to permit the name time to sink down into his subconscious and rummage about there. The answer came up almost immediately, "Cybernetics," he said.

The heads of all those sitting around the table suddenly jerked in his direction as though they had been pulled with string and General Augstadt's square features began to acquire colour.

Dr. Ferguson nodded and then said, "Now let me ask you this: have you ever heard of Operation Foxglove?"

"No."

The general looked both relieved and indignant, glaring about the table challengingly as though daring anyone to have heard of it, but Dr. Ferguson said smoothly, "We hoped you would not." He lifted his pince-nez towards the group, "Have I your permission then?" and collected what Hero could only characterise as a series of grudging half nods, with the exception of Wiener, whose head did not move in the least and whose gaze simply remained unwaveringly watchful.

"You may not remember," Dr. Ferguson began, speaking directly to Hero, "that in addition to being internationally acknowledged as the greatest expert in the field of communication and control of mechanisms of machines and living creatures, Professor Constable is also head of the Department of Cybernetics in the advanced engineering school at Columbia University, where he lectures upon the subject and has established his laboratory as well. To refresh your memory, here is a photograph of Professor Constable," and Ferguson reached into a folder and produced a glossy print of a striking face, which he handed to Hero.

It was a lion's head with a mane of bushy grey hair, bulging brow, and small, intense eyes. The nose was vigorous, but the mouth was rather too small for the noble proportions of the rest. Hero had the curious feeling that it might be petulant and then dismissed the thought. No man ought to judge another by an immobile face imprisoned upon a photographic print. The chin was ample and stubborn. The pose was slightly off profile, towards three quarters, and the whole attitude was aggressive. Hero laid the picture on the table before him.

Dr. Ferguson cleared his throat and continued: "Operation Foxglove is the application and development by the Department of Defense of the government of the United States, of a recent theory evolved by Professor Constable, partially confirmed by preliminary laboratory tests. It has been given a number one Defense Department priority by the President of the United States himself."

Well, Hero thought, one now knew how high was up.

"General Augstadt here," Ferguson was continuing, "is in charge of Operation Foxglove, which, I might add, is top secret and so restricted that its nature will not even be discussed at this meeting. Am I right, General?"

Augstadt replied belligerently, "You bet you are," and once more challenged with his truculent look all those at the table but particularly the newcomer. If Hero had been inclined to wonder how a project of such importance came to be in the hands of a bruiser like the general he no longer did so, for it seemed to him that perhaps this would be just the man. The scientists and back-room boys would get on with their work, but whatever Operation Foxglove was, it would be kept up to scratch by this Teutonic-sounding martinet, and anything which got in its way would be subjected to rough handling.

"Then," Dr. Ferguson continued, "it will be sufficient for our purposes to say that Professor Constable has been working closely with General Augstadt and the Department of Defense upon this project while, however, insisting upon remaining in New York City and continuing his experiments from his own laboratory at Columbia University. "I might add," and here a curiously innocent expression came into his mild blue eyes, "that while the Defense Department as well as the Federal Bureau of Investigation has made Constable's laboratory as nearly impregnable as you might imagine, from the point of view of security, Professor Constable has been and is something of a problem child."

The nods and expressions from those about the table, plus the audible snort from Wiener testified to this as being probably the understatement of the year.

Through Hero's mind went the thought: *this is all just A B C security stuff, what the devil have they got me here for?*

Thereafter Wiener spoke up. He said, "I think it is only fair, before we go any further, to point out that at the time Professor Constable consented to become part of Operation Foxglove his past, his antecedents, his habits, his associations and associates were thoroughly investigated by my department, and nothing whatsoever in any way against him was turned up." And then, in reply to a questioning glance that Hero threw him, he added with a slight withdrawing of thin lips that could have been meant for a smile, "No affiliations at the extremes of either wing."

"Exactly," agreed Dr. Ferguson. "I think I am right then, in saying that his collaboration began more than a year ago and has continued ever since, despite the fact that three months after having begun, Constable suffered a shattering personal blow. His only daughter, then aged ten, was discovered to be suffering from leukaemia and died shortly after." He reached into his portfolio again, produced a second print and handed it over to Hero. "This is a picture of Mary Constable."

With the photograph in his hands, Hero found that he was able to react to it emotionally, while at the same time through the medium of his ears his mind was occupied with what Dr. Ferguson was saying. He felt touched by her at once.

The camera had caught a lovely little girl with hair falling to her shoulders, nose yet unformed and freckled across the bridge. But the studio portrait revealed a sweet clarity at the temples and a gentle tremulousness at the mouth. She resembled her father, but whereas Hero had thought to find some petulance in his expression, there was none in that of the child. The modelling of the lips was extraordinarily tender, with just the subtlest shading of a humorous quirk which would grow into that compassionate tolerance that some women acquired towards men, and Hero knew that it was this that had probably reached him. His stepsister, Meg, of whom he was extraordinarily fond, had it too. And the photograph showed also that the eyes of Mary Constable were brimming with intelligence and the joy of living. It must have been very hard to lose her.

How hard, Dr. Ferguson had been explaining and Hero's ears and mind absorbing.

It appeared that Professor Constable and his wife, Jane, had been childless until a late age, indeed almost too late, for she had been forty and he fifty-seven when their daughter had been conceived and born. As often is so the case with the children of older parents, Mary Constable was a felicitous, charming, highly talented, and intelligent child. Professor Constable's enjoyment of and love for her could hardly be imagined. Indeed, she became the focal point of the next ten years of Constable's life. Her illness and death had left him incalculably desolate and a markedly changed man. He had sufficient strength of character to avoid going completely to pieces; he maintained an interest in his work and the project upon which he was engaged, but for the rest, life had gone out of him. Ferguson then proceeded to a character sketch of Professor Constable and his relationship to Operation Foxglove.

It all hooked up with Ferguson's previous remark that with regard to security the professor had been something of a problem child. It appeared that not only had Constable refused to submit to the sequestration demanded by the government of someone working upon such a secret and vital project, that is to say to accede to himself and his family living in a closely guarded compound such as was inhabited by many of the atom scientists and others, but he had refused even to transfer his activities from New York to Washington. Far from being a one-sided man, or head-in-clouds scientist crank, Constable, at least before the death of his child, had been gregarious and life loving. He enjoyed art, music, the theatre, and the company of friends and simply would brook no interference with his usual way of life.

And even while Hero was wondering how Constable had been able to make this stick, in view of the weight and pressure which alone could be wielded by the group in that room, not to mention the priority rating given to the project by the President, Ferguson was telling him:

"Constable is that genuinely *rara avis,* the indispensable man. He had them all," he said, with that blandness and innocence of expression which could make a vulgarity or bit of slang sound like scripture, "by the short hairs. If they wanted what Constable had to give they had to take him on his terms or not at all. He took the line that his job was to develop his theory to the point where it would work in practice and to this he was giving his time and efforts. Hence, security was neither his problem nor his concern. The government had no choice but to accept."

Having concluded, Dr. Ferguson leaned back in his chair and asked, "Is that about the straight of it, gentlemen?"

Wiener grunted, "Hell yes! And doubled in spades!"

General Augstadt shifted his chair noisily and said, "If I had my way with the son-of-a-bitch . . ." but then held himself in check.

Ferguson looked over at the general and favoured him with his sweet and engaging smile. Hero gathered that some kind of small contretemps had taken place, the nature of which he could not guess.

But what were they all driving at? What were they coming to? How and in what manner had this potentially dangerous situation suddenly blown up and above all why had he been called in? The truth, when revealed quietly and succinctly by Dr. Ferguson, proved that in this day and age it was the fantastic that became the commonplace and the impossible the probable.

"This," continued Dr. Ferguson, "placed rather a burden upon these gentlemen here, to put it mildly. Constable refused to co-operate and even warned them against any visible interference in his affairs, threatening to resign from the project if he felt himself to be under surveillance. This naturally has not prevented the responsible authorities, that is to say Army Intelligence and the FBI, which, in our country, is charged with the duties of counterespionage in the United States, from maintaining their own checks upon his movements. It has thus come to their attention and they have brought it to mine in my capacity as president of the Society for Psychical Research, that for the past four months Professor Constable has been attending spiritualist seances in a certain house on the upper West Side, where he has become convinced that he has made contact with his dead child."

This sentence, having been spoken, seemed almost to take shape and squirm like a living thing on the table before them. And having dropped it there Dr. Ferguson straightened in his chair, cleared his throat once more, put on his eyeglasses, took them off, opened his portfolio, shuffled some papers, and closed it again.

Hero now knew why he had been summoned, though not yet of the urgency or the danger.

CHAPTER III

Brainwash from Beyond?

"Voice or physical?" Hero asked. All heads swivelled in his direction, as though they had only just at that moment become aware of his presence. The smallest edge of a half bitter smile curled the corners of Wiener's mouth and seemed to say as plainly as though he had spoken aloud, *Just what I expected; well, here we go.*

This time Dr. Ferguson kept on his pince-nez and regarded Hero over the top of them with just the slightest expression of anxiety as he replied, "Both. Professor Constable has heard a voice purporting to be that of his daughter and seen and been in physical contact with a figure which he believes to be a materialisation of her."

General Augstadt said, "Gee-*zuss* Christ!" Young Ferris laughed and drew a reproving look from Wiener.

Hero asked, "Who is the medium?"

Ferguson consulted one of his dossiers, "I have here two reports. One made by the FBI," and he nodded towards Wiener, "the other by me. The facts tally in essentials so I will summarise. The medium is a Mrs. Sarah Bessmer, who operates in conjunction with her husband, Arnold Bessmer. The woman is a trance, voice, and materialisation medium who works psychometry, clairvoyance, clairaudience, slate-writing, table-tipping, and the production of ectoplasm." Here Dr. Ferguson again peered over the tops of his glasses for a moment and added mildly, "She has also seen the inside of several gaols for brief periods. They came originally from Los Angeles, where they conducted a spiritualist church and where, of course, they would be tolerated. They moved away from there some fifteen years ago and established themselves in St. Louis, where they operated successfully for six years or so and managed to keep out of trouble. Some eight months ago they came to New York and leased a brownstone house off Central Park West in the Nineties. Through recommendations from clients in St. Louis and Los Angeles, they had no difficulty in finding an opening here. They worked entirely privately; sitters were accepted only after personal introduction and reference by someone known to them, plus an interview with the prospective new client."

Hero murmured, "Always useful, that."

"I beg your pardon?" said Ferguson.

"Sorry," said Hero. "Please go on."

"Their seances are limited to three evenings a week and twelve to fourteen sitters."

Ferguson looked up from the report and said, "I might add that the Bessmers are highly regarded in spiritualist circles here. There is considerable competition to be accepted into their seances. They number amongst their sitters several members of the Society for Psychical Research who have enthusiastically endorsed the reliability of the phenomena which Mrs. Bessmer has produced.

General Augstadt uttered one scathing word: "Clowns!"

"Some four months ago," Dr. Ferguson continued, "Professor Constable received notice from the Bessmers that they had a message for him from someone on the 'other side.'"

"How was this communicated to Professor Constable?" Hero enquired.

Dr. Ferguson coughed and looked momentarily embarrassed, "Through one of our members," he replied. "A Mr. Charles Woodmanston. He is a long-time spiritualist and one of the most enthusiastic supporters of the Bessmers."

Almost without realising it Hero found himself gazing at Wiener, who answered his unspoken question with, "My pigeon.

An idiot who still wears spats and Arrow collars. A supposedly harmless old fool."

"A not unfair description," commented Dr. Ferguson, "to which, perhaps, I ought to add, that he also favours a pearl stickpin in his tie, checkered waistcoats, and is a bachelor. He is, I believe, a man of about my own age. He wrote to Professor Constable asking for an interview, claiming that he had a message of great importance for him and went to see him."

"What did Constable do?" Hero asked.

"He was polite and eased him out. The second time, however—and Woodmanston was able to see Constable again—he told him that the message concerned his daughter Mary, and it contained some nursery reference which, Professor Constable believed, was known only to his family. His curiosity aroused as well as torment over the loss of his child increased, Constable agreed to go to a seance. Mrs. Constable refused to do so and has steadfastly maintained this refusal. Professor Constable, however, went in company with Mr. Woodmanston and received a message. Still half sceptical, he went again and then again because Mrs. Bessmer, supposedly through her controls, was apparently able to produce the dead child's voice speaking to him directly. Constable was now wavering and it was shortly after this at a seance, which was also attended by Mr. Woodmanston, that he received final, convincing, and positive proof of his daughter's return."

Hero asked, "What was that?"

Dr. Ferguson looked up from his papers and sighed. "The hand of Mary Constable," he said.

"What!" cried Hero, and he sat up in his chair as though the seat had been electrified. "Not the living hand . . ."

"No, but I'm afraid as far as Professor Constable is concerned, the next best thing. His daughter's hand cast in wax and perfect in every detail. During the seance the person of the dead child was ostensibly materialised. A bowl of liquid wax had been prepared and another of cold water. The materialised spirit said, 'I am here, Daddy, I am with you again. Believe in me, Daddy. I have come back because I love you. To help you to trust me I will leave you my hand.' The materialised spirit then thrust her hand into the bowl of wax and thereafter into the cold water. Professor Constable afterwards felt his forehead brushed by a kiss and everyone heard the words whispered in a child's voice, 'Good-bye, Daddy. I'll come to you again. Trust me.' When the lights went up there, resting upon the table between two bowls, still wet from the cold water, was the transparent hand and wrist of a child, the fingers curled in an attitude of supplication as though reaching out to her father. Professor Constable broke down and wept."

"Was there any light during this manifestation?" Hero asked sharply, "Or was it conducted in total darkness?"

"Total darkness."

"From whose notes are you quoting?"

"Mr. Woodmanston's."

"Is he accurate?"

"In the sense that he writes down everything he sees and hears, yes."

"—Or thinks he sees and hears," Hero said. His mind was playing like the flickering of heat lightning around the production of the wax cast. Sixty years ago, at the turn of the century, no less a personage than Sir Arthur Conan Doyle had believed in it. The essential problem it posed was, that if a human hand were dipped into wax and allowed to harden it would be impossible to withdraw the hand from the cast without breaking it. But a spirit hand, that could dematerialise . . . ?

Hero knew how Sir Arthur Conan Doyle had been hoaxed with a crude substitution of an already prepared cast, but then, so would Frank Ferguson. It was not for this he had been summoned. The whole story had not yet been told, and, indeed, the watchfulness of all the others and their air of expectancy confirmed to him that this was so. Hero asked, "Have you a photograph of the hand?" and felt there was something chilling about the gravity and the heaviness with which Dr. Ferguson withdrew four glossy prints from his portfolio and handed them to him.

They showed a delicate wax cast of the hand of a child taken from four different angles, the narrow tube of the end of the wrist, the back of the hand, the palm and the fingers half curled, the little finger almost bent in what was indeed, as Mr. Woodmanston had described, an attitude of supplication; a loving hand from the other side reaching out to one who had remained behind. From the shape and position of the cast it would be absolutely impossible for any living flesh or bone to have been withdrawn from it without shattering it.

But there was something else about the photographs which bid for Hero's attention and which, as he began to examine them more carefully, sent a curious thrill of dread and apprehension down his spine; he felt his mouth suddenly dry and his throat constricted. He took up the picture which showed the hand palm upwards, fingers towards the camera and scrutinised it closely and as he did so was aware that Dr. Ferguson had reached into his breast pocket for an object and was pushing it over towards him silently. It was a small magnifying glass.

Hero took it automatically and focused it between his eye and the photograph. Faint, but unmistakable, there were fine lines, loops, and whorls at the tips of the thumb and fingers.

Hero cried harshly, "Those are fingerprints?" and he could feel the thumping of his own heart. Dr. Ferguson sighed and looked almost guilty as he replied, "Yes, I am afraid they are."

"Whose?"

"The kid's, all right." This statement was even more startling because it came or rather almost exploded from the young man known as Ferris. It was the first time since the introduction that he had spoken.

"Are you sure?" The cry wrung from Hero was almost one of anguish.

Augstadt bawled: "They can't be! It's impossible!"

Dr. Ferguson gestured towards Ferris with the glasses on the end of the black ribbon and said, "Mr. Ferris is a fingerprint expert."

"They match up," Ferris was saying. "There's no doubt about it; not any. We have checked and double checked and had confirmation as well from the bureau in Washington. We can show you photographic enlargements of the prints, and you can compare them with those of the Constable girl yourself."

Hero again examined the photograph with the hand lens, "Are they on the inside or the outside?" he asked. "It's not entirely clear from the picture."

"On the inside. It doesn't show too well there, but the wax is transparent."

A thought flashed through Hero's mind which made him recoil with horror and brought a sickish expression to his lips for a moment, which reflected in his eyes as he glanced at Dr. Ferguson.

The old man met his gaze levelly, but the expression in his young-looking blue eyes was enigmatic. He said, "I know what you are thinking of, my dear fellow, but I am afraid it won't wash even if it could have been done that way. Mary Constable's body was cremated two days after her death."

Hero threw a question at Ferris, "Where did you get the fingerprints of the little girl to compare with these inside the cast?" But it was Wiener who answered.

"They're on file. Whenever anyone accepts a government job with security involved we take the fingerprints of the entire family as a precautionary measure," and as he saw still an expression of query on Hero's face he added, "Well, say that one of them were to disappear . . ."

Dr. Ferguson said to Hero, "Do you wonder that Professor Constable is convinced of the life after death survival of his child?"

Hero replied, "No, I do not."

General Augstadt burst forth angrily, "Do you mean to say you believe that a high-dome like Constable would go for that kind of crap? A scientist?"

Hero turned to Augstadt, "Have you ever attended a seance?"

Augstadt glared at him and said contemptuously, "I wouldn't be caught dead in one!"

Wiener's yell of glee bounced off the ceiling and startled them all into a break in the tension and soon they were all shouting with laughter with the exception of the general, who looked about him indignantly until the penny dropped suddenly and brought a kind of sickly smile to his face. "Well, you know what I mean," he finished lamely.

When the laughter finally subsided, the tension had been considerably relaxed. Dr. Ferguson leaned over, picked up the photographs, and stacked them with his fingers. "You are probably wondering how we acquired these," he said. "Our friend, Mr. Woodmanston, persuaded Professor Constable to permit this hand, which incidentally, is kept under glass I believe, in his home, to be photographed for the archives of the Society, as well as the fingerprints verified." He then said to Hero, "Could you reproduce this phenomenon under the same circumstances as the Bessmers have?"

Hero replied, "No, I could not, at the moment."

"Neither can we," said Dr. Ferguson. "I was hoping you might have encountered something of the sort abroad. Do you think you might be able to devise a way?"

Hero reflected carefully and said, "Perhaps. I should want to attend one or several seances at the Bessmers and study the situation. If given time . . ."

"Exactly," Ferguson agreed, "but unfortunately there is no time, or, shall I say, very little. And this brings me to the final stage and the most unhappy one of the dilemma in which we find ourselves in connection with Professor Constable." He produced a number of typewritten sheets which he opened and began to thumb through, peering at them once over the tops of his glasses.

There was now a rustle and a quickening of interest on the part of those gathered there and Hero inferred that all that had been said and taken place before had not touched any of them deeply, but that which was now about to be discussed concerned them all very greatly.

"If I may state the situation up to this point in its simplest terms," Dr. Ferguson said, "perhaps oversimplified—the manifestations observed and credited by Professor Constable and others attending the seances are either genuine or false."

The general delivered himself of a strangled snort and Wiener seemed about to speak when Ferguson stopped him with a gesture, "Wait," he said. "We are not taking sides but merely stating a simple syllogism. And, I might add, that if these phenomena were to be proved genuine nothing very much would matter any more; not nations, not individuals. The whole world would be changed overnight. On the other hand, if the second premise is true, then all of the difficulties and dangers which have brought us together here this morning come into play and we must decide how to cope with them immediately . . ."

Dr. Ferguson withdrew several of the sheets from the portfolio and continued, "Once more, to save all of you time, I will try to state the case for Mr. Hero." Indicating the papers, he said, "We again have our good and, as Mr. Wiener has remarked, idiot friend Mr. Woodmanston to thank for this. He is an ardent and convinced spiritualist, who has kept, and keeps, an accurate diary of everything that transpires at the seances he attends, which he writes down later and sends to me urging publication in our monthly bulletin. Thus, I have here a record of everything said as well as done at the seances attended by Professor Constable, including a series of messages purported to have been spoken by Mary Constable, at first a disembodied spirit and later, after the manifestations of the hand, by a supposed materialisation of the dead child. There are some thirty-nine of these messages here, which I will not attempt to read out individually, since you gentlemen are familiar with them. I will turn them over to Mr. Hero for study. But I will simply suggest to him that anyone of intelligence reading these messages consecutively from the first through to the last, will be forced to suspect that a powerful intellect has been and is in the throes of taking over the mind of Professor Constable preparing him either to sell out the secret of Operation Foxglove, or even, we are gravely apprehensive, to defecting with it."

Hero felt the sweat break out from under his armpits and the drops rolling coldly down his flank.

"The messages," continued Dr. Ferguson, "proceed with such subtlety, leading him on step by step, that one would feel almost more comfortable crediting the supernatural with their authorship than the natural, or even the child Mary Constable herself. One thing is certain, from wherever they have emanated they are far beyond the scope of the Bessmers."

"Lord!" breathed Hero, "Occult brainwashing."

"Something like that," Ferguson commented, "but far more effective than any psychological hocus-pocus." He continued, "You heard the first message at the time the hand was first produced, begging her father to trust and love her and offering him proof of existence. This line was continued for a time, along with physical manifestations in which Professor Constable was actually caressed by a small creature seen in the dimmest of red lights, though he was not allowed to touch her according to the rules laid down by the spirit itself. She discussed life in the hereafter with him, and later Professor Constable came regularly to these evening seances for a rendezvous with his lost daughter. I might add that he is charged a stiffish fee for attendance at these sessions, since 'physical manifestations' are supposed to take so much more of Mrs. Bessmer's powers."

He paused, and Hero murmured, "Not to mention the ploy that you are more inclined to believe what you have had to pay for."

Wiener looked up sharply. Dr. Ferguson nodded, "Exactly," and went on. "After about a month the tenor of the messages begins to change. Mary is no longer happy on the other side as she once was, nor are the others, her little playmates, the dead children who have 'crossed over.' It is the state of the world and its tensions, of nations pitted against nations that has troubled them and is keeping them from enjoying the delights on the other plane. Here, for instance, is one direct plea aimed at the heart of a father: 'You want me to be happy, Daddy, don't you? What you are doing is making me sad. You always said you would do anything to make me happy. Good-bye, Daddy. I will try to come and see you again soon, if they will let me.'"

"Bloody," said Hero, half under his breath.

"The next time she returns the tune changes. 'They' on the other side did not wish her to come to her father because there was something that he was doing which would make things worse in the world and would give more pain and suffering, not only for those on the earth but for those who had transcended. From then on a campaign develops and is intensified. It never directly mentions Constable's activities but by constantly sowing doubts in his mind seeks to turn his manner of thinking through the love for his child. Restored to him apparently by a miracle she now threatens to withdraw from him once more, or be withdrawn by 'them,' to be lost forever in the limbo beyond the farthest galaxies." At this point Dr. Ferguson peered over his glasses again and said, "You know, to a man who has contributed to communication with satellites whirling millions of miles away through space, the picture of his daughter exiled to this awful void might be very real indeed."

Hero suddenly turned to General Augstadt and said, "Have you noticed any difference in Professor Constable lately in connection with his attitude towards his work?"

"You're goddam right we have," the general said. "What the hell do you think we're here for, sweating it out listening to all this baloney? What I want to know is, why we don't just bust into that house, clean the lot of them out, and bring Constable to his senses before he sends us all down the drain?"

As though continuing an interrupted debate, Wiener restored his chair to level and said to Ferguson, "I am afraid I am with the general there, Frank. Or at least let me put a couple of operators into that house and find out what the hell, before we read that Constable is in Moscow via Brownsville, Mexico City, and

East Berlin. Why the devil you want to keep fooling around with this spook stuff when . . ."

Dr. Ferguson refrained from replying either to General Augstadt or Wiener and instead said to Hero, "Fortunately, for the time being, I have managed to persuade these gentlemen that they must be patient and do nothing of the kind. FBI operatives attending the seances would gain no knowledge whatsoever and might very easily be led to expose themselves. Any attempt to break up Professor Constable's contact with his daughter, or brutally shatter his illusions, will lose him to us. He would never forgive us. It would be the end of Operation Foxglove."

With a curious twist of his head on his neck and bitter writhing of his lips, General Augstadt said, "And if he spills his guts to the Russians it'll be the end of the free world, and you can bet your ass on that."

That sentence trembled before them all like a flashing of doom, but Dr. Ferguson merely shifted to a more comfortable position and waving his spectacles at Hero, said mildly, "You see, my dear boy, how you come to have quite a problem on your hands and why I have taken the liberty of sending for you."

CHAPTER IV

Invention of Peter Fairweather

"Just what is it that you expect me to do?" Hero asked Dr. Ferguson.

They were alone now, at the window of his private office, looking down on Fifth Avenue bathed in bright spring sunshine, the equally teeming transverse of Forty-second Street, and the semi-hypnotic stop and flow of the traffic as the lights turned red and green.

The meeting had broken up on the grudging acquiescence of those present that Hero should be given the opportunity to investigate the Bessmer seances, for they had been compelled to admit Dr. Ferguson's contention that any ordinary operative was simply not competent to understand or judge what was going on. Hero was completely unknown to anyone on this side of the water; he was the most experienced investigator of occult phenomenon on both sides of the Atlantic and could pursue his work unhampered. Ferguson had indicated to the group exactly the cover he proposed to provide for Hero and to which the latter had concurred. It was clever, because with any luck it would lead him directly to Constable. In the meantime the Army as well as the FBI would step up its surveillance of Constable's movements and take all precautions possible without either irritating or alarming him. Hero was to report, as a safety measure, directly to Wiener by a telephone call at eight in the morning and eight in the evening as well as personally, should there be any developments he felt might be beyond him. The way Saul Wiener had made this last condition, Hero had no doubt, amounted to the casting of one large vote of no confidence. Yet they were all helpless, impaled on the horns of the dilemma. There was nothing else they could do for the moment.

Dr. Ferguson let Hero's question lie for a moment, while he continued to gaze down upon the vibrant Avenue, filled with life, so far removed from the problems of death and when finally he turned to reply, Hero was aware that there had been a change from the impersonal chairman, who had so coolly stated the case a few minutes before, to a man with an intensely personal concern. "I want you to save my friend," he said.

"Oh," said Hero and looked swiftly down the line of further pitfalls presented by this new development.

"Sam Constable has been my friend for thirty years. When Wiener first came to me for information about the Bessmers and the seances that Constable was attending, I already knew about it and what was happening. If I had let them do what they wanted to do—well, you heard them—they would have destroyed him. That is why I sent for you."

The secretary appeared at the door, "Mr. Woodmanston is here, Dr. Ferguson."

"Good. Ask him to be so kind as to wait, we shall only be a moment." When the door had closed Dr. Ferguson continued, fixing Hero with his look of deep concern. "I want you to ascertain whether or not the Bessmers are complete frauds; I want you to find out if you can, the source of the messages from Mary Constable and the brain behind them and who is delivering them; and above all I want you to find, or work out for me, a way of producing a duplicate of the dead hand of Mary Constable, fingerprints and all, under the same conditions as the Bessmers have done. For that, my dear boy, is the only way we shall bring a man of Constable's nature and calibre back to sanity." And then he added, half to himself, "If there is any sanity to bring him back to."

Hero said, "You will leave the entire matter in my hands, no matter who may be hurt, including Constable?"

Ferguson said, "Yes. We must. But I don't want Constable hurt. I have no other choice but to trust to the confidence I have in you."

"I'll try," Hero said.

Dr. Ferguson nodded, then moved to his desk to push a button but paused with his finger poised and said to Hero, "Are you satisfied with your cover as I have outlined it?"

"Yes."

"Very well, I will present the broad picture and leave it to you to do the embroidery." He pressed the buzzer and the secretary appeared with Charles Woodmanston in tow.

"My dear Charles, how very good of you to come."

"Frank, my dear fellow, I am honoured that you should call upon me."

Mr. Charles Woodmanston was a sparrow of a man, impeccably and tastelessly dressed in a style gone out a half century before. He had shoe-button eyes and a small, dark, spiked moustache that was obviously dyed, for the rest of his thinning hair, carefully parted in the middle to show a line of pinkish scalp, was white. His shoes beneath cream spats had pointed toes, his waistcoat was cream-coloured too, his tie was an ample purple foulard, the tiepin this time was not pearl but a jewelled butterfly, and as he half bustled, half minced into the room he moved like a dancing master.

Oh, oh! Hero thought to himself, *I know you.* For in and around the seance rooms of London he had met the British counterparts of the little man, well-to-do dilettantes with nothing to occupy their birdbrains. They were the favourite pigeons of the spiritualist gangs, and also the source of most of the information gleaned by the fake mediums and later bounced back at astonished clients.

"Dear boy."

"Dear fellow."

Ferguson and Woodmanston were clucking politenesses at one another like a couple of hens, except that it was obvious to

Hero that Mr. Woodmanston was a boob and Dr. Ferguson was not.

"May I present a friend of mine from London, dear Charles, Peter Fairweather."

Woodmanston extended a moist hand and said he was charmed; Hero countered that he was delighted. Woodmanston allowed that it had been many years since he had visited that that wonderful city; Hero suggested he might find it greatly changed—.

Dr. Ferguson broke in upon the inanities, "Peter lectures on applied psychology at Cambridge."

"How exciting," said Mr. Woodmanston, and Hero was aware that his little eyes were questing from one to the other and his head cocked birdlike on one side.

"I have asked you to come here to meet Peter because I have— we have a favour to beg of you."

Mr. Woodmanston swelled perceptibly. Like all useless little men he yearned for importance. "My dear Frank, you have only to name it. I am all ears."

Hero found himself compelled to look at Mr. Woodmanston's ears, which were rather large and stood away from his head.

Dr. Ferguson motioned them into chairs and said, "Have I your permission, Peter?" and then to Woodmanston, "I am afraid this recital is going to be rather painful to my friend."

Mr. Woodmanston tut-tutted and said, "Oh dear, oh dear."

Dr. Ferguson began, "Mr. Fairweather has recently been the victim of a tragedy and has suffered a great personal bereavement."

Mr. Woodmanston's face lit up as though another battery of lights in the room had been turned on. Dr. Ferguson launched into the story.

It was to the effect that for more than a year Peter Fairweather had been engaged to marry one of his students, an attractive girl called Ruth Lesley and with a few sentences Ferguson was able to imply that this was no ordinary match, but a mating of minds as well as persons. There had been nothing to interfere with their marriage, since Fairweather had a large and independent fortune, but Miss Lesley had wished to complete her course and take her degree before marrying. However, they were as close to one another in every way as it was possible for two human beings to be. And here Dr. Ferguson, never relaxing the suave dignity of his narration and elegant choice of words, managed without ever saying so to convey just how close. Six weeks ago Miss Lesley was suddenly stricken with a cerebral haemorrhage and within twenty-four hours was dead. Her fiancé came very near to losing his reason. When he had somewhat recovered from the shock, he found he was no longer able to continue his work in the surroundings which reminded him of his loss, asked for leave of absence and travelled to the United States in an effort to forget.

"Not to take up too much of your time," Dr. Ferguson concluded, "Peter has had several extraordinary experiences which led him to consult with me, both in my capacity as the head of our Society as well as an old friend of his father's. Peter, would you care to go on from here—if you feel up to it?"

During this narration Hero had been seated, his hands folded between his knees, staring blankly ahead. It seemed to take two or three seconds before Ferguson's words aroused him and then he appeared to be still stumbling through the fog of his thoughts as he said, "The dream I had. It was too vivid—too much so. She was there in the room—a tall girl and so very gentle—and speaking to me. Not like an ordinary dream, do you understand, but as though she had come back." And he regarded them both, his face etched into bleak lines of misery.

"And then the feeling that she is somewhere about close by . . . She couldn't simply have disappeared like that, could she? So much love, so much of *her* to be wiped out overnight with nothing remaining. If she is trying to reach me I ought to help her, oughtn't I?" Hero broke off and looked at the two others as though he had just discovered them in the room for the first time. He said, "I do apologise, I am behaving like a bloody fool."

Mr. Woodmanston had been exchanging knowing glances

with Dr. Ferguson and he said now to "Fairweather," "My dear sir, not at all, not at all. We who know understand you so very well. Believe me, sir, there is help for you." He looked to Ferguson and gestured with his hand, making it into the shape of the hand of Mary Constable.

"Does he know about . . . ?"

"Yes," replied Dr. Ferguson, "he does. I was hoping, perhaps, I might persuade you to introduce . . ."

"Of course, of course," the little man was all aglow with excitement. "He must attend a seance at the earliest opportunity. I am sure he will get the most satisfactory results. I can see the contact is almost there now. I am sure the Bessmers will accept him, I will introduce him as a friend of yours."

Dr. Ferguson said blandly, "As a friend of *yours,* my dear fellow, would I think carry even more weight."

"Yes, yes, of course," agreed Woodmanston. "As a friend of mine." He looked suddenly dismayed. Would Mr. Fairweather consent to being interviewed by Mr. Bessmer? The Bessmers didn't like to accept anyone without a personal interview.

Hero suddenly seeming to come to life, said, "Of course. I'll do anything you say." And then, "Can they really help? Will they be able, if she is there, to let me through to her?"

Woodmanston's neck stretched inside his high, stiff collar with pride and importance, "One can never *promise* in such matters. I can only testify from the evidence of my own eyes and ears to the marvels they have achieved. But you shall see for yourself. I may perhaps be able to arrange for an interview this very afternoon. Where can I reach you?"

Dr. Ferguson coughed and said, "You may leave a message for him here. Peter is not anxious to have his whereabouts known. As you can imagine, he would hardly welcome the attentions of the press."

"I will telephone Arnold and ask him. You will hear from me." To Hero he said, "Be of good cheer, Mr. Fairweather, I know you can be helped!" He threw them both a look of triumphal confidence, clapped his hat upon his head, and departed.

Dr. Ferguson said, "My dear boy, the loss to the British stage when you decided to become a spook hunter . . ."

"What a pathetic little fellow," Hero said.

"Useful! He will leak most of that to the Bessmers, particularly the part about your independent fortune—and, incidentally, whatever it does cost you, agree to pay and it will be defrayed."

Hero said, "What would mediums do without clots like that?"

Ferguson replied, "They would have a thin time. You know that type. They give away information about themselves and others so that they can get it back via some trumpet in the dark, or big Chief Wampum speaking Hongkong pidgin English, to feed their starved little egos. By the way, I believe the Bessmers do have an Indian control."

Ferguson's attitude indicated that the interview was concluded and that he was about to turn to other things. "I think it would be best if we were not seen together more than occasionally, if at all. Remember, you are Peter Fairweather. Telephone in that name this afternoon and we will have a message for you. I am sure Woodmanston will be able to arrange it. Whenever you feel the need to speak to me privately, go to the reading room and call for the text of the tablets of Shamshi-Adad, translated by Von Schweringin. That always fetches me to see who is asking for them. They are perfectly filthy. He was a dirty old king who lived in the time of Hammurabi." The light blue eyes suddenly illuminated boyishly, "Wiener would love that," he said. "Still . . ."

Hero prepared to leave, Dr. Ferguson accompanied him to the door. He said, "Good-bye, my dear boy, and be careful. Don't get yourself hurt."

But there had been a certain absent-mindedness about the caution. Hero, as he made his way to the lifts, was left with the feeling that if Dr. Ferguson could be helped clear of the problems resting upon his shoulders, the full extent of which Hero was even then not wholly aware, since he did not know what Operation Foxglove was, he would not be too greatly upset if Hero *was* hurt.

The house on West Ninety-first Street, a few doors from Central Park West, was three-storeyed, a brownstone affair as like to its neighbours in the block as peas in a pod. It had a tall flight of steps leading up to an outer front door, glass panelled, giving onto a second set, opaque and more formidable. There was also a downstairs entrance, gained through an area way with access through a grilled iron gate, obviously the servants' and delivery entrance. It was five minutes to four that afternoon when Hero mounted the steps and pushed the doorbell to keep the four o'clock appointment he had been advised was arranged for him. He passed through the glass doors, but there was an appreciable wait before one of the heavy double doors was opened by a manservant. After the bright sunshine without, it was dark and gloomy inside the hall at the bottom of a staircase. The man appeared to be middle-aged, stocky, but powerfully built. He wore dark trousers and a white coat, his head was as bald as a wrestler's and wrestler was the impression that Hero gained; his build and the way his hands and wrists hung down from the sleeves of the white jacket.

Hero said, "My name is Peter Fairweather, I have an appointment to see Mr. Bessmer at four o'clock."

The man said, "Okay. Wait in the parlour; I'll tell him." He did not bother to show Hero into the room, he merely indicated it with a gesture of his head and then went shuffling off down the hall, passing through a door at the rear.

It was Hero's first introduction to an old-fashioned American drawing room. He found it most depressing and his mind leapt to an adjunct, easily made, of another American bit of nomenclature, funeral parlours. There was the musty smell of velvet curtains two-thirds drawn; there were tables and cabinets in mahogany. The furniture was red plush, darkened by age and dirt. There was a marble mantelpiece over a fake fireplace with photographs of ugly people in the lumpy clothes of yesteryear on the walls. Two large rubber plants added the dark of their shiny leaves to the gloom. There was a bookcase with some bound volumes, but before Hero could inspect their titles there was a rustle and a sniff, and Arnold Bessmer was standing in the doorway. Hero had not heard him approach.

Hero was surprised. Somehow he had made up his mind that he was about to encounter one of those figures familiar around the London seance rooms, weak-eyed, weak-chinned, smarmy, and insignificant. The man was tall and vigorous, heavy-jawed, with a pair of compelling dark eyes. He had blue-black hair, cut stand-up, shoe-brush fashion. What was astonishing about his face was that the mouth was a woman's, soft and shaped. Later, when he smiled, Hero saw the glint of a number of gold teeth. He was dressed in a dark suit and wore a bow tie.

He strode into the room with his hand outstretched, "Mr. Fairweather!"

Hero once more was startled. His voice was deep and extraordinarily beautiful, like the bass note of an organ. He was as repellent to Hero as a reptile, the bowed mouth above the heavy jaw was almost too much to take, yet the deep voice and the sombre, magnetic eyes had a curious appeal. Hero was certain that women would find him irresistible. He was equally certain that this man was no fool and that not for one second while he was in that house must he, Alexander Hero, think of himself as such but only as Peter Fairweather in search of his lost love.

The man's grip was hard, but his hand was cold. "It is good of you to see me so soon—a stranger," Fairweather said.

"We never turn a stranger from our door," boomed the man. "A friend of Charles Woodmanston's is a friend of ours. I am Arnold Bessmer. You are in deep trouble. You have come here seeking help. The Church of the Breath of Jesus and the Holy Ozone has never refused to assist a true believer."

The absurd and ridiculous-sounding names rolling sonorously from the diapason of Bessmer's cavernous chest surprised Hero too, for it was the first time he had encountered that kind of bluff, if bluff it was, and he wondered if this was what they had called themselves before they were chased out of California. He also wondered whether it had been thrown at him as a test to see if he would balk at it. He managed to repeat in a hoarse whisper,

"You are very kind," and sought to bring the glaze back into his eyes again.

"Come and sit down here," intoned Bessmer, "and we shall see what we can do for you—if it lies within our power." The sonorous voice rang with sincerity. He steered Hero to a chair at the table in the centre of the room and sat down in one opposite. There was a carved cigarette box of Chinese jade between them. It was expensive. On the table as well were several ash trays, a large leather Bible, a lamp, and a framed photograph of a girl who looked like a Hollywood starlet, inscribed, "To the Bessmers. God bless them," with an indecipherable signature. Bessmer sat with his hands folded for an instant. "The burden upon you is a heavy one," he said.

Fairweather made no reply beyond a faint inclination of his head. He was thinking of the last day that he and Ruth Lesley had walked in the dusk, and the perfume of her hair.

"Perhaps you would care to smoke to ease you?" Bessmer suggested and reaching into a pocket produced a gold cigarette case, which he snapped open.

Fairweather said, "No thank you." He feebly slapped the side pocket of his jacket saying, "I have a pipe—but I would rather not."

"Your bereavement is still very close to you."

Fairweather looked at Bessmer as though he had read his thoughts, and said, "I don't know what to do or where to turn, or what to say."

Bessmer said, "I am an ordained minister, you may unburden yourself to me." It sounded like a peal of Sunday bells.

Hero allowed him to coax the story out of him piecemeal, letting slip pertinent details here and there as though torn unconsciously from an anguished memory. And during the recital, locked away in a small corner of the mind that was being Peter Fairweather, Alexander Hero was wondering where the bug was. In the cigarette box? Bessmer had offered him a smoke from his own case instead of from the table. In the lamp? Or not at all? The interview before the seance simply cried for the hidden microphone, and Hero had a moment's vision of the wrestler moistening his pencil tip with his lips and taking down the pertinent facts he was revealing in some room in the house. Or the medium herself, with her ear to a speaker, memorising the life and times of a dead girl and a desolate lover. The house was quiet except from below, where the kitchen must be, from whence came the muffled clash of dishes and the clink of silver and Hero was aware that stealing into the mustiness of the parlour was a hint of frying onions; a homely touch, he thought.

With one hand Bessmer toyed with the jade box and then opened it. There was nothing inside with the exception of a dozen or so cigarettes. Was a microphone in the lamp then? Or one of those modern, ultra-sensitive ones buried in a picture frame or the back of a chair, which could pick up a whisper at ten feet? It was always the same problem, casing the premises of spiritualists, to achieve an unhindered inspection.

Fairweather continued his stumbling confession of love for a lost girl, but with a kind of careful cunning that he was certain was not lost upon Bessmer, to speak in unrevealing ambiguities, dropping hints and facts as though unaware that he was doing so. Bessmer listened, his dark eyes moist, the absurd pouting bow of his mouth tremulous with sympathy.

The presence of the dead girl was all about him, Fairweather concluded, so strong that it was an unbearable agony to be able to come no nearer. Mr. Woodmanston had said . . .

As Fairweather trailed off, Bessmer sat for a moment with his head bowed, and then, looking up and fixing Fairweather with his gaze said heavily, "We of the Holy Ozone claim no miraculous powers. We can be no more than a link between those who seek and those who have passed over and wish to return. You understand that it is *they* who decide, not we." He paused.

Fairweather said faintly, "I think I do."

"My wife is a unique and wonderful woman. The spirit is with her, the power is in her. She is the instrument through which they can come from the other side, those poor wandering ones who seek to be reunited with those who love them."

In the locked away corner, Hero thought to himself: *Different country, different bloke, same pitch. The price ought to be coming up shortly.*

"We have seen some wonderful results here. A bereaved father has found his loved daughter; a son has been restored to his mother; a missing will has been located. When the power in Sarah Bessmer is strong, as it sometimes is, the spirit materialises into flesh; the father holds his daughter clasped in his arms; the mother presses her son to her bosom. Perhaps you, too, could once more enjoy the presence of the one for whom you seek. Afterwards these manifestations leave Mother weak and drained."

Peter Fairweather said, "You give me hope," and Alexander Hero thought, *Here it comes!*

The organ fugue of Bessmer's voice droned on, "We ask nothing for ourselves, for this work, for this would not be right to suborn God's gift to suffering humanity. All contributions go to the Church of the Breath of Jesus and the Holy Ozone for the propagation of His word that the dead shall rise again. Contributions are voluntary, the amount to be determined by the members."

Peter Fairweather whispered huskily, "I would like to contribute," and then added, "I am a stranger; perhaps you could suggest what might be acceptable."

Bessmer never batted either of his compelling eyes as he murmured, "Shall we say twenty-five hundred dollars? There would almost certainly be a manifestation, perhaps even a reunion."

Alexander Hero almost broke through the cover of Peter Fairweather with a gasp at the unabashed impertinence of the fee named and barely controlled himself. Almost a thousand pounds! Members of seances in London might be clipped a fiver for a visit and if hooked be milked for fifty or a hundred. The sum mentioned was utterly outrageous and yet implied that it was a guarantee of goods delivered. Woodmanston in his excitement must have spilled everything, including the fact that the wealthy Fairweather would be in New York for only a short while. The Bessmers must have decided that the bird must be plucked quickly, or not at all.

Fairweather swallowed Hero and murmured, "I'd give anything to know she was here and happy."

Bessmer moved his chair, "The church funds are paid in cash," he said. "Perhaps when you come this evening—there is a seance tonight at nine o'clock. Bring this card with you." He pulled open a drawer, took out a slip, and initialled it. He was standing, and Fairweather was, too, his hand clasped in that same hard, cold grip. "We shall try," said Bessmer. "We shall try our utmost." And a few moments later Hero found himself outside the house, walking towards Central Park West, looking at a card which read, "Services of the first Church of the Breath of Jesus and the Holy Ozone. Admit one," and the date and the scrawled initials, "A.B." One thing was certain. The Bessmers were no small-time operators. Hero thought it quite possible he might find himself with his hands full.

CHAPTER V

The Shaking Tent of the Ojibwas

"They want," Alexander Hero said, "twenty-five hundred dollars in cash. I think it is a try-on. If I can't produce it they are rid of me and no harm done. If I can, they'll make a quick kill. I couldn't get hold of Dr. Ferguson."

Saul Wiener accepted this almost absent-mindedly, pushing a button, and, when a girl came in, said, "We will want twenty-five hundred dollars, Miss Jurgenson, in fifties and twenties." And then as the girl, noting the sum on a pad, went out, he added as an afterthought, "unmarked, please."

They were in the New York regional office of the Federal Bureau of Investigation, on the northeast corner of Third Avenue and Sixty-ninth Street, diagonally across from a huge, plush, new block of flats and, as Hero learned from the chatty driver of the glittering behemoth of a yellow cab that took him thither, only two blocks away from the Russian Consulate. "Handy, ain't it?" the cab driver had said. "They don't know who's watching who." Hero thought he was probably right.

Wiener was one of five special agents in charge (known as ASAC for short) concerned with counterespionage, sabotage, subversion, domestic communism, etc. His office was large, quiet, and air-conditioned. The walls were panelled in walnut veneer on which hung a framed photograph of J. Edgar Hoover and a large blue and gold plaque of the seal of the Federal Bureau of Investigation and the Department of Justice under which it operated. Hero took in the three words on a ribbon below the scales of justice, apparently the motto of the bureau. They were,

"Fidelity. Bravery. Integrity." Hero was well aware of the reputation of these quiet-appearing agents. They were as courageous as lions.

The desk was large, a flat-topped affair of walnut on which was a photograph of a pleasant-looking woman and two attractive children, a boy and a girl, of about nine and twelve. In addition there were two large, black, glass ash trays and a paperweight which consisted of a miniature missile on a launching pad. There were "in" and "out" baskets for mail and two telephones. To the right of the desk, on a small table, there was a squawk box with some dozen switches for inter-office communications. The visitors' chairs were of green leather, deep and comfortable. The wall-to-wall carpet was of green too, soft and thick. The curtains at the windows were in good taste. The sixth-floor window looked out upon Third Avenue and the gloriously glittering doorman of the apartments opposite, whose uniform, Hero judged, had been designed to be a combination of one of Napoleon's marshals and an admiral's aide.

Wiener was moody to the point of appearing glum, though he maintained a careful politeness towards Hero. He played with the Phi Beta Kappa key which he swung on the end of a gold chain until the secretary returned with the packet of money which he took without comment and slid across the desk towards Hero.

Hero said, "You don't seem to be shocked at the amount. I am."

"Nobody is shocked at prices over here any longer," Wiener commented. "It depends what you are getting for it. If those crooks can come up with a dead fiancée who never existed, I'd say it was cheap."

Hero said, "What if they aren't crooks? The man claimed he was an ordained minister."

Wiener's loud snort of contempt was so obvious that he tried to turn it into a cough. He reached into a folder, pulled out a large filing card containing a photograph in the upper left-hand corner, and sailed it across the desk to Hero.

The photograph was of the young Arnold Bessmer, without as much flesh; there were the same compelling eye, heavy jaw, and too pretty mouth; the details noted on the card were uninspiring. Briefly, Arnold Bessmer, then twenty-seven, had indeed been an ordained Baptist preacher but had been unfrocked and expelled from the Church at the conclusion of his trial for molesting a fourteen-year-old girl in La Jolla, California, for which he had served four years of a six-year term at San Quentin; two years off for good behaviour.

Hero slid the card back and suggested mildly, "He may be a swine but not necessarily a crook. If he is a crook, why do you let him operate?"

Wiener said, "I know you think we are pretty uncivilised over here, but we do have laws and, strangely enough, abide by them. To begin with, the Bessmers are not involved in any inter-state crime and are smart enough to keep from running foul of state laws and city ordinances against fortune-telling. Until there is a complaint against them for fraud there is nothing anyone can do. If they produce your girl friend for you, you might like to lodge one. If we could have nailed them we'd have done so long ago. That's why we have had to go to Ferguson." Wiener then closed his lips with an almost audible snap and Hero felt it was to keep from adding, *And God help us, that is why we have agreed to rely on you.*

Hero said, "You know, it is a common mistake that many make and you must not fall into it. People somehow come to regard me as a policeman. I am not. I am an investigator of occult phenomena, and my job is to sort out the possibly genuine from the obviously false."

Wiener looked even more morose. "I'd forgotten," he said, "you British still believe in ghosts, don't you?"

"If you want to argue from the individual to the general," Hero observed, "so do you Americans." And when Wiener flashed him a look he said, "Constable, for instance."

"Oh, Christ!" said Wiener.

"And the hand," Hero continued, "the hand of a child dead almost a year. Can you make one?"

Wiener moved at his desk with a gesture of impatience and regarded Hero with even greater disfavour. "Christ Almighty," he drawled, "what about the hand?" he repeated. "Isn't that what Ferguson says you are here for? Isn't that all a part and parcel of that crap of tambourines, musical instruments, and trumpets floating around in the dark, with the medium supposed to be tied to a chair?"

Hero nodded. He said, "By and large it is pretty revolting, isn't it? But one never really knows, does one? One has to take each case as it comes, as though none had ever happened before." He reflected for a moment and then said, "You know, it was your ancestors who really started it all."

Wiener looked at Hero sharply, "What's that?"

"Ever heard of the shaking tent of the Ojibwas?"

"No! What do you mean by my ancestors?"

"If you won't think me impertinent," Hero said, "it seemed to me that you probably had some Indian blood—American Indian."

Wiener looked intensely annoyed. "How did you know?" he asked.

Hero said, "I do apologise. The first time I saw you—it seemed to me—I guessed. You confirmed it."

Wiener suddenly shouted with laughter, and his whole attitude of morose suspicion fell away from him as he regarded Hero with amused eyes. "I suppose that's how they do it," he grinned. "Great-great-great-great-grandfather Wiener was a pack peddler before the Revolution. He married a Mohawk girl, First-Flower-That-Comes-After-the-Snow. I am probably the only Indian Jew in the five boroughs. I don't go around talking about it, but I suppose in a ridiculous way I'm proud of it. I have even learned a few phrases in the Mohawk language, in honour of the first flower to poke its head up through the snow." He nodded towards the framed photograph, "Look at the cheekbones on the kids. They've got it too." Then he added, "What was the shaking tent of the Ojibwas?"

Hero replied, "Well, they were Canadian Indians I believe. You will find it in the reports of several of the French missionaries who first penetrated into the wilderness there. The medicine man would let them tie him up with deer-hide thongs and place him in a closed wigwam with a small fire going inside. Soon the whole tent would begin to shiver and shake, and smoke would come pouring out of the top, after which the voice of the Great Spirit would be heard prophesying. Later when they opened up the wigwam, the medicine man would be lying there still nicely packaged."

Wiener, amusement not yet faded from his eyes, asked, "How was it done?"

"Oh well, I suppose the fellow was as adept at getting in and out of rope ties as any of the experts today," Hero explained. "It is really no trick at all. After which he probably chucked some resinous gum onto the fire, shook the tent, and disguised his voice."

"Well," said Wiener, "there you are."

"Yes, I know," Hero agreed. "There wasn't much to the stunt. What was never really explained was the remarkable nature of the prophecies they were able to make. Really some rather extraordinary things of which they could not possibly have had any foreknowledge—at least so it would seem. The evidence of the missionaries is quite explicit on the subject. Perhaps the primitives were a little closer to—such things. A sort of vermiform appendix of the shaking tent has come down to us in the mediums who claim to have an Indian control."

Wiener was looking serious again. He said, "You really believe in some of that stuff, don't you?"

As seriously, Hero replied, "I don't believe in anything. I am paid to keep an open mind. When I come across something that cannot be explained I keep at it until I find out how it is done."

"And if you can't?"

Hero said, "Regrettably, up to now I always have. But I am still hoping."

"Do you know the urgency of the matter? Do you know yet what Operation Foxglove is? You haven't asked me."

Hero said, "I didn't wish to annoy the general. I thought that if you wanted to tell me you would."

Wiener played for a moment with the fraternity key, denoting accomplishment in the more rarified intellectual strata during his university days. He said, "We have had a pretty good report on you from abroad. We could not accept—" he hesitated here.

"A pig in a poke from old Ferguson," Hero concluded for him.

"Exactly," Wiener agreed, momentarily holding the dossier which he had not opened but which Hero gathered contained as much of his life as was public and probably a good deal that was private. "You don't appear to have had any traffic with our friends from the other side of the iron curtain. There seems to be no reason why you should not know about Operation Foxglove, and, as a matter of fact, there are probably a great many why you should."

Wiener squared away the several dossiers on his desk before him, one on top of the other. "I will show you the dope on Ma Bessmer later," he said. He fell silent for a moment and then shifted in his chair so that he faced Hero and began to speak in a voice that was pitched in a lower key, almost as though he felt that on this subject the walls of his own office were not to be trusted.

"There are probably a half dozen nations working on the same problem at this very moment. We know the Russians are and probably your people and the Italians, who are good at that sort of thing. But Constable has got it. He has evolved a wholly new theory upon which he is still experimenting which makes the practical electronic adaptation a possibility. General Augstadt's Operation Foxglove, with the co-operation of Constable, is on the verge of realising these possibilities. And, by the way," Wiener digressed suddenly, "a word of warning: don't sell General Augstadt short. He gets things done. Thanks to him Operation Foxglove is at least several months ahead of schedule."

Hero said, "Yes, indeed. I was certain that General Augstadt—" and as he hesitated Wiener concluded for him, "Couldn't be as much of an imbecile as he appeared to be!" For a moment the two men smiled bleakly at one another.

Wiener continued. "The field of cybernetics, as you know, embraces the control of the mechanisms of machines as well as living creatures. Constable has concentrated upon the former side of it which ranges from automation to the issuing of commands to satellites."

Wiener remained sunk in thought for an instant and then continued, "I am no expert, but it isn't difficult to see that as the mechanical brains and nervous systems of missiles and satellites become more and more complex, approaching more close by to the organisation of the human nerve centres, they also become more vulnerable. Professor Constable has shown the way to intruding upon the commands taped into a missile or established by ground radio and persuading it to disobey these commands and in some cases to reverse them."

The shock waves of the implication struck Hero full force. "Good Lord Almighty!" he breathed. "He turns them into homing pigeons."

"Exactly," Wiener nodded. "Hostile missiles are to be persuaded to return whence they came, or splash into one of the intervening oceans. Constable is close to achieving the breakthrough."

The contingencies began to make Hero's head swim. Wiener coolly enumerated some of them. "If every nation had the device, all the hardware would be scrapped and we'd be back to even Stephen again; fighting with ground armies or dropping bombs from aircraft, and we have all just about found a way to stop that. But if the Russ gets it before we do, or he gets it and we don't, we are all dead ducks, and it's win, place, and show to old man Spengler."

Wiener waited for his words to sink into Hero and then said quietly, "Unfortunately, just as we are on the verge of achieving success—we are about a month or two months away, with Constable absolutely indispensable to the project, somebody works his own racket on him."

"Eh?" said Hero, startled, "his own . . . ?"

"Cybernetics," Wiener said, "the other end of it."

"Good Lord!" Hero cried. "The human mechanism."

"Someone has found a way to enter into communication with the brain and nervous system of Professor Constable and initiate a series of commands running counter to those taped into him by love of country, normal habits of patriotism, personal welfare and security, honesty, and the inborn reactions of a gentleman. Someone has been ordering Professor Constable either to spill his secret . . ." Suddenly Wiener's voice rang harshly, "*Our* secret, or defect to the other side of the curtain with it."

Hero said softly, "But you don't know who."

"Who but the Commies?" Wiener said in a tone that was almost an irritable snarl.

"Or Mary Constable?" Hero suggested.

Saul Wiener hit the folders before him with his fist in angry impatience. His dark hair seemed to be standing straight on end, his eyes snapping venomously from above his high cheekbones. "Jesus Christ!" he shouted. "Are you still insisting . . . ?"

"Oh no." Hero cut him short, "I was only naming the alternative. Or behind Mary Constable, another? A lot of people believe in God, you know, and in the risen Christ and His miracles."

Wiener said with cutting scorn, "God via the Bessmers?"

"God in any way He wants to, if there is a God or ever has been." Hero's voice suddenly took on some of the harshness of Wiener's, "What would you do if it turned out that it *was* Mary Constable?"

Now it was Wiener's turn to face implications and he was suddenly horrified by what he saw. He groaned, "Christ Almighty," and then said, "God knows, I never wanted you in on this case and don't want you now."

Hero said more quietly, "I can sympathise with your feelings but I am afraid as things stand now you no longer have any choice in the matter. It has rather moved out of your sphere."

Wiener was contrite as quickly as he had become angry. He said, "I am sorry. I apologise. I can see your point, of course. We are not accustomed to dealing with abstractions or people's beliefs, or even the possibility that a dead child could return to urge her father to betray his country."

"I have not said or intimated she has," Hero declared. "I am only taking the lawyer's stand. Until I know how that hand was materialised and can duplicate it, the case against Mary Constable remains not proven."

Wiener asked somewhat stiffly, "Will you play ball with us?"

"Certainly," Hero agreed. "As far as I am able. I have told Dr. Ferguson that I must be allowed a free run to handle this in my own way and he has agreed."

"*He* has agreed!" Wiener said sarcastically.

Hero suggested, "It is Dr. Ferguson who has engaged me. He is the one for whom I am working." Then as Wiener's glance went swiftly to the packet of money resting close to Hero's hand, he continued, "He gave me to understand that you might be difficult but you would co-operate."

Wiener's boyish smile broke through again and he said, "Very well then. We will let it go at that. But you do understand now the urgency?"

"Oh, by the good Lord, I do!" said Alexander Hero. "I do indeed. Better even than you could ever think."

CHAPTER VI

Mr. Fairweather Encounters His Fiancée, Deceased . . .

It was nine o'clock that same evening when Hero pulled the doorbell of No. 12A West Ninety-first Street and was admitted by the same manservant, now wearing a black alpaca coat. He took his time inspecting the card that Hero presented and carefully counted the packet of bills handed over, giving the Englishman a better look at him, noting again the thickness of the neck and traces of cauliflowered ear. This would be a rough customer in a fracas. Hero had no doubt that in the dark of the seance room this troglodyte would not be far away and prepared for anything. If someone were suddenly to grab or create a disturbance he would probably regret it.

Not that anyone of those gathered already there in the parlour into which Hero had been shown was the kind likely to start any trouble. There were eleven of them, and Hero made the twelfth.

As he appeared in the doorway Mr. Charles Woodmanston minced over, twittering like an excited tomtit as he elbowed his way through the gathering to Hero's side.

"My dear fellow! Delighted! How splendid that you were able to come. So pleased I could arrange it. I do hope there will be a contact. I am as excited as though *I* were expecting a message. Allow me to introduce you to everyone here. Mrs. Bessmer, I understand, is resting. You will meet her when she comes down."

He fingered Hero's arm, gently tugging and guiding him. Hero then smiled inwardly over the fact that both Hero and

Fairweather were conscious of the lingering aroma of those earlier fried onions.

Woodmanston rattled off the names. There were a Mr. and Mrs. James Rimbaud, Mr. and Mrs. Harold Clark, Mr. Holworthy, Miss Agathey, and a Miss Forsby, a Mrs. Hennessy, and Mrs. Small, two widows, a Mr. Weitzenkorn. But for the twanging of their American voices, they could have been the counterpart of any group of sitters from London, Birmingham, or Leeds. In one way or another all of them were weak people, whose faces or attitudes showed that they were unable to cope with the realities of life and death and needed the kind of delusions to be found in a seance room.

Hero evaluated them swiftly. They were genuine.

The two married couples were there for a mother and sister. Weitzenkorn was a forlorn, bald, little man, sixtyish, who had lost his wife. Both the formidable widows were refusing to let their departed husbands rest in peace. Miss Agathey, who was in her eighties, was being advised by the spirit of her brother, who had always looked after her and her affairs and since his death had apparently continued to do so, no doubt, Hero thought, approving any contributions she felt inclined to make to the Church of the Holy Ozone. The other spinster was Miss Forsby, and Hero was not able to ascertain immediately what brought her there or what contact she sought. It became clear, however, when Arnold Bessmer entered the parlour, wearing a long tail coat and a minister's collar. It was Bessmer, of course.

He moved amongst them unctuously shaking hands, enveloping each with a phrase delivered in the deep organ tones. "Friend Holworthy—come to visit your spirit mate again—we missed you at the last meeting, Mrs. Hennessy. So did your husband. Ah! My dear Miss Forsby. Fetching as ever, I see—Friend Weitzenkorn, I hope we shall have something for you tonight."

His roving eye picked up Hero standing beside and towering over Woodmanston. He came over and engulfed Hero's hand in both of his. "Dear new friend Fairweather. I hope we shall be able to help you. I *feel* we will. I have prayed. Sarah feels the magnetic fluid flowing strongly tonight. She will be here in a moment."

Bessmer raised his voice and addressed them all. "Are your minds clear? Are your thoughts of grace? Think sweet thoughts of your loved ones. Call to them. Prepare to tune in to infinity."

Hero had an impression, a strong one, clear, unmistakable, trustworthy. The messages from Mary Constable, those subtle, progressive, step-by-step temptations were not the creation of Arnold Bessmer. The man was clever and no doubt dangerous, but it was the crude, bare-faced shrewdness of the carnival pitchman, crystal-ball or palm reader, who has learned how to size up a crowd or an individual in an instant and prescribe for them. He could dish it up for the mugs, but his was not the intelligence to steer the brain of a Samuel Hale Constable.

And not that of Mrs. Sarah Bessmer either. Hero was staggered when she came into the room. Not because she was so different from what he expected, and the mind picture of her he had created, but because she so exactly fitted it. His imagination, of course, had been made up of a composite of many other mediums he had known both in London and the Continent and had exposed: gross, vulgar, cunning women of low origin. They were almost a breed.

She was of average height but powerfully built, with huge hams of fleshy arms which, Hero knew, in women could be deceptively strong, and he looked to her wrists, hands, and fingers to see whether he could detect muscles that ought to be there. They were; little lumps between thumb and forefinger. Her features were gross, her head large, lips fleshy; she had a strong Roman nose and dark, impudent eyes behind gold-rimmed spectacles. Her hair was iron-grey, profuse, and combed high on her head, the style of 1900, when women wore rather revolting puffs in their hair known as "rats," to fill it out and around which their pompadours were piled. Most mediums he had known wore their hair in this fashion. It was of course most useful for the concealment of small objects.

She was even dressed as he had expected her to be, in black

satin over what was probably a considerable amount of whale-
bone or steel in the form of old-fashioned corsets from which her
flesh bulged. She exuded an odour of mustiness and camphor
balls. And she had eaten a great deal of the onions which had
been cooking.

Woodmanston approached her as though she had been the
Pythian goddess, twitching, fluttering, and scraping and introduced Peter Fairweather as her new sitter.

Her brash gaze took in Hero fully through the lenses of her
spectacles for an instant, and she said, "Pleased to meet you. I can
see spirits all about you, young man. I feel like I got the power
tonight."

She was uneducated and probably semi-literate. No subtlety
here. She moved off among the others saying, "It oughda be a
good meeting. I feel the power." Then she asked, "Are we all
here?"

Her husband answered for her, "No, not yet. We are waiting
for our dear friend, Professor Constable."

The bell pull at the street door clanged. A silence fell upon
those in the room. They heard the manservant pad to the entrance and open it. A moment later Professor Constable entered
the parlour.

And one makes thirteen, Hero thought to himself. *What a
good thing I'm not superstitious. So that is Professor Constable.*

There is always some slight shock when a person heretofore
seen only as a photograph suddenly comes to life. Hero experienced it now, at the sight of the lion's head with the bushy grey
hair that had once been red, the fiercely intelligent eyes, and the
stubborn chin.

Constable was clad in baggy, unostentatious clothes and a neu-
tral-coloured tie, knotted untidily as though in haste or by one
who did not care for dress. He was there now in the same room
with them, this big man, the figure around which was collected
all the fuss and worry, the secrecy and the plotting. Behind the
ample, curved dome of his brow he carried the knowledge upon

which rested the safety of almost half the people on the face of the globe.

And yet, at the same time, he was not there. His eyes appeared to take in none of them, as though all of his thoughts and concentration were turned inwards. No one addressed him; he spoke to no one. He simply disappeared as it were, by melting in with the others who now all turned their backs as they faced the far end of the parlour where two pairs of curtains were drawn back, revealing sliding doors which were rolled open to admit them to the room behind the parlour, at the back of the house. It was a more spacious one, where obviously the seance was to take place.

Hero followed them through, lagging behind, the better to be able to study and memorise the layout of the place.

It was not unfamiliar. At the far end was the cabinet he had expected. Few if any "materialisation mediums" would operate without a cabinet, including those utterly revolting ones who produced ectoplasm by regurgitating cheese cloth, or extruding it from the body orifices. The cabinet was an enclosure some ten foot square, extending from floor to ceiling, made of heavy, black cloth curtains. These curtains were now open to reveal a chair, a small, three-foot table on which reposed a tambourine, a kind of speaking trumpet, a dinner bell of good size, and a small accordion. Facing the cabinet and some five yards from it at its farthest point, was a semicircle of chairs for the sitters. Hero counted them. There were fourteen. Bessmer himself, then, would be in their midst.

There were windows on either side of the cabinet, but the blinds were drawn as well as curtains pulled. Over on one side of the room was a large cabinet radio-gramophone, the lid of which was open. Hero could see that it was loaded with records, ready to drop and play one at a time when activated. Who would the activator be? The all-in wrestler, of course. The burly servant had already rolled shut the sliding doors behind him and had taken up a post by the instrument and Hero saw that handy to his position were several light switches as well.

Woodmanston, who had appointed himself Hero's guide, said, "Shhh. They don't like anyone to talk from now on."

Hero nodded. He had not said anything.

The others were already seating themselves round, leaving only the central area clear, though Professor Constable had ensconced himself in one of these chairs. He sat hunched down, legs extended forward, hands thrust into his trouser pockets, chin resting upon his chest, hearing nothing, saying nothing, caring nothing about any of those present.

Bessmer sat down next to Constable and motioned for Hero to take the seat on his other side, with Woodmanston occupying the last vacant chair on Hero's right.

Bessmer suddenly turned to Hero and asked, "You ever attend a seance before, friend Fairweather?"

Peter Fairweather replied in a voice husky with anticipatory nerves, "No. You must tell me what to do."

"Don't do anything until you are told," Bessmer said. "We never know what is going to happen. Do what the spirits say. I'll help you." Then he added, "I have prayed for you, brother. Amen."

There were murmurs of "Amen" from others in the semicircle.

Sarah Bessmer came down through the rear of the room, her step firm, and trod to the front of the cabinet where she faced all of the sitters, her heavy features expressionless except for the glitter of her eyes behind the lenses of her spectacles. She addressed them: "I said I felt the power tonight. It is there. I can feel them in the air all around me, waiting. I'll do my best—for all of you."

"Amen," intoned Bessmer.

"Amen," the others echoed, all except Constable, who never moved or shifted from his inward gaze to his outer surroundings.

Mrs. Bessmer was not yet finished. She lifted her powerful, fleshy chin somewhat and said, "We got a new sitter here tonight. Mr. Fairweather. He will want me tied up, to the chair, no doubt, for proof like. So there can't be any complaints. Is that right, Mr. Fairweather?"

Peter Fairweather seemed to dissolve into a jelly of fright and embarrassment. "What? What?" he jittered. "Of course not! I mean, whatever you say, whichever way is the best."

"Well, I want to be tied up," Mrs. Bessmer said, with sudden, odd truculence. "Then afterwards if anyone comes around saying there has been any hanky-panky—well." Her big chin came up higher on the word "well," and involuntarily Hero looked over in the direction of the manservant standing by the gramophone with his finger on the light switch.

Bessmer said ringingly, "Are you sure you want to, Mother? It don't seem right when you give so much!"

Mrs. Bessmer replied, "Shut up!" and her mouth closed like a trap upon the words and she added, "I said I was to be tied tonight. Mr. Woodmanston, will you come into the cabinet and do it, please?"

Woodmanston leaned over to Peter Fairweather and whispered proudly, "I'm always the one who ties her. I know how. You watch." He rose and went to the cabinet with Mrs. Bessmer, where, from behind one of the curtains she produced a length of heavy clothesline cord, some twenty feet of it. Mrs. Bessmer sat in the chair by the table, and little Woodmanston bound her to it by the legs, arms, and chest, winding and rewinding the rope about her lumpy figure, stopping only to fashion an intricate knot, then continuing until the last foot of cord was exhausted and she was trussed up like a mummy. He returned to his chair next to Peter Fairweather, glowing with satisfaction and pride. "There," he said. "No doubts, eh?"

Alexander Hero chortled within himself and thought: *Thirty seconds and you'll be out of there. If I tied you, Mother dear, you would never budge in a month of Sundays.* Hero, of course, would have used a spool of thread, that anathema of the fake medium. For with the first bit of strain applied, or struggle to evade, the thread would snap and with it the proof. No mediums

Hero had ever known would permit themselves to be bound by the wrists or thumbs with ordinary sewing cotton.

Bessmer now arose and, looking to the semicircle, said, "Messages? Any sealed messages?"

Four of those present reached into their pockets and produced envelopes of thin paper, of the kind usually devoted to airmail letters.

Bessmer collected them, inspected them briefly, and then showed them to Fairweather. "They have been sewn up with coloured silk," he said, "so that they cannot be tampered with or opened. They will be returned in the same condition. The spirits maybe will answer the questions sealed inside." He went to the cabinet and deposited the envelopes on the table.

Alexander Hero thought, *The good Lord give me strength! That chestnut in this day and age. And all the envelopes supplied, of course, by the Bessmers.*

Bessmer pulled the black curtains closed carefully, returned to the group and sat down. "Join hands," he said and groped for Constable's on his left and took Fairweather's on his right. Fairweather felt Woodmanston's hand, like a small bird, creep into his, the one still free.

"Lights, Pratt," Bessmer said, and the manservant flipped the switch and plunged them into what first seemed like total darkness.

So that was the bruiser's name, Hero thought. From his vantage point over by the wall he could probably see more of them than they of him.

Bessmer said to Fairweather, "Just sit quiet. You must not be impatient. Sometimes it takes a long time before anything happens."

"Yes," whispered Peter Fairweather, "I will." Then added, "I have prayed that she will come." The blackout was not complete. Somewhere in the room there was a small, red glow which diluted the density of the murk, yet did not enable one to see beyond distinguishing occasional outlines or shapes indicating some shadow deeper than others. But in a sense it was a light that would enable those who gave evidence later as to what they had seen or felt to swear that it had taken place under illumination.

"Music, Pratt," Bessmer said.

Another switch clicked; a motor whirred; the gramophone gave out those internal noises preparatory to dropping a record onto the turntable and allowing the needle to enter upon grooves. Church bells chimed loudly. There was an organ introduction and then a male voice choir launched into a hymn, "Shall We Gather at the River?"

"Let us all join in," Bessmer boomed. Nervous voices and quavery ones took up the tune.

In the dark, Peter Fairweather went back to that Cambridge he had known first as an undergraduate and later when he had returned as a lecturer and bent his mind to the days of the first advent of Ruth Lesley and how all that had come to be between them had happened.

He imagined her first in the hall, her brown head lowered over the notes she was taking, the tendrils of hair showing on the nape of her neck and felt the first thrill of recognition—a woman who might possibly become beloved. When she raised her eyes to his and he saw her fully, he knew.

When first Hero created in his mind the person of Ruth Lesley, the face and figure of his stepsister, Meg, daughter of the Earl of Heth, swam into his ken; good Meg, his sometime right-hand girl and partner with her expert knowledge of photography, assisting during some dangerous investigation. He found himself remembering the sudden desperate pressure of her arms about his neck at the moment of his departure, when they had kissed good-bye and her whispered injunction, "Be careful! Take care of Sandro for me."

Deliberately, and for reasons which he himself did not understand, Hero denied Ruth Lesley the appearance of Meg and reached further back into subconscious recollection of a time when a brown-haired girl had once appeared to him in a dream and kissed him. He had not known who she was but they had walked together hand-in-hand, through a meadow of spring flowers.

The sweetness and tenderness of the moment had filled him simultaneously with joy and melancholy. He was then perhaps ten years old. Who was she? Who had she been? He never knew. She never came again. But the echoes of her loveliness sometimes rang faintly through Alexander Hero, during the years as he grew from boy to man.

Her he made into Ruth Lesley, now grown and at last come back to him, that perfect, unattainable woman whom every man harbours in some corner of his mind. Even when love comes and the lonely heart is eased, the faint echo of that other from the long past childish dream may still whisper faintly.

The hymn had finished; the gramophone clicked off. The silence that followed was disturbed by an ugly sound that broke into the fantasy that Hero was setting up. It was a kind of strangled moan and issued from the direction of the cabinet. Irritably he recognised it as in all probability Mrs. Bessmer about to go into her so-called trance.

Arnold Bessmer gave Hero's hand a squeeze, apparently meant to be one of encouragement and whispered, "Sarah's starting." Again he ordered, "Music, Pratt," and when the next record dropped and turned out to be "Lead, Kindly Light," he said, "All sing."

The noise (which Alexander Hero knew provided excellent cover for whatever "Mother" might be getting up to in the cabinet) enabled Peter Fairweather to return to his imagined love.

This scene was no longer the lecture hall. He invented a golden afternoon of bicycling together down a narrow, country lane and stopping to rest, sitting side by side on a bank in quiet reflection and enjoyment of their surroundings, the immediate greenery, the distant woods, the hum of insects, the quivering of leaves and grasses in the wind. And then they would turn to regard one another silently, filled with that extraordinary exultation and joy of contemplation. After that they would come to-

gether to search one another for the innermost meanings of what
they felt through touch and caress . . .

Alexander Hero stood apart for an instant and contemplated
the lovers entwined upon the bank. If thoughts indeed carried
electric charges and the gross woman behind the curtains could
receive, then the person of Ruth Lesley and her lover must be
communicated. What surprised Hero was the desire he experienced to return to this creation. It was as though he had given
her life and she awaited him there on the green, mossy bank of
the mind where winds are always soft and scented and the girls
the attainable enchantment.

But if she had been endowed with life, she had been doomed
to death too. Within himself, broadcasting to whoever might be
tuned in, Peter Fairweather now created that sense of utter misery and desolation of a world gone dark, of an endless groping
and wandering through that darkness in search of the forever
lost. His darling was dead, the warm flesh cold, closed the melting, tender eyes, vanished the sunny laughter, the gentle voice.
Where was she? Where had she gone? The yearning and the
quest surged once more through Peter Fairweather and constricted his aching throat. In the most curious kind of self-hyp-
notism the longing for the dead chimera brought the sting of
tears to Peter Fairweather's eyes in the dark.

The record had run out again, and when the singing
stopped a low moaning and whimpering came from the direction of the cabinet and continued for what seemed an age. Then,
suddenly and startlingly the tambourine thumped and rattled,
the squeeze-box wheezed the opening strains of "Nearer My God
to Thee" and the trumpet, suddenly glowing with phosphores-
cence, emerged from the cabinet, apparently unaided, and
floated around in the air in its vicinity.

Bessmer squeezed the hand of Peter Fairweather again and
whispered, "Shhh. The spirits have come." Alexander Hero remained in abeyance, grimly disgusted. Fairweather continued to
be filled with the yearning and sadness that had been conjured
up.

A rat-ta-plan of raps issued from the direction of the cabinet accompanied for an instant by a burst of eerie laughter. In the darkness one of the women suddenly exclaimed, "Oh! Something touched me!" Hero felt a chilly current of air and experienced what seemed to be the feel of an icy hand brushing past his ear and started in spite of himself.

"Shhh!" whispered Bessmer again. "Don't move. They're all around us. They're looking us over."

Hero didn't doubt this and was amazed that even experienced as he was his senses had tricked him. But his nose had not. He had recognised the faint, stale, musty odour. There were some murmurs and little shrieks and cries from other sitters and once a chair scraped heavily. Even with that faint red glow of light and the eyes accustomed to it, there was nothing to be seen. Then things quietened down again, except for the somewhat heavier breathing of the expectant sitters. Hero wondered what Professor Constable was thinking. Apparently none of the exploratory spirits had approached him.

Then, out of the darkness, again from the direction where the cabinet was located, was heard a deep voice with tinny, metallic overtones provided by the trumpet through which it was speaking. "How! Me Big Chief Thundering-Cloud. Me come here from Spirit land say-um how."

From the direction where pathetic, bald-headed, little Mr. Weitzenkorn was sitting came an answering "How," and there were several more scattered "Hows" in the manner of "Amens." Hero didn't have to suppress a smile; it was all too tragic. Peter Fairweather was still miles away at the bier of Ruth Lesley.

Bessmer whispered to Fairweather, "That's Sarah's Indian-control, Chief Thundering-Cloud. He was killed at the battle of the Little Bighorn."

"Me got-um messages," intoned the invisible chief. "Me read-um. Me tell-um." The voice then assumed the tone of one reading: "Miss Agathey ask if brother got-um books other side. Brother, he say got-um plenty books. Everybody got-um plenty everything other side."

The sere voice of Miss Agathey was heard, "Oh thank you, Chief! I am so relieved. Howard always did enjoy reading so much. He'd have felt lost without his books."

Big Chief Thundering-Cloud was on his second round. "Mr. Weitzenkorn say to wife, Leah, you happy? Will I be able to see you sometime? Wife Leah, she say I happy. You maybe see me sometime."

Hero wondered why Constable, himself, and perhaps others there had been promised materialisations, whereas some were confined to receiving secondhand replies to their written queries and came by the answer almost as soon as the question. Obviously the cash contributions of the latter had been smaller.

"And the messages are in sealed envelopes," Bessmer's penetrating whisper reminded Fairweather. "And they will be returned unopened."

Fairweather remained at his mourning but Hero's thought was: *I'll bet they will. And in the meantime "Mother" is having a ducky time reading them right through the envelopes with a pencil torch.*

There were several more messages and replies, after which he took his leave. "Me go now. Princess Devi come. How!"

There was a rather delicate tinkle and rattle of the tambourine bells, followed by a high squeaky voice saying, "Hallo, everybody! I'se here. It's little Princess Devi from spirit land."

Bessmer again sibilated an explanation. "Mother's Hindu-control. She's only twelve years old. Child bride, you know. When her husband the maharajah died she had to commit *thuggee* on his funeral pile."

Fairweather laid a wreath of roses upon a fresh turned mound, but Alexander Hero thought that Saul Wiener would be probably glad to learn that an intellect that could confuse *thuggee* with *suttee* certainly could have had no part in the subtlety and danger of the Constable messages. He was also happy to note that the little Hindu child bride talked baby talk with the accent of a Louisiana mammy, which was probably as close as Mother Bessmer could come.

The squeaky voice prattled on. There were many spirits there who had come from far, far off to see their loved ones. Not all would be able to be seen or felt; only those who had progressed. Princess Devi pronounced it "pwogwessed." Hero wondered why Professor Constable had not thrown up yet and felt that shortly he himself might.

Princess Devi delivered several spirit messages too in her imbecilic voice. One was for the Rimbaud couple: "Baby Bobby is well and happy; everybody on the other side admires his beautiful, big, blue eyes."

In the darkness came a sob and a woman's voice, "Oh, it's true! It's true! Everyone said he had heavenly blue eyes; they were the most wonderful colour."

"There is a very strong spirit here," squeaked Princess Devi. "Ooo, she's strong! She wants to come through to see someone here. It's for a Mr. Fairwevver. Oh, Mr. Fairwevver, are you here for your spirit friend?"

Peter Fairweather at first did not connect the name with himself. He had been far away, plodding homeward in the dusk from the grave of the girl he had been about to marry. Then he became aware that at his side Woodmanston was tugging at his hand frantically and whispering, "That's you, Fairweather! It's for you!"

Princess Devi repeated, "Mr. Fairwevver, are you here?"

Fairweather felt Bessmer's breath on his ear as he said, "You have been summoned, Mr. Fairweather. There is a spirit come for you. You must respond."

Peter Fairweather said, "What?" And then, "Yes, yes, I am here. This is Peter Fairweather speaking."

The tambourine tinkled once again but more faintly, as though it were receding and the horrid, baby voice of Princess Devi, too, was more distant. "There's a spirit come to see you Mr. Fairweather. I'se a-goin' now. Listen! Listen! She wants to speak to you."

In the darkness the ensuing silence of the next few seconds seemed thick and enveloping, like a canopy through which no sound could penetrate. There was not even the exhalation of the sitters to be heard, as though they all were holding their breaths.

A soft, thrilling voice penetrated from nowhere. "Peter! Peter dear! Can you hear me?"

Peter Fairweather was shocked and startled. The speech was that of an English girl. It was the voice of Ruth Lesley as he had imagined her, as he had thought of her, as he had remembered her ever since.

Alexander Hero was equally staggered. Here was no vulgar ventriloquist or frowsy swindler speaking through a tin trumpet. Every accent, every syllable had fallen familiarly on his trained ears.

"Peter! Dear Peter! I can't see you. Where are you? I have come from so very far away."

Peter Fairweather rose from his chair, snapping the chain of hands. He spoke her name, "Ruth!"

"Peter! Come to me."

At his side Bessmer said softly, "She's calling you. Go to her."

Fairweather cried, "Where? Where?" He was confused and filled with the strangest kind of turmoil. "Where is she? Where can I find her?"

"Come to me, Peter!" The call was even softer and more sweetly sounded.

"In the cabinet," Bessmer said. "Go to the cabinet."

"Yes, that's it," Woodmanston urged, his voice almost cracking with suppressed excitement. "Go to her."

As though to help him find her the red light seemed to glow more brightly for an instant or two, driving back the deeper shadows and revealing the outline of the cabinet, the curtains of which seemed to have acquired some motion.

Peter Fairweather gave himself up completely to the strange dream that had suddenly burgeoned and enveloped him and he moved forward with the step of a somnambulist. He paused once more before the slightly swelling curtains and now could hear the heavy breathing and faint moaning that denoted the medium.

"Peter! Peter, hurry!" The thrilling whisper was so faint that none but himself could have heard it. He parted the curtains, stepped inside, and was enveloped by the blackness therein and for a moment was not certain of his balance, as though he had plunged into a nightmare abyss and was falling—falling.

There was a rustle and once more the whisper of his name, and then Ruth Lesley was in his arms, her body pressed to his, her arms enfolded about his neck, her mouth upon his, expressive of all the hunger and longing and overwhelming love that they had known.

The reuniting was a singing ecstasy into which Fairweather felt himself sinking, as though he was tumbling through the universe of stars. There was nothing held back in the embrace. She was all there. She was all his, as she had always been from the very beginning and now promised to continue throughout eternity.

"Peter! Peter!"

"Ruth!"

And then no longer words but only the sweetness of contact. Unaware, instinctively Fairweather's fingers began to grope. There was a low, sweet laugh and then as suddenly as he had been caught up in the embrace he was alone. There was no one there. With his hands he tried to push the darkness away from him and to find her again, but she was gone, and as he felt about, his fingers suddenly encountered rough, coarse hair and then the large beak nose and the fleshy face of the medium, and he touched the cords that bound her. She began to strain and moan and cry out and Fairweather could feel that her face was wet with perspiration. Almost in panic he reached for the flap of the curtain, opened it and staggered into the faint red luminescence which, from where he stood, outlined the shapes of the other sitters in their semicircle, like a court of doom. Somehow he managed to regain his seat.

CHAPTER VII

. . . *As Well As the Late Mary Constable*

Peter Fairweather, merging with Alexander Hero, shrank back into the welcome darkness confused, disturbed and furiously angry.

He felt the movement of both Bessmer and Woodmanston reaching for his hands and submitted unwillingly, for the touch of both was horrifying, particularly the moist fingers of Bessmer, which were squeezing his almost with affection.

Hero had been profoundly moved and shaken both physically as well as emotionally. For the moment the two characters of Peter Fairweather, the Cambridge lecturer on applied psychology, and Alexander Hero, psychical researcher and investigator of the occult, had become inextricably merged.

He realised that there are some women, usually inexperienced, whose kisses are fresh, hard, and impetuous, whose mouths convey only innocence; and others whose lips are so soft, clinging, melting, and sensuous that thoughts become tumbled and disarranged and the senses reel as though the act of love had already begun. It was such a girl that he had held in his arms in the darkness of the cabinet and such a kiss he had received. He had been overwhelmed and excited to the point where his normal cold and accurate powers of observation, so greatly needed at this seance, had been interfered with; he had practically been seduced.

That alter ego of his, Peter Fairweather, into whose character he had so completely immersed himself, was badly shaken too. The mental creation of the nonexistent Ruth Lesley had been so fully rounded and completed that she had taken on almost a life and death, and for a moment Fairweather-Hero wondered whether the very power of his yearning for this imaginary person might not have been communicated to some wandering, errant spirit who had appeared to assuage his loss. Then his rage returned, fury at himself for being so naïve but even more anger with the Bessmers for taking him for the kind of noddy on whom a stunt could be pulled such as used to be worked on imbecilic and nasty old men at the turn of the century, for whom "spirit brides" were produced with whom they sat kissing and fumbling in the dark.

Yet, as reason began to put the brakes on his whirling brain, he saw no reason why human nature should change in a matter of fifty years or the tricks used for gulling it. Through Woodmanston and himself, a character had been built up for the Bessmers of a bereaved young man, distraught beyond reason and wealthy as well, who appeared a setup for a physical manifestation. Aware that his stay in this city was limited, they had simply soaked him for all the traffic would bear and then delivered the goods. But who was "Ruth Lesley"? What was the source of the hellfire which in a few brief seconds she had poured into his veins? And whence had she come?

One thing was certain. If there had been a real Peter Fairweather as well as a Ruth Lesley, Fairweather would be coming back for some more of the same. And with the return of the memory of the kiss and the first slight intrusion of his normal sense of humour, Hero realised that he had not yet wholly succeeded in dissecting Fairweather from Hero and which wanted what.

He heard Woodmanston whisper, "Did you find her?" And at the same time Bessmer asked, "Was there someone there? Did you hold your girl in your arms?"

The remains of Peter Fairweather answered, "Yes—yes, I think so. It was Ruth." And then had the good sense to add, "Will she come back? Can I see her again another time?"

"Maybe," said Bessmer. Moans and gasps and a retching sound

came from the direction of the cabinet. "Music!" commanded Bessmer, "Mother needs more of the power." Another hymn invaded the airless seance room. "Everybody sing. Sing for Mother," Bessmer shouted.

Sing to cover up whatever the old bag is up to now, Hero thought. One thing was certain, she had been in her chair and bound all the time he had been in the cabinet.

With his pulses slowing and blood cooling, Hero could now give his attention to recording for the filing cabinet of his mind what he could remember of Ruth Lesley and his experience.

She had been tall. From where she had come to when she was in his arms, her brow just at his chin, he judged that she was some five foot eight inches. She was slender too. The memory of the position of his arms about her told him that and she was young, for there had been the pressure of firm breasts against his body. This was the recipe for the dead Ruth Lesley that had been given to the Bessmers. Her hair had been silken, but as to its colour or how she wore it, there was no clue. Her flesh had been soft, warm, and supple, and as he forced his thoughts back over the fantastic moments, Hero tried to remember what she had worn but could not. His hands had felt a garment of some smooth material, but whether it had been a frock, a sheet, or a nightdress, he could not judge.

And beyond this and the memory of the sensuality which in that brief time had held nothing back from him, that was all. He might encounter "Ruth Lesley" in the street, in a shop, in a restaurant and never recognise her. He regretted now that he had not had upon him a certain small device that enabled him to see in the dark, as undoubtedly Mother Bessmer was doing. But it had been important at this first visit to behave and observe exactly as the other sitters, to see and hear and feel what they felt.

Something was knocking at his memory, demanding to be heard—something he had overlooked, neglected. It came to him then, the sense of smell. Ghost literature was full of scents of the sea, of the grave, of brimstone that accompanied visitations. He remembered now. There had been a fragrance about her.

There had been no mistaking the fetor of Mother Bessmer in the close confines of the cabinet, but when the girl had been in his arms there was a redolence as intoxicating as her person. It was hardly a scent at all but, and here he smiled in the darkness at his own extravagance of thought, a distillation of starlight and sunlight, fresh, delicate, somehow far off and intangible, as though the spirit of Ruth Lesley had brought with her some hint of the mysteries of those other planes where dwelt the dead.

"*Rubbish!*" said Hero to himself.

"*But that's what it smelled like,*" insisted Peter Fairweather.

"Blast!" Hero swore under his breath and wished he could kick himself for having permitted himself to be so thrown.

The singing and the music had stopped again, and the discs of the tambourine were shivering. The sickening voice of the Princess Devi control was heard, "I'se here again. I'se been all around the world. I'se got some more messages for people here." She delivered them to the couple named Clark and to Mrs. Hennessy and Mr. Holworthy. They were ambiguous, vaguely comforting, except the one to Holworthy to say that "Annie," his spirit friend, could not be there that night but might come to see him another time.

Hero had a sudden blind and utterly ridiculous stab of jealousy. Did Annie, when she showed up, do the same thing for Mr. Holworthy that Ruth Lesley did for Peter Fairweather? And as he realised the utter stupidity of the emotion his gorge against himself rose again.

"Ooh!" gurgled Princess Devi. "Hallo, Mary! Don't you look pretty tonight. All pretty for your Daddy, ain't you?"

The anger drained from Hero, and he was cold, and alert.

"Princess going to give pretty Mary a kiss—there!"

The room suddenly resounded to a young and silvery laugh. It did not emanate from the moronic Princess Devi. It was the infectious laughter of a child. Hero was conscious that all his nerve ends were throbbing.

Princess Devi spoke once more. "Daddy Constable, your Mary is here. I'se going now. Come to see your Mary, Daddy

Constable. But you mustn't touch her. If you are a *good* Daddy, Mary will kiss you. Good-bye now," and the tambourine rattling became fainter and was gone. Nothing stirred, no one moved. Someone or something whispered "Daddy! Daddy!"

Like a person who sits in a theatre and is aware, yet not wholly so, that the lighting has been subtly changed, Hero experienced the feeling that it had, before he was certain or saw what was now revealed. There was a faint, phosphorescent glow before the cabinet whose outline was now dimly seen, and settled in front of it upon the floor, her legs curled beneath her, her hands in her lap was the figure of a child. At least this was the firm impression made upon Hero by the shape, for it was too dark to judge or note any detail.

There was a noise at Hero's left, and then dimly he perceived the hulking body of the professor, risen to his feet and shambling forward towards the materialisation of his dead daughter.

The room had gone quiet now except for the usual noises of the entranced medium, and even these had been reduced to a faint whimpering. For an instant, the bulk of Professor Constable was silhouetted against the diffused and concealed red lighting. He sank to his knees before the figure which had emerged from the cabinet.

"Mary!" he cried, and in his voice was all his love and yearning for his child. "You've been so long coming . . ."

"I'm here now, Daddy!" Fairweather/Hero marvelled. The voice of Mary Constable was that of a well-bred child and had the true, eager breathlessness of the very young girl.

"Don't move, Daddy, I want to kiss you. In case They won't let me come again. Hold still now."

There was a change in the position of the faint figure before the cabinet and then a light cry, "Oh Daddy! Prickles!" followed by the silver laughter and Professor Constable laughed too, as though he were alone in the room.

The hair at the nape of Hero's neck was beginning to rise. Evidently "prickles" was a family joke, perhaps when Constable had not shaved closely enough. There was a slight sound as though there might have been the lightest of kisses and a sob from Constable.

In God's name! Hero thought, *Why do they force him to this in front of all of these yahoos? Why don't they let him into the cabinet for his rendezvous, decently concealed from view?* That he should even question this became an immediate indication to Hero of how addled he was. Witnesses were wanted to corroborate both what Professor Constable had seen and heard, to confirm his conviction as to the return of his child.

From the very beginning, when the affair had been unfolded to him, Hero had wondered why the series of messages from Mary Constable had been passed to her father in open seance, to the point where Woodmanston was able to record them or remember them when the lights went up. Hero now realised that the messages, even if heard individually or put together and read in sequence, would mean nothing to any of those there for none of them knew the project upon which Constable was engaged or that in any way he was a security risk. It was not until Dr. Ferguson had reread the sequence of messages *after* the FBI had come to consult him regarding Constable's attendance of the seances that anyone had suspected the brilliance and subtlety of the plot. A layman hearing or reading them would put them down to the kind of thing usually encountered in spirit messages—talk of "them" on the other side, the happiness or unhappiness of those passed on and their reflections upon the sordidness of life upon earth compared to the goodness and advancement upon the other planes. This was stock spiritualist stuff. Nobody would notice that it was being given a dangerous twist and that not so much a brainwashing was going on as a laundering of Samuel Constable's ethics and honour to the point where he could no longer recognise them.

The voice of a child again penetrated the darkness. "They were angry today, Daddy. It's so awful when They're angry for They're so good and wise and I must obey Them. They said you must work for us over here, Daddy, or I should not be allowed to come to see you. They said you would know how."

"Mary!" Constable cried, without either shame or embarrassment, "my darling!"

"Daddy, I love you! Don't let Them take me away. They only want the world to be good. They have sent you another message."

"What is it, Mary?"

"You *are* your brother's keeper. I don't understand it."

"My God!" said Constable. "I do."

"Good-bye, Daddy! I must go now."

"Will you come again, Mary?"

"I don't know, Daddy. You must make Them let me by obeying them. You want to see me happy, don't you?"

"Will you kiss me again, Mary?"

"Not any more, Daddy. They don't want me to."

Her voice had become perceptibly fainter. "They're calling me. Good-bye, Daddy! Help me."

There then came a great, gasping cry from the medium in the cabinet which startled all of the intense and silent listeners into shifting and rustling in their seats. When the shock had been assimilated, the faint figure before the cabinet was gone and Professor Constable had risen and was groping his way back to his seat, and there was the noise of his heavy body settling into it. Hero felt the breeze of his passage on his cheek. And there was a second sensation for an instant, half realised, half imagined, perhaps, and it filled Alexander Hero with the utmost horror. It was olfactory. In his nostrils was the faintest suspicion of the curious scent that had clung to the hair and garment of Ruth Lesley, as though some of the lingering fragrance had been picked up by Constable.

Was it real? Or was it a memory smell, left in his nostrils as sometimes odours remain with one long after their cause has been removed. Which? Hero's mind for an instant entertained the thought: *Were Ruth Lesley and Mary Constable by some strange transformation one and the same? Tall, slender, sensuous woman into small, gentle, tender child?* He reflected it. Was the little girl then truly a phantom?

"Lights!" bawled Bessmer, so loudly and unexpectedly that one of the women near by screamed, and Hero felt his nerves jump. With dramatic suddenness all the lights came on, dazzling the pupils of their eyes and simultaneously, through some release, the four curtained walls of the cabinet fell to the ground, revealing the table with the instruments still on it and Mother Bessmer roped to her chair, head lolled back, her face slightly empurpled, her tongue protruding, eyes rolled up within the lids so that only the whites showed. She seemed to be half retching, half strangling. There was no one else in the vicinity, and there appeared to be no place where anyone could have gone.

"That's all," said Bessmer. "The power has gone out of her. Untie her. Some water, Pratt."

Woodmanston rushed to release her bonds. Bessmer held up her head as Pratt arrived with a glass. And Mother Bessmer came to, with a "Where am I?" performance.

Alexander Hero tried to collect his scattered wits. The seance was over.

Hero wanted out. He needed fresh air. And above all, he wished to be gone from that room and away not only from the Bessmers but from those people who would now, he was certain, paw over his experience, question him about it, drag it forth and certainly destroy whatever curious beauty and excitement still lingered in his mind from it. Also he had the feeling that he would not be able to look Constable in the face for the moment and hoped he would be gone quickly or that he himself could make his escape, even though a part of his mission was to learn more about him. With the lights up the man *must* be embarrassed.

There was some milling about, under cover of which Hero felt he would be able to leave quietly, particularly as an admiring cluster was beginning to form around the grim figure of Mother Bessmer, who was mopping her face with a handkerchief. The ubiquitous Pratt had already removed the props and folded up and taken away the curtains of the cabinet and the room had become quite ordinary, though nonetheless repulsive. The double doors between the seance room and the parlour had been rolled back. Hero knew that he ought to be prying about where the cabinet had been, looking for means of egress, sliding panels or trap doors, but he thought that would do the next time. He began to edge unobtrusively towards the door. He never made it. There was yet another trial stored up for him.

"Hey there, friend Fairweather!" Bessmer was bellowing. "Not so fast. I guess maybe I forgot to tell you the custom around here. Now we have refreshments. Come along back here and enjoy yourself."

It was true. Pratt had produced some trays of sickly-looking fruit punch, sandwiches, and highly coloured petits fours. Those present were already helping themselves and standing about with their glasses in one hand, cakes in the other, munching and chatting as though five minutes ago they had not believed themselves in communication with the beyond.

Worst of all, Professor Constable was amongst them, balancing some punch and a sandwich. Mother Bessmer was stuffing herself and Hero heard her say, "When the power goes out of me I get gosh-awful hungry."

The reason for the party was obvious. Relaxed through the social contact and flattered to be allowed to remain and meet the Bessmers upon equal footing, the sitters would be off their guard and in the chit-chat reveal unconsciously further information about themselves, their families or their problems, which would be used and thrown back at them at the next seance, to bind them more tightly in the toils of the pair. As to why a man like Constable should permit himself to be dragooned by the Bessmers into remaining for their ghastly social, Hero was certain he was afraid to leave for fear of offending them. And Hero reasoned that it was probably at just such gatherings, while he was still emotionally upset, that Constable would let fall those items that he was convinced were secret between only his daughter and himself. There might, in fact, be almost an unconscious compulsion upon him to do so.

"Have you met Professor Constable, my dear Fairweather?"

Charles Woodmanston was saying and made the introduction which Constable acknowledged with no more than a sharp glance from under his thick eyebrows and a half grunt. "The Professor had a splendid contact tonight. Really splendid! The dear little creature was quite plain and the voice as clear as ever. You must tell us about yours, Fairweather. It isn't often one gets to go inside the cabinet. We are dying to hear. Was there a manifestation?"

It was agony for Hero to reclaim Fairweather again and caused him to stammer, "Yes—well, I mean I'm not sure—I think so. There was something or someone. It is the first time I have ever . . ."

Holworthy chimed in, "It takes a bit of getting used to, but you'll be coming back again."

"We hope so. We hope so," interposed Bessmer jovially and the dreadful party spirit accelerated.

Fairweather stammered, "Yes indeed. May I?"

"Of course! Delighted!" boomed Bessmer and clapped Hero fraternally on the shoulder. "Mother, Mr. Fairweather's going to be one of our regulars while he's here."

Hero was aware that Constable had thrown him another look from beneath his brows. He still felt embarrassed in the presence of the man, if for no other reason, then, for him; embarrassment and something very much like a deep pity. It was bitter to be compelled to see him in these surroundings, submitting to whatever was required to maintain what he was convinced was his contact with his child.

Hero managed to enter an orbit that took him away from the neighbourhood of Constable, even though it landed him with the two widows, who were somewhat disgruntled because the messages from their husbands that night had been slightly cavalier. Thereafter he positioned himself near the door of the parlour, so that when released he might be one of the first to escape. He tried to close his ears to all the familiar shop talk about ectoplasm, secondary planes, clairvoyance, astral bodies, and spirit magnetism and pull himself together.

Arnold Bessmer clapped his hands and then held up his arms for silence. "All right, friends, that's all. It's been a great evening. I hope everyone is satisfied. I think you will all agree with me that Mother Bessmer has earned her rest tomorrow and Sunday. We will meet again at the same time on Monday night. Pratt will give you your cards on the way out and arrange for your contributions. Go to church on Sunday, folks, and pray. God bless you all. Good night, good night."

Hero was first to the door as he had planned. The man Pratt was seated at a small table with the white, initialled cards. He handed one to Fairweather with his name on it.

"About the contribution . . ." Fairweather said.

The chunky bruiser looked up and said, "A grand from now on, the boss says." And again Fairweather was simply staggered by the impudence of it. He managed to stammer, "A-all right. I'll have it Monday," and turned away.

"In cash," the man called after him.

Hero found himself hauling in great gulps of the pleasant night air into his lungs, but he was still badly shaken by the implications of the operation and the colossal and unmitigated nerve of this pair. Nor was he one iota closer to the brain or the body behind Mary Constable, or who or what had made her hand, or how. He descended the stairs and, through sheer mental confusion, instead of turning east, where a few steps would have brought him to the broad avenue paralleling the park and he could have picked up a taxi back to his hotel, he turned to the right, westward, down Ninety-first Street, past the rows of silent, old-fashioned, brownstone houses such as he had just quit, in the direction of Broadway. His hands were shoved deep into the pockets of his light topcoat and, as he walked, he was thinking furiously.

He had not gone far when he was aware of footsteps behind him. His ear picked up their rhythm and he noted that they were hurrying. He tried walking somewhat faster and the footsteps behind him quickened too. Someone was definitely trying to catch up with him.

The street was well lighted, there were passersby on the other side, moving in both directions and Hero did not consider any possibility of an attack upon him. He was not anxious to be accosted but short of breaking into a run there was no avoiding his follower, so he slowed sufficiently to let him come abreast.

"Ah, Fairweather," said Professor Constable, "I see you are going my way."

CHAPTER VIII

Nightcap with Professor Constable

It was a wrench for Hero to pull himself back into the personality of Fairweather. He had formed something of a dislike for this weak-minded, mooning fellow and had shed him with relief upon gaining the street, only now to have to summon him back hastily with all his memories and clad, he hoped, in not too transparent a tissue of lies. He was also aware that to hoax a pair of semi-literates on what a Cambridge lecturer might be like was one thing; to pull the same wool over the eyes of a man like Constable was another.

As they fell into step side by side, Constable said, "Wood-manston tells me you lecture at Cambridge. What subject?"

Hero was grateful now for the intelligence of the cover which had been suggested. He had spent four years up at Kings a decade ago, involved in a most erratic selection of reading. Ten years marks but few changes in a great university, and somehow one keeps track. Hero answered, "Applied psychology," and then added, "Churchill College. We're the upstarts." Hero had reasoned swiftly: Churchill College had been founded in 1960. If Constable had been to Cambridge it was unlikely he would have been there recently.

"What was *your* college?" Constable asked.

"Kings," Fairweather replied. Hero was on firm ground there, for he remembered it inside and out.

"How's old Underhill?" Constable asked.

"Retired," Fairweather replied. "He conducts interminable quarrels through the columns of the newspapers."

"He was my tutor in hydrodynamics some thirty years ago. He must be over eighty now. He was never entirely sound, you know," Constable commented.

Fairweather said, "That's what Professor Heisinger said, when he reviewed Underhill's latest book. They are having rather a row in *The Times* at the moment. Everyone's hoping they will meet in public."

Constable laughed, and it had the ring of a man at ease in whom not unpleasant memories had been aroused. He continued to chat amiably about places and people he had known during his time of study at Cambridge, as they crossed Amsterdam Avenue and on to the corner of Broadway. There they stopped and stood for a moment, in that kind of pregnant, embarrassed silence of two people who did not know how to take leave of one another, who did not particularly wish to do so, but because they were strangers could not manage to bridge the gap.

Constable threw Fairweather another of those curiously penetrating looks and after a moment's hesitation said, "I understand that you had—a contact tonight."

Hero was now certain that Constable had deliberately followed him and wanted to talk to him. It seemed too good an opportunity to miss. He replied, "If you mean was there someone—yes. I am almost certain of it. I have never experienced anything like it . . ."

Constable said, "I wonder if you would care to have a nightcap with me. There is probably some beer on ice. I don't live very far from here. I'd be delighted if . . ."

"How very kind," said Peter Fairweather. "Gladly."

Constable hailed a taxi and they rode in silence to 113th Street and a narrow, three-storeyed house of white stone with bow windows, situated between Broadway and Riverside Drive. The professor let them in with his key and led Hero up a flight of stairs to his study located at the back. He said, "Make yourself comfortable, I'll see what's in the fridge. There ought to be some beer, if that's all right with you, and Jane usually leaves something to eat." He grinned suddenly, "I don't know about you, but the Bessmer offering doesn't do much for me."

It was the first time that Constable had mentioned the pair by name and Hero was surprised at the offhandedness and even slight mockery in the tone. The scientist said, "Cigarettes in this box, cigars in that one. Help yourself. I shan't be a minute."

Hero heard him descending to the kitchen and pantry below and turned his attention to the study. This was a fair-sized room which took up the whole width of the house, one entire side of which was lined with books from floor to ceiling. It was attractively furnished and contained a large, flat-topped early American desk, some antique chests of drawers, several deep leather chairs, a leather couch, and two steel filing cabinets. On the walls were two paintings by Henri Lebasque and a Grandma Moses. Near the desk there stood a pedestal on top of which there was a glass case of ebony wood. Inside the case was a support of black velvet and upon it, palm upwards, the fingers shaped in a curiously moving attitude of supplication, was the perfect wax cast of the wrist and hand of a young girl.

The Englishman would have given much to have been able to make a close examination of it but dared not, for he had no way of knowing how long Constable would be and he must not be caught showing unusual interest, since he was not supposed to know of its existence or what it purported to be. Instead he wandered about looking at the paintings, the man's-world knickknacks, including the usual photographs of conferring of doctorates with Constable at the receiving end and one even that he was able to recognise as taking place at Cambridge.

As Hero knew, the science of cybernetics was still so recent that specific literature upon the subject was limited and was represented more by its components, physiological and mechanical. There were books on anatomy and a number of treatises on the nerve systems of animals and humans, as well as the latest publications on electronics, computers, servo systems and automation. There was a book on cybernetics published in 1948 by a mathematician, Norbert Wiener, and Hero smiled to himself at the coincidence of names and wondered what the FBI Wiener would say to his swift penetration of Constable's citadel. The remainder of the library was diverse and showed interest in all forms of literature from classics to plays, poetry and modern novels. Returning to the scientific section, Hero reflected how small was his own knowledge of the subject and wondered whether he had been neglecting something which in any way might be made to apply to his own curious profession.

A familiar name caught his eye in gold lettering on a green spine, "S. H. Constable" and he pulled down the book and opened it to the title page, *"The Machine, Master or Servant? A Study of Communication with the Inanimate by Samuel Hale Constable, Wykoff Professor Industrial Engineering, Columbia University."* This was followed by a formidable string of degrees and fellowships. The publication date was 1959. Hero thumbed through it and found himself in a welter of equations and diagrams, most of which at first glance were unintelligible to him, but the reading of a paragraph or two of the text showed a clear style. He felt that probably no one had progressed further in this field than Constable—at least he had not heard of anyone.

The beginning of a chapter on the ills to which giant computers were subject so fascinated Hero that he did not even hear the return of Constable, until the scientist appeared in the doorway, bearing a tray containing four bottles of light lager beer, glasses, and a dish covered with a moist napkin. He set it down on the desk, came across, and looked over Hero's shoulder to the book in his hands.

"That!" he snorted angrily. "The damned thing's out of date. I've told my publishers to withdraw it, but they're idiots. Here, if you're interested . . ." He went to one of the filing cabinets, pulled open a drawer and produced a thick, typewritten manuscript which he threw onto the desk, and for a moment Hero wondered, horrified, whether the man could be so unsecurity-minded as to have produced Operation Foxglove.

Constable soon relieved his mind. The script turned out to be an updating of the same book, and he picked out the chapter which Hero had been reading, to which was attached a wholly different set of charts. "Here," he said, "you can see the difference. The entire input system has been changed because of the expanded memory section." And with a finger he traced a portion of the chart as though it were as clear as day to Hero, instead of an almost unintelligible tangle of symbols for leads, wires, connections, and transistor posts.

For a moment Constable himself was lost in contemplation of his work muttering, "The damn fools! If they don't hurry *this* will be superseded." He slapped the pages together again, tossed the batch into the filing cabinet drawer, and rolled it shut. "Let's eat," he said.

He removed the napkin from the dish, revealing appetising sandwiches of roast beef, chicken, and cheese, and he had one of each with evident enjoyment, as did Hero, washing the food down with long, smacking draughts of lager, emptying half a glass at a time. When they had finished he said, "Will you have a cigarette or a cigar? I like a pipe myself."

Fairweather slapped his side pocket and said, "If I might also . . . ?" and produced his briar.

"Good man!" said Constable. "Here, try this mixture." He pushed the tobacco jar across. Both men filled, tamped, and lit.

Constable said, "I should be interested if you wouldn't mind, in hearing something of your experience tonight." He again threw the from-under-the-brows look at Hero and added, "I understand that you recently suffered a—an unhappy bereavement."

Fairweather reflected that Charles Woodmanston was better than radio or television for spreading news. Aloud he said quietly, "Yes. I lost my fiancée shortly before we were to have been married." There would be no theatrics for the professor.

"Was she there tonight?" asked Constable.

"Yes—I think so."

"But you are not certain? You were not absolutely sure?"

Fairweather took time before replying. He sucked at his pipe, blew out a cloud of smoke, examined the stem and then he said, "When it's the first time—when in one second all of your preconceived notions are overthrown; when you are required to make the transition from the world of the living into a universe perhaps of the living dead, you rather tend to doubt the evidence of your own senses."

Constable nodded. He said, "It's a shock at the beginning." Then he repeated, "Was she there?" And this time Fairweather thought he detected a note almost of entreaty. He thought: *he wants to be told she was. He must be told. This is why I have been asked here.* Aloud he replied with quiet simplicity, "I thought so."

"Materialised?"

"Perhaps."

"Her voice?"

"As nearly as I can remember. It was a whisper."

"Touch?" Constable queried.

And now to Fairweather there was no mistaking the anxiety on Constable's heavy features or the importance he placed upon the reply. Fairweather hesitated for a moment and then let his voice drop the merest fraction of a decibel, "I felt contact . . ."

"Like flesh and blood?" said Constable, and his voice too was lowered and intense, "And the fragrance . . ."

The suppressed Alexander Hero sent up a warning to his alter ego Fairweather. Wasn't he making a grave mistake in humouring Constable? Wasn't he with every confirmation of his own supposed experience solidifying Constable's belief in the phenomenon that had been produced for him? Wasn't this the very reason that Constable had followed him and asked him to his home, because there must yet be some infinitesimal lingering of doubt somewhere in his mind, something gnawing at him which yet prevented him from taking that last, fatal step into which he was being lured?

The dilemma was intense and fraught with a most awful danger. Yet he knew that if he denied the contact and maintained scepticism he would very soon be shown the door. For it would not be what Constable wanted to hear. And after all, his job was to remain there as long as possible, get to know the man and learn all he could about him.

"Like flesh and blood," Fairweather repeated.

"What happened?" Constable asked. Petulance had crept into his voice. "I am never allowed inside the cabinet with her as you were. She tells me I am not to touch her. Were you caressed? Did you feel the brush of lips past your cheek? Did she whisper intimate secrets of the past to you, that only the two of you could have known?"

Fairweather reflected that there was no need at this point to arouse the conflict of jealousy in Constable by revealing the full extent of the "contact" that had been his. "Yes," he said. "I am very badly shaken. I don't know what to think or believe."

"Ah, you don't! Neither did I at first. But believe me, sir, I wanted to as much as you. Is it incontrovertible proof you must have before you can be certain? Then look behind you."

Fairweather turned about in the deep chair, not permitting his gaze to fall anywhere and looking rather as though he expected to see an apparition.

"In the cabinet," Constable directed and arose. Fairweather did likewise and the two went and stood on either side of it. "That," said the professor, "is the right hand of my only daughter, Mary. She was ten years old when she died, a little over a year ago. I asked for proof of her return. She left me this."

Fairweather said nothing, but regarded the thin shell of the wax hand with morbid fascination. It was translucent and pearly in colour and seemed to shine on its background of black velvet. It was innocent and touching and yet a wicked mystery, a problem he did not know how to solve, a challenge, and an enigma. It seemed that in every investigation he should be dogged by one phenomenon that appeared to be inexplicable, that he should be teased by a glimpse of that long sought breakthrough that would change the world if only it could be proven beyond any dispute or doubt. What kind of proof was there here, except that as a magician himself and expert at illusions of every kind, he could think of no way to produce or duplicate it?

"They had prepared for it. There was a bowl of melted wax and another of cold water. She came, I saw her figure. She plunged her little hand into the wax . . ."

"Was there light?"

"Eh?" said Constable. "There was at the beginning when she came. Perhaps later there wasn't. But I heard the splash of water and she laughed and said, 'Don't 'plash Daddy.' It was a secret little thing between us when she was a baby and I used to splash her in her bath. After she said good-bye, the lights went up almost immediately, and the hand was there upon the table, dripping wet as though the spirit had hardly departed from it."

He continued to look upon the object without speaking. "Would you like to examine it more closely?" Constable asked. With a small key from his chain he unlocked the cabinet and lifted out the black velvet base with the hand. He passed it to Fairweather, who marvelled genuinely at its perfections, the slenderness of the wrist, the fine markings of the lines of the palm, and the delicacy of the tapering fingers curled so naturally.

"The fingerprints are hers," Professor Constable asserted, giving each word a special emphasis.

Hero had no need of a magnifying glass to see the lines of the loops, whorls, and ridges etched upon the inside of the cast. Something of which he was not quite certain was bothering him. He asked, "Were your daughter's palm prints taken at the same time as the fingerprints were?"

Constable replied, "No, they never do. What difference would it have made?" Then he continued, his voice suddenly harsh with emotion, "Perhaps I ought to tell you. The child was cremated. I couldn't bear the thought of her . . ." He left the sentence uncompleted. But when he took the hand from Fairweather and replaced it there was an expression of satisfaction on his face. "Proof positive," he said as he snapped the lid down and relocked it. Then suddenly looking at Fairweather sharply he said, "There have been spirit hands before this. Did you know?"

Alexander Hero almost replied, "Yes, I did."

"No," Fairweather answered.

"Kluski in Vienna, around 1910," Constable said, and there was scorn in his voice. "They were crude fakes as were the ones that fooled Conan Doyle. Marjorie, the Boston medium of forty years ago, was better," he continued. "She produced fingerprints." Constable then laughed loudly. "They turned out to be those of her dentist, a man still living at the time."

Hero was astonished that Constable had already read and reviewed all the cases of prior wax spirit hands and the methods by which they were produced. Yet it was what any intelligent man would have done. His surprise was that the scientist had taken the risk of a disillusioning discovery. And, of course, the damnable thing was that the gamble had come off, for as he himself knew none of the prior cases were applicable to the manifestation of the hand of Mary Constable.

Professor Constable rapped the cabinet with his knuckles, "But this child was dead and ashes. This is her living hand from another plane."

He's caught, Hero reflected. *Bemused, trapped.* The old story of the man of science hoisted upon the petard of so-called scientific proof. Yet, might not he himself, Peter Fairweather, have been similarly taken in had he been real and there had been a genuine Ruth Lesley? Or Alexander Hero, for that matter, for all of his knowledge, prying, proving and testing and the most curious unexpected and unapposite thought suddenly crossed his mind. What if something were to happen to his step-sister, Meg? Would he then be the same cool, reasoning, sceptical brain?

"Well, what do you think?" Constable asked.

Fairweather tapped some loose ash from his pipe and said, "Quite frankly, I am afraid I was bothered by Chief Thundering-Cloud and little Devi, and I am wondering how you . . ."

Professor Constable threw back his great lion's head and roared with laughter. "Oh," he said, "we don't pay any attention to Mother Bessmer's little jokes."

Hero was startled by the astonishing ambivalence of the man

and his ability to see so clearly one part of the picture. Yet, Hero knew that the most difficult and unapproachable of the converts to spiritualism were those who were able to admit the occasional hoax but remained all the more steadfast and unshakeable in their beliefs. Amongst them, Sir Arthur Conan Doyle, Flammarion, and Sir Oliver Lodge, who time and time again had their noses rubbed into the truth and yet refused to see. He decided to test this out still further.

"The contributions to their church . . ." he said and then hesitated significantly.

Constable looked at him almost quizzically, out from under his bushy eyebrows. "Did they sting you?" he asked.

Hero said, "Twenty-five hundred dollars."

A look almost of satisfaction came into Constable's face and he said, "Well, you've probably got it. I pay them a couple of hundred dollars a week." And he added with some asperity, as though suddenly angry that he had allowed himself to reveal financial details, "Man, how can you put a price on the return of the dead? If you had a dying child would you quibble over the doctor's fee? Mother Bessmer . . ."

Fairweather had a moment of revulsion himself at the thought of the woman and cried, "Mother Bessmer! You never knew my fiancée, sir. Why would she choose to come to me through such a . . ."

Constable did not let him finish, "Hell's fire, man!" and he pounded the desk with his fist, "You never knew my daughter! She was . . ." His face had become suffused from the choler with which anger had afflicted him, and he was unable to speak of his child as he would have wished, to tell what she was like and what she had meant to him. Instead his lips trembled and his brow furrowed and when he continued, something quite different came out. "It's the power, man!" he cried. "The old bag's got the power. She didn't ask for it, but she's got it. It's no chooser of persons when it comes. Anybody might have it—you might have it yourself, only you wouldn't know about it unless you tried it, or discovered it by accident. I haven't got it. God knows

I've tried. The spirits have to have the power to enable them to communicate and come through. She supplies it. What difference does it make whether or not she stinks? Here . . ." He concluded abruptly, went over to the door, and flipped the switch leaving the room in total darkness.

Hero thought: *Good Lord, what's the man up to? Is he going to try something on?*

Constable's voice cut through, "There are five lamps in this room. Can you see any of them?"

"No."

"Would you know where they were if you had not seen them, if you had entered the room in the dark?"

"No."

The switch clicked again, the lamps glowed. "Now you see them all right. Power, man! They won't shine without power and as long as the voltage and wattage is correct *they* don't give a damn where the power comes from."

All the anger had suddenly gone out of Professor Constable's face and was reflected by a most curious and indefinable expression as he shambled to his chair, slumped into it again, and sat with his head sunk on his chest and his long legs extended before him, just as Hero was aware that the word "they" seemed to be lingering in the air between them, as though it had taken form. It was "they" who were threatening to banish Mary Constable.

Alexander Hero looked down upon the man in the chair and saw through to the appalling conceit and overweening ego that was leading him to prepare to sell out his country and his people to satisfy the father hunger in him, the loss of his own immortality in the person of his daughter. It must have been like playing God for this man to reflect upon the power he was conferring upon one nation and one people. He must have thought himself as sitting atop Olympus making a Jovian decision. But the sell-out would not be a matter of conscience but of selfishness.

Constable pulled himself out of his thoughts and his posture, looked over at his guest and said, "You're not convinced, are you?"

Fairweather replied, "I shall go back again on Monday."

Constable said, "I'll see you there. It is difficult at first, until you come to know. I saw your face when the lights went up. You will have proof with all the little things, the things she will say, the secrets between you that no one else could know—such things as Mary tells me."

Fairweather nodded and said, "Yes. I heard," and then added, "What a curious thing for a ten-year-old child to say."

"What?" Constable said sharply. "What was that?"

Fairweather said, "You *are* your brother's keeper."

Constable flared up, outraged. "It wasn't *she* who said it. It was They."

Fairweather simply looked the silent question at him without speaking.

Constable chose to answer Fairweather's unspoken "And who are They?" by another question. "What do you or I or anyone know of what lies in the beyond, except what those who have passed over have told us? If I can flip a message to the stars and the farthest galaxies beyond to throw a solar switch, so can whatever or whoever or whichever is out there communicate with us. Why wouldn't the spirits of the dead retain their consciences? Do you remember the lines from Elizabeth Browning's *Aurora Leigh*, 'When we disavow being keeper of our brother, we are his Cain'? I was being reminded." He looked at Fairweather gravely, sucking on his pipe and then removed it pointing at him with the stem, "Do you know how awful it is out there; how far, how cold, how dark, how lonely? You, my friend, must have your moments of terror when you peer into the human mind. Could you imagine some of the horror of space into which we probe, the heat, the chill multiplied to infinity, like the nonboundaries of the universe?"

Hero thought: *He is terrified of what they have threatened to do to the spirit of his child. They will win unless I can stop it.*

"You were very kind to come," Professor Constable was saying.

Fairweather realised that Constable was standing and the interview was over. He too arose. "Perhaps we can have a chat again another time," Constable concluded. "I shall be most interested to know what results you obtain on Monday."

They moved towards the door and had to pass by the cabinet from which shone the pearly, translucent hand, and for an instant Constable's gaze rested upon it becoming melting, fond, and relaxed. He pointed at it with his pipe stem and said with a little smile that was almost mischievous, "You cannot explain away that, you know." Then they passed on to good nights at the door, where Constable said, "It's just half a block over to Broadway where you will be able to pick up a cab."

The door closed behind him and Hero walked up the hill from the river in the direction indicated. He looked at his watch. It was half past two in the morning. Thirty seconds later his tooth hit him a wallop that staggered him, nearly knocking him off the kerb of the pavement. It was a swooping, swinging pain that came out of nowhere to assail him full force, and whose impact was not diminished because it was unexpected and he had quite forgotten about his dental problem. He had been told that it might blow up, but no one had forewarned him of this kind of stabbing agony. As he pulled himself together to continue to Broadway, he was already mentally in the chair of Dr. Hofstetter, the dentist whose address his own surgeon had given him, should continued treatment be necessary in New York, and was deciding to call first thing in the morning for an appointment, when the pain left him as suddenly as it had come.

When he reached Broadway there was only the slightest mandatory echo throbbing in his cheek. Constable had been right, there were plenty of cabs cruising at that late hour. He stopped one and directed it to his hotel. By the time he arrived, there was not so much as a lingering trace any longer of that sudden, colossal toothache.

CHAPTER IX

Nihil Est Demonstrandum

Sleep, however, would not come. Too much had happened to him, too many impressions had crowded in upon him since he had stepped off the plane at Idlewild less than eighteen hours before. And now to this was added the realisation that he had just spent considerable time in the company of a man who was contemplating an action which was fraught with the most terrible consequences for the Western world and could affect the lives of millions of innocent persons.

Vis-à-vis Constable, the full horror of what he proposed to do and the changes it would bring to free nations had not registered. He had been intent upon maintaining his cover; Constable had appeared no more odd or abnormal than any bereaved human grasping at the straw held out by the charlatans of spiritualism. But now that he was alone, the monstrous enormity of the possible conspiracy was making its impact and he remembered attitudes, expressions, things unsaid but nevertheless present in the man's mind during his interview with the Professor, against the background revealed by Ferguson and the Intelligence agents. Samuel Hale Constable was not just another sorrowing father *cum* chuckleheaded, purblind scientist diddled by a pair of modern Cagliostros. He was a time bomb fused to go off at any moment to the enslavement or destruction of an entire civilisation unless one could put a stop to it by bringing him to his senses before it was too late.

The implications brought him leaping out of his bed, chilled, his teeth chattering. He was angry for letting himself be manoeuvred into this position, as well as with Ferguson for his bland assumption that Hero would be able to solve the problem with a wave of his hand. He also resented Ferguson's protection of Constable. Action should have been taken long ago. Hero recognised the academician's approach to the situation. Wars were never any of their concern until they had become history. If Constable was planning to defect or pass on his discovery to the Russians he was no better than any other traitor and deserved to be seized and confined.

At this point Hero paused to laugh bitterly at himself. He had been thinking along the same lines as General Augstadt. However, Hero's sudden appreciation of the dilemma had done nothing to alter it. It was just as important to the West that Constable complete his work for the Americans as it was that he be kept from spilling it to the Communists. In the end, Ferguson was right. The man must be brought around to accept disillusionment by a demonstration that his "proof" was no proof at all. But how much time was there left?

Hero wanted to talk to someone and for a moment contemplated putting in a transatlantic call to his stepsister. In addition to her skills with cameras she had a cool, analytical mind and was devoted to him. He resisted the temptation which he knew arose out of panic and instead, to calm his nerves, sat down and wrote her a promised letter.

"Megs darling:

If you are expecting to hear about New York, Fifth Avenue, its shops and smartly dressed women—*pas ce soir*, Josephine. So far I have seen the interior of several offices, and two private houses, one of them the lair of a very nasty pair of pseudo-spiritualists fitted out with most modern equipment, and that is all. The rest of the cast includes the usual clots, fish-eyes and barmies you run into at a seance, and that is my America to date. Oh yes, there is a colour television set in my room, a telephone in the Aunt and the maids and valets carry walkie-talkies.

"Those with whom I am working regard me as being weak-minded, loony, or some new kind of British queer and consider my intervention in this affair a major catastrophe. They have no use for sperrits or those who hunt them and for the moment are suffering me like the idiot child about whom there is not much one can do.

"By now you will have penetrated the fixed grin and twigged that I am up against something that has me worried stiff. I cannot even write you about it. The problem, briefly: produce not only the improbable, but the potentially impossible and within from 24 to 48 hours. The loser's end on this one is not even to be thought of. The least of them is that I return to London with my tail between my legs having been made to look a proper charlie to my American friends. And after that, the balloon goes up.

"No, my pet. There is nothing you can do but prepare a rosette of crêpe to adorn my brow for brains gone West. I have racked them and racked them. Tomorrow I shall pay a visit to Paul Cryder. The Elliotts, who run that shop in the Strand, put me on to him. Their opposite number here. I don't expect much will come out of it. Once you begin grasping at straws, that's what you get—straws. On the other hand, he might just show me something so elementary that I shall feel even more of a simpleton than I do now, but a relieved one. Put down that suitcase, sis. 'Have camera, will travel' doesn't apply here. How I wish it did.

"On this note of tender yearning I retire to my patent, Jumbo Inner Vi-Spring Bridge Suspension Bed with Dream-Flote Mattress,

Love,
SANDRO."

Hero felt somewhat better after he had signed and sealed this. Even summoning his stepsister to mind for a one-sided conversation on paper relaxed him. It was significant of their relationship that he had written her nothing about the kiss in the dark and the disturbing effect it had had upon him.

At eight the telephone at his bedside rang. Surfacing heavily,

Hero answered it. It was Wiener, making the morning check they had agreed upon. He asked sharply, "You all right?"

"Yes, yes. I got to bed late last night."

"What was it like?" Wiener's anxiety was evident.

Hero had not yet had time to think what he would say, or for that matter even to be clear in his own mind what he felt. He replied, "Inconclusive."

Wiener echoed, "Inconclusive!" He sounded neither happy nor friendly. "I like that! Maybe you'd better drop by."

"Right-o. If you don't mind, I'll have a bath first and some breakfast!" He had drawled this lazily and deliberately, designed to irritate. A better footing than being ordered around by Wiener would have to be established.

"No, no! Sure, sure! When you're ready. I'll be here."

Washing and shaving, Hero reflected upon the report he must make about the events of the night before, including his meeting with Constable. But how much and in what manner? At the end of his breakfast coffee he had not yet reached a conclusion. Discussing the often weird facets of his profession with laymen always presented problems.

There was not so much as a nudge from the tooth which had dealt him such a nasty one the night before or rather that morning, and he even dared experimentally to poke his jaw to see whether it might start up. It didn't. Under the circumstances it seemed silly to bother the dentist. Time enough for that another day, and he put the matter out of his mind.

It was, as Hero had expected, a wrangle. After listening to what Hero had had to tell him of the seance, Wiener, with every evidence of angry and disgusted impatience, was for direct and immediate action. "We take the place," he said. "If we pick the brat up by the scruff of her neck and hold her under Constable's nose, where does he go from there?"

"Out of Operation Foxglove," Hero said.

Wiener stared at him.

"And what if there isn't any brat?" Hero added.

Wiener spat into a wastebasket and said, "Oh, Christ! You make me sick!"

Hero said, almost sympathetically, "I'm afraid a lot of people feel that way about me—if not at the beginning of an investigation then usually halfway through, which is why I insist upon the stipulation that if I take on a job I cannot be dismissed from it win, lose, or draw. Have you the patience to look at this with me, from my point of view?"

Wiener looked sulky, but it was himself with whom he was irritated. He said, "I seem to spend my time insulting you and then apologising. Are all of you British so equable?"

"Speaking for myself, only in connection with my own field. If you were to question my golf handicap or my taste in wines . . ."

Wiener laughed. "All right, I'll listen to you. Start talking."

"If I were asked to define occultism," Hero said reflectively, "I would say it was compounded of wishful thinking, sleight-of-hand, music-hall tricks, the evidence of idiots, coincidences, unreliable reports, greed, human gullibility, and—the unexplained and to a certain extent the unexplainable. Precognition, clairvoyance, thought transference, extrasensory perception and hallucination—do you know how much there remains unanswered where the psychical and psychological appear to merge?"

Wiener drawled, "You're doing the telling."

"Up to now, in my opinion, there has not been a single case proven of the dead returned or the existence of a spirit world."

"Why do you say up to now?"

"Because for me, the next case always remains open until I can shut the door. Until I am able to show how that damned hand was made, the case of Mary Constable remains unproven."

Wiener's thin lips were curling again.

"Besides which," Hero continued, "let's say you rush the place. You still have to get through the door and into the seance room, by which time you would find nothing. Those are slick operators. You might pick up bits of apparatus for working spirits, such as lazy tongs, cheese-cloth drapes, phosphorescent paint, and maybe a trap door or two, but you would not find Mary Constable. And her father would continue to believe, even if the Bessmers were sitting in gaol for fraud or fortune-telling, or whatever you wanted to book them for. He would never forgive you for the raid."

Wiener was looking reflective. "Believe it or not," he said, "the same idea struck me after my infantile outburst, but I was damned if I was going to admit it to you." Hero grinned at him, and the smile was returned. Wiener had a lightning turn from cold to warm which was attractive. He continued, "But supposing you were to grab the little girl next time, always providing that you did not take hold of a handful of air, and turn up whatever it was—child or midget, for Constable's inspection?"

"We don't grab," Hero said.

Wiener commented, "Hell's bells!"

"All it precipitates is an unholy and messy row," Hero explained, "a lot of milling about in the dark, screaming, and clutching, and you accomplish little, except getting your hands into some butcher's tripe they have been selling as ectoplasm or catching the medium wandering about in her nightgown. In the end all you achieve is notoriety. If you chase one medium the clients simply go to another. What we try to do is educate the public."

"And you're aiming to educate Constable?"

"Yes," Hero replied, "I am." And then he added, "Besides which, the Bessmers have a very unpleasant-looking chap working for them and I, not being a story-book detective with muscles, would wind up on the pavement with a thick head and would never get back in again. I can't see much point in that."

Wiener said, "The estimable Pratt, eh?"

It was Hero's turn to look surprised. Wiener smiled sourly and said, "Just because we agreed not to queer Constable's pipe dream doesn't mean we have been sitting around on our asses." He opened a side drawer to his desk and took out a folder. It was bulging with photographs on one side and documents on the other. He said, after consulting it, "Besides the Bessmers there is a cook, Annie Riley, who lives in the house. She's all right. Came from an agency. Previous references O.K. Pratt is an ex-wrestler and ex-con. He came here with the Bessmers from St. Louis. He would give you a roughing around. Otherwise everybody who comes into the house goes out. Clients, applicants, sitters, post-men, delivery boys, you name 'em, we've got 'em."

He pulled out the batch of photographs and shoved them over towards Hero, who at a glimpse could see what they were; day and night shots, the latter made by infra-red light, linked to-gether, of people entering or leaving the Bessmer establishment, either by the front door or the service entrance, with the time of arrival and departure marked. Hero was amused to find amongst them a daylight shot of himself the afternoon before, arriving to apply for admission, as well as night photos of himself coming and going to and from the seance.

"Would you like to order a dozen?" Wiener asked. "We'll give you our special discount."

Then he nodded with his head towards the pictures of the sitters which Hero had spread out. "We've checked on all of them," he said. "They're okay as far as that goes. Ordinary boobs, particularly your friend Woodmanston. We rather thought he might be behind some of this, but he isn't." He frowned and then with a direct and enquiring gaze at Hero he said, "We can't find any trace of either a child or a young girl inside the house, or coming or going."

Hero said, "My ear wouldn't deceive me. It wasn't Mother Bessmer speaking."

Wiener grunted, "Uhuh." Then he looked quizzically at Hero and said, "Well, what about your girl friend? You're not going to try to tell me they can materialise someone who never existed!"

Hero was glad he had held back the information about the shattering embrace and the kiss of "Ruth Lesley" and had merely reported contact of voice and touch. He could imagine what Wiener's shafts of sarcasm would have been. Aloud he said, "I mean to have a dekko at the lady on Monday. I'll have a look at Mary Constable at the same time."

"How?"

Hero produced a small, black tube from his pocket. "Sniper-scope," he said. "Not too efficient, but it works. Mother Bessmer must be using some similar kind of device. The room is probably gimmicked with infra-red or black light. That's how she moves about."

Wiener gave a sigh of relief. "You do believe it's a Commie job, don't you? You were kidding about all that crap about materialisation and the hand?"

"I do certainly think it's a Commie job," Hero said. "I think it is a brilliant, subtle piece of work put up by a bigger intelligence than you will find in that house. But I also wasn't kidding about the crap or the hand. What one thinks doesn't count. It's what one knows that matters."

Wiener said, "The Russian Consulate is just a block or so from here. By God, I'll bet they're laughing up their sleeves at us! Except this will probably have been handled by another crowd, especially infiltrated for it." He hesitated and tapped his teeth with a pencil. "The one thing that puzzles me—that has always puzzled me from the very beginning—is why the Bessmers? Why work through a pair of cheap crooks like that with the whole goddam world at stake—for them just as it is for us."

"I can tell you that," Hero said. "It's because there isn't anything better. That's what most mediums are like, nearly all of them, vicious, vulgar, and rotten. Occasionally you find an amateur who acquires a following and indulges in some cheating just for kicks and prestige. But the Bessmers are your rank and file. And the point is it works; is working. They have hooked Constable, haven't they, so it's good enough." Then he added, "I saw Constable after the seance. As a matter of fact I went home with him and we stayed up until two-thirty."

Wiener sat up in the chair at his desk and said, "Did you now? Well, that's what I call right cosy." But the way he said it showed that for the first time he was impressed with Hero and his abilities. "Is he going to defect?"

Hero said, "Not yet. That would put him out of touch with

the Bessmers and hence out of reach of his child. He would have no guarantee of ever being able to make contact with Mary Constable on the other side of the Iron Curtain. As long as the Bessmers are allowed to work unhindered he will stay."

"Will he sing?" Wiener asked.

"I beg your pardon?"

"Talk," Wiener elucidated, "Make contact with the Russian Embassy some fine day and spill his guts."

"Yes, he will," Hero replied. "Unless we can manage to stop him. It's the hand, you see. He's convinced it's genuine. You can raid that house three times a day, send the Bessmers to gaol, and even confront him with an impersonation, but until you find a way to duplicate . . ."

Wiener cried, "Great God Almighty! A man with Constable's brains and savvy . . ."

"Not to mention ego," Hero added. "You forget the fatal conceit of these chaps. They carry their God around with them whose initials are Q.E.D. They will build an altar in the shape of a gigantic machine, three storeys high costing millions, to be able to chant 'Quod erat demonstrandum' and worship. And at the same time they can be deceived by a magician vanishing an egg or producing a bunch of paper flowers out of their left ears."

Wiener said, "Oh come on, Hero, the mad professor is science fiction and you know it."

"It would be simpler if he were," Hero declared. "All he is endeavouring to do is what man has been trying ever since he came down out of the trees—to banish death. You still pay undertakers to comb the hair, rouge and lipstick the faces of the dead, embalm and dress them to look lifelike. On Sundays we troop out to cemeteries to gaze upon a slab of stone or a mound where the body lies buried. What are we thinking of, the spirit or the flesh?"

Wiener did not reply.

Hero's gaze went to the two children in the photograph on the desk of the FBI man. Wiener followed its line and his eyes suddenly narrowed as he got the message of the glance. Hero said, "Inside Samuel Constable's skull there is an extraordinary

amount of sophisticated grey matter, but his arms still yearn for
the feel of his child. She was taken from him and he desired her
back as she was, warm flesh and blood. They have turned his own
weapon against him and written Q.E.D. to the thing he wanted
most—the resurrection of his child."

Wiener was looking gloomy. "And what do you propose to
do?"

"Change the initials," Hero replied, "to N.E.D."

"Meaning?"

"*Nihil est demonstrandum.*"

Once more Wiener dropped the monosyllable, "How?"

"If I can make a wax hand for him, complete with fingerprints."

Wiener broke in impatiently, "If, if, if! Do you know how it
is done?"

Hero said quietly, "No, but I'm going to find out. That's my
business. That's why Dr. Ferguson sent for me."

Wiener came to a decision. He said, "All right, I won't push
over your applecart—yet. But I want a *quid pro quo*. I'd like you
to arrange to take me to that seance next Monday night. I want
to see and hear for myself."

"And grab?"

Wiener smiled. "If it will make you feel better I'll promise
not to, or create a disturbance . . ."

Hero said, "It will cost money. Particularly to arrange it without an interview with Bessmer first. I think it would be better."

Wiener said, "We've got money."

Hero agreed, "It's a deal!"

Wiener suddenly stuck out his hand, "O.K. Come on, I'll take
you to lunch, then. We'll go to Pietro's on Forty-fifth Street and
let you see what a real American charcoal-grilled steak looks like."

Hero felt that for the first time, at least for the moment, as
though they might be working together.

CHAPTER X

The Magic Shop of Paul Cryder

Hero found what he was looking for in the close-packed Manhattan directory, which afforded the information "Cryder, Paul. Magic eqpt. 43a Cedar Street" with a Worth telephone number. He picked up the instrument to announce himself and then, for no reason he could think of, replaced it and decided simply to drop by instead.

His next impulse was to commandeer a taxi and let himself be wafted in comfort and without strain to the address given, but he conquered that one too. His batteries had been nicely recharged by the charcoal-grilled steak and beer at Pietro's upstairs restaurant, cosily entered through the kitchen, and he was inclined to experiment with the American subway, to familiarise himself more with the city as well as to compare it with the London Underground.

He got out the pocket map and guide to New York he had purchased, and found that Cedar Street was in the downtown, financial section which would correspond to the City in London, only a few blocks between Broadway and the river and not far from that famous street know as Wall, the alley inextricably linked with the Yankee dollar. He ascertained that there was a Wall Street stop for the Lexington Avenue subway and fared forth to a meeting with Paul Cryder, internationally known dealer in magical equipment, stage illusions, etc., known, that is, in the ever shrinking world of stage magicians.

While the steel monster roared, shrieked, and screamed its way downtown beneath the city, swaying, shaking and rattling most alarmingly at what seemed like a maximum speed of a hundred miles an hour, Hero summed up in his mind what he knew about the Cryders.

It was an old firm, perhaps the oldest one in existence, which was why he entertained hopes that somewhere in their files or library, or even tucked away inside the skull of the surviving Cryder, Paul, would be something about wax hands. Perhaps the late Harry Houdini, who had performed such signal service in America in exposing fake mediums, had experimented with this manifestation and left some word behind. If so, Cryder would be the man who might know.

The Cryder firm was founded in 1843 by one Leon Cryderski, a Polish itinerant stage magician and sleight-of-hand artist, recorded as having given exhibitions several years before in New York and Philadelphia. Severely injured in a theatre fire which cost him the flexibility of his hands so necessary to his profession, Cryderski then opened a magic shop on Cedar Street and his descendants and heirs had occupied the premises ever since. As with the Elliotts in London, the shop had enjoyed bonanza days at the turn of the century, when magicians and magic shows flourished and great names among the prestidigitators could fill a theatre for an evening. In the modern era, interest in such shows had slacked off, practically to nonexistence, and like other such firms the Cryderski heirs would have fallen upon hard times.

Somewhere along the line the Americanisation of the name had taken place and the "ski" dropped. The incumbent Paul Cryder would be the great-grandson of the founder. The Elliotts had known him shortly after World War II, when they had visited America. He would be in the neighbourhood of fifty-five now.

The train decelerated into Wall Street from full speed to stop in ten seconds and Hero made his escape before the automatic doors, which closed almost as soon as they opened, could catch him. Once more in the open air and the continuing warm sunshine, Hero orientated himself, soon found the narrow canyon of lower Broadway, paused a moment to admire Trinity Church, humbly tucked away among the skyscrapers like a flower growing in a forest, walked the block or two to Cedar Street, and turned to his left towards the river.

Cedar Street was a backwash left behind by a city that had raced northwards. It contained murky business premises, hardware stores, and dingy cafeterias. Hero passed shops selling cut-rate radios, sporting goods, and stationery. The Cryders' place was located between the store fronts of a dealer in stamps and one in plumbers' supplies.

The sign over it, CRYDER'S MAGIC SHOP, must still have been the original, regilded, but painted in the script style of a century ago. The business indeed had fallen upon evil days, for the windows were so covered with dust and grime as to be almost opaque and contained little but those horrors sold to imbeciles and juvenile delinquents, such as sneeze powder, false noses and moustaches, exploding cigars, and boutonnieres that enable one to squirt water into someone's face. A few tricks in dust-covered boxes were on display, but mostly the goods were of the type described by a fly-specked card: BE THE LIFE AND SOUL OF THE PARTY. The establishment had veritably run badly to seed.

Hero opened the door and went in, setting off the discordant jangle of an old-fashioned bell attached to a spring above the door to signal the arrival of a customer.

His first impression was of a small, narrow shop with the counter running its length to a curtained-off partition at the rear. Behind the counter were stock shelves from floor to ceiling that contained mostly dusty cardboard boxes, the contents identified by handwritten labels. It smelled of old age, dust, and blocked drains.

There was movement at the curtain; it was pulled aside and a man entered. He was short and stout; a few sparse hairs were stretched across an all but naked skull and he was wearing a green eyeshade. He was clad in a black alpaca jacket with paper sleeves pulled over the forearms. The eyeshade made it difficult to determine the exact colour of his eyes, but they were quite light and probably blue, behind the lenses of horn-rimmed glasses. His cheeks were flabby, and his mouth had a discouraged sag. His attitude was desultory, as of one who never had much to expect from customers these days.

"Mr. Cryder? Paul Cryder?"

"Yup. What can I do for you?"

For a moment Hero debated whether it might not be wise for him to appear simply as an anonymous customer, or even give a false name, so as not to involve himself. Then he vetoed the notion as unnecessarily devious as well as probably futile. His first impression of Cryder was of a man made sullen and unco-operative by failure, and if he were to get anything out of him it would only be upon the basis of his friendship with Phil Elliott, as well as his own standing as an amateur magician.

He therefore replied, "My name is Alexander Hero. I'm over here from London on a visit. Phil Elliott said I was to come in and see you." Therewith he produced his personal card as well as another testifying to his membership in the Inner Circle of the Magician's Club of Great Britain.

"Say, Phil sent you, did he? That's mighty nice of him. Are you a member of the profession?"

His attitude had changed. The lethargic despondency had fallen away, the droop went from his mouth and the light-coloured eyes seemed to produce an avid glitter.

"Amateur," Hero said and then added, "I am in need of some help."

Cryder's interest remained at heat, for his visitor had said nothing to indicate he might not be a customer for some apparatus. He said, "Well, well, well! I haven't seen Phil since shortly after the War. Come along in back with me and we'll see what we can do for you."

He held the curtain aside for Hero to pass through. Hero was astonished to see what lay behind the partition. The area was half a dozen times the size of the shop and was a warren of aisles and shelves with costumes and magical paraphernalia for stage illusions hanging from the ceiling. Hero recognized the expensive equipment for at least a score of the larger vanishings presented by the great magicians of another day. Apparently the

THE MAGIC SHOP OF PAUL CRYDER   115

Cryder establishment took up and owned the space behind the smaller shops on either side of it and stretched far into the rear as well. Here was money tied up and for a moment wholly inconvertible. Hero wondered what Cryder lived on. There would not even be a Christmas sale. People who wanted to buy magic sets for their children would get them from uptown toy and department stores.

Over to one side in a corner was an old-fashioned roll-top desk with an electric light and a green glass shade suspended over it from the ceiling and a muddle of account books, papers, and letters on it. A swivel chair stood in front of it and another straight one at the side. That part was apparently Cryder's office. Just beyond it, deeper in the area, a flight of wooden steps led upstairs, and if the front of the shop suffered from despondency and neglect, the rear was in far better shape; clean and well looked after as though Cryder's sense of values had not wholly deserted him. There was no doubt that he was equipped to supply everything magical from the self-lighting cigarettes and fans of cards used by imitators of Cardini to the vast stage machinery and props needed to vanish an elephant before the eyes of an audience.

"Sit down, sit down," Cryder was saying, indicating the straight chair and settling himself in his own and rocking back in it. "Smoke?" He shoved over a half-filled box of dry-looking Romeo and Julietas.

Hero patted his side pocket and then reached in and produced a pipe and pouch. "May I?"

"Sure, sure! I forgot you Englishmen go for pipes. Go ahead, light up." He selected a cigar, obviously treating himself in anticipation of a sale, examined it carefully, removed the band, bit off the end which he spat out and lit up. "How are things over there?"

Hero saw no reason for not being truthful with Cryder and besides he wished to establish sympathy and a rapport. He had loaded and fired his pipe and he made a face as he stuck it between his teeth. "Bad," he replied, "if it weren't for amateurs."

Cryder wagged his head and said, "I know, I know, ain't it the truth. Over here even they don't even care much any more. Well, anyone Phil Elliott sends me will be treated right. Can I interest you in something?"

Hero's mind had been judging, sifting, analysing, cataloguing. Cryder was a common little man, probably still devoted to his business but now frustrated and no doubt in financial difficulties. Whatever had been originally European, had been lost in a few generations. His speech and psyche were American. His cordiality was purely commercial. Otherwise there was little Hero could make of Paul Cryder. If there was more to the man it was nicely concealed behind the lenses of his spectacles, the green celluloid eyeshade and the burning cigar. He kept his paunchy little body tilted backwards in the swivel chair and using one foot as a lever kept it moving slightly from side to side. Hero completed his inventory with the word "nervous."

"Well, yes," he said, "there's something in which I am interested, and I am, of course, prepared to pay for any information, advice or help you can give me in addition, naturally, to the equipment."

Cryder waved his cigar affably and said, "Sure, sure, sure! Anything you say. You'll get a right price. What's on your mind?"

Hero was conscious of an inner trembling as he launched into what he hoped would be the beginning of a solution. "I want," he said succinctly, "to make a wax hand."

The axis of Cryder's chair squeaked and grated. "You want to make a wax hand," he repeated.

"Not solid," Hero said. "A glove cast in one piece."

The mechanism of the chair protested again. "Not solid, a glove cast in one piece," echoed Cryder. Then he added, "I guess that ain't too much of a problem. What's it for?"

"Materialisation," Hero said feeling certain that Cryder would understand without further elucidation.

"Materialisation," Cryder repeated.

"In one piece," Hero continued. "And produced on the spot." And then he added, "With fingerprints."

Automatically Cryder repeated, "With fingerprints," and then looked up sharply from under the visor of his eyeshade and asked, "You in the medium racket?"

Hero nodded and replied, "In a way."

Cryder said, "There was that medium up in Boston, what's-her-name, that done it. Marjorie. But that was a long time ago. I suppose we could dig it up."

"Yes," Hero said, "I know. They were the fingerprints of a living person. I want to make a wax glove with the fingerprints of a person who is dead and buried."

"You want to make a wax glove with the fingerprints of a person who is dead and buried."

"Yes. Do you think you could do it?"

"Do I think I could do it."

Hero suppressed his irritation at Cryder's apparent habit of repetition but this time the little man added nothing to the repeat and the squeaking and groaning of the chair had stopped as well. It was now in the forward position and Cryder was sitting up with his hands in his lap and his head sunk forward on his chest, as though in deep reflection, searching his mind for an answer. But his silence continued beyond normal expectation, almost to the point of embarrassment. Hero did not wish to break in upon whatever train of thought or memories of past magic he was evoking with a "Well?" and yet as the silence lengthened he felt that he ought to speak, say something or even do something to break it.

It was shattered most unexpectedly and violently by the jangle of the bell attached to the front door of the shop.

Cryder started as though his mind had just returned to his body from a far distant journey and he dropped cigar ash onto the front of his black alpaca coat, which he brushed off hastily as he leaped to his feet and said, "Excuse me. I won't be a minute," as he went out through the curtain.

Hero heard light, stiletto heel taps and the lilt of a feminine voice and then Cryder saying, "Oh, hello, Tina! You back? We got a visitor." After that his voice dropped to something indistinguishable.

The curtain was pushed aside and a girl preceded Cryder into the room where Hero had risen to his feet in anticipation.

It was her eyes which first hit him so hard that he was left breathless, though later he knew that it was all of Tina Cryder which had set up the disturbance within him. They were the colour of the clearest of light aquamarines, enormous, and set startlingly in a tiny, piquant face, beneath a thatch of lustrous dark hair which must have been long enough to reach to her waist, for she wore it most astonishingly, parted in the middle and in two plaits coiled into large buns at either side of her head, in the Austrian fashion. Her skin matched her brunette colouring and was fine in texture. The effect of the pair of translucent eyes blazing at him from the dark countenance was shattering.

And, in fact, the first look she gave him upon entering the room was both challenging and appraising.

There are some encounters between male and female the conclusion of which is settled even before their hands have touched or their voices mingled. Sight has transferred seemingly all that each needs to know for the chemicals of craving to begin to react. Everything seemed to stir at once within Alexander Hero as he saw the sudden augmented glow in her eyes, and the expression of her parted lips.

"My daughter, Tina," Cryder said.

When she moved towards him, her hand extended, Hero saw that, though tiny, she had an exquisite figure, beautifully proportioned. She was like a little doll, except that her carriage, her attitude, her expression were adult and feminine. For all of her small stature she was a ripe woman and, to Hero, instantly and wholly desirable.

The introductions were not yet completed and her hand was already in his, firm and warm, and she was looking up searchingly into his face.

"This is Alexander Hero from London, England," Cryder concluded. "A friend of Phil Elliott from the Inner Circle."

Hero for an instant was uncertain whether her grip did not suddenly tighten and gropingly wondered whether it could be his fortune that she was trying to send him the same message as he to her, that first acknowledgement and awareness which, if put into words could only be expressed by, "We've found one another."

"Alexander Hero," Tina Cryder was saying, "I'm very happy to meet you." She had just the faintest of accents in her speech, but Hero could not tell what it was, only that it was charming. Could it be Polish? But why?

Cryder said, "Mr. Hero's been asking about a wax hand for a materialisation. He's in the medium business." As the girl turned to him with an enquiring glance he added, "All in one piece, a glove like, but with fingerprints."

Everyone was very still now, and the silence reminded Hero of the one he had just endured when Paul Cryder had sat so long without saying anything.

"The fingerprints," Cryder concluded, "would be of someone who was dead and buried, like the spirit came back." Then he added, "Would you know of any stunt like that?" and turning to Hero he explained, "My daughter knows some of this stuff better than I do. She's travelled four years as a magician's assistant. The Great Scarlett. She's been all over. I guess you've been to London too, ain't you Tina?"

Tina said, "Oh, Father!" as though in modesty, but Hero had the impression that for an instant she was genuinely annoyed and wondered why. Strange, he thought, the tricks fate plays on postponing meetings. He had been out of London on an investigation in Norfolk* during the time that the Great Scarlett, who specialised in the materialising and vanishing of dozens of white doves, had appeared at the Savoy.

"She wants to be a regular actress," Cryder was saying.

* Too Many Ghosts.

"Have you tried the library, Father?" Tina Cryder asked sharply.

"Eh? What?"

"I said have you tried the library?"

Even in asperity her voice appealed to Hero. It had a breathy catch to it that to him denoted sexual mystery and at the same time he thought, *she wants to speak to her father alone*. It was also quite possible that he was embarrassing her for some reason with his talk of the theatre.

"No, I ain't. He's only just come here."

"Then we ought to try that first."

Cryder said, "Tina's got something there," and then to his daughter, "Why don't you take him upstairs and fix him up with a drink while we check?"

The stairs led to a large drawing room. It was furnished with early American antiques, probably acquired by the original Cryderski. It contained also a grand piano, a record player, and the ubiquitous television set. There was a room opening off it towards the front of the building that must have been Tina's bedroom, for she disappeared into it for a moment but left the door open, and he could see her doing some arrangement with her hair and face. Presumably another door towards the rear led to her father's apartment. She returned, walking thoughtfully, her gaze cast down and avoiding Hero's following glance. She went to a cellarette at the side of the room, opened it, and asked, "Scotch?" But in doing so her eyes looked upwards into those of Hero, the ice-blue fire within them blazed once more, and it started all over again—the entanglement, the excitement, the desire and the foreknowledge that somehow it was to be gratified.

"Yes, please."

She poured the drink from a decanter, splashed it with soda, and brought it to him.

How old can she be, Hero thought. *Twenty-seven? Twenty-eight? The woman's psyche in the doll's body. She will have to stand on tiptoe when she kisses me. It's French, the accent. More French than Polish. But her father speaks like a guttersnipe.*

Where did she learn? With the Great Scarlett? And how many others besides him? What, jealous already, Hero? If I cannot quench the fire in those eyes with tears . . . Thus his thoughts racketed, unruly, uncontrollable.

"I'll go and help Father," Tina Cryder said. "He sometimes gets lost amongst his own books. I hope we'll be able to find something for you. Do make yourself comfortable."

Hero watched her until the top of her brown head had disappeared down the stair well, and he listened until he could no longer hear the click of her tiny feet.

Holding his drink and sipping from it occasionally, he cased the room. The walls were covered with photographs of famous magicians of the past, most of whom Hero knew by name or reputation and they were all signed to one or another of the various generations of Cryders; funny, old-fashioned theatrical pictures, some of them already fading yellow. On the grand piano were two framed cabinet portraits, one of a magician in Chinese make-up inscribed "To Tina, who never missed a cue. Affectionately, Fang Wu." The other was of the Great Scarlett and Tina together, she wearing tights, holding his top hat and wand, he unfastening his scarlet cape and it was signed, "To Tina, with all my love. Will Scarletto."

Hero knew Wang Fu to be one of the last of the great illusionists, recently retired, working cabinet, sword and vanishing tricks. He was a German Jew named Karl Boehmer and glancing at the figure of the girl in silken tights he saw how perfect she would be for the work. She was probably something of a contortionist and could roll herself up to fit into the tiniest places in the traps and boxes. Most likely she had started very young. And now that there were no longer magic shows or acts, other than a few night-club performers doing sleight-of-hand, what? She would try the stage, of course. Had that been the basis of her irritation with her father, that she had had less of the luck or the talent than she had hoped? A strange pair; a curious set-up. He only knew that he wanted to see more of Tina Cryder, and he was quite well aware that at the first look into those astonishing and fantastic eyes she had driven every thought of the non-existent Ruth Lesley and the girl who had all but seduced him in the dark of the cabinet out of his head.

In the library, at the far end behind the shop, containing some two thousand volumes on magic of every kind, from the earliest incantations and illusions practised by the primitive priesthoods to subjugate the tribes, down to modern volumes revealing the secrets of the great stage magicians and which were never allowed into the hands of non-professionals, father and daughter were snarling at one another.

Paul Cryder was pale, sweating and his knees had a tendency to tremble. "Who's the guy?" he demanded. "What is he, a copper? What's he come snooping around here for, asking about a hand with fingerprints of a dead one? You said there wouldn't be any trouble. What's this Limey doing sticking his nose in? Who's he working for?" And then he added, "Who are you working for? What the hell are you up to?"

Tina Cryder's face was high-coloured with fury, and the expression of her mouth was no longer pleasant.

"What do you care?" she cried. "You got paid, didn't you? Well, I'm getting mine." She no longer had an accent.

Cryder's voice rose by a pitch, tingled with hysteria, "But I told you I don't want any trouble. I did a job for them friends of yours, like I do for anyone in the business and ask no questions, and that's an end to it. But you're mixed up in something, and now this guy coming around, and he wants the same thing. I want to know what's up, what's cooking. I don't want my ass in no sling. Who's this guy?"

Tina Cryder's face was a study in contempt. "You're chicken!" she spat at him. "You're chicken yellow. Where would you be if I hadn't got you the ten grand for the job? You don't want any trouble! What do you think anyone pays ten grand for a job for? For a gag?" Then she said, "For Christ's sake don't lose your nerve. All you've got to do is to keep your mouth shut and your shirt on. I'll find out about this guy." She could have told him all she already knew, but in his present state of funk decided not to do so.

"How will you find out?"

"By going out with him."

"What makes you think you're going out with him?"

"He's going to ask me."

"Why?"

"Because I want him to."

Paul Cryder looked at his daughter, his glance still burning with hostility, "Well, whatever you're up to, keep me out of it. I done my job. That's all I know, understand?"

Tina did not reply. She was thinking of an Englishman named Peter Fairweather, his mouth and the hungry encirclement of his arms. She was wanting him with that peculiar all-enveloping, all-pervading greediness that had been her characteristic from the very first, ever since she had been old enough to have wants and desires of any kind whatever.

Cryder said, "What do we say to the guy?"

Tina Cryder mounted a travelling step-ladder that served the shelves just beneath the ceiling and pulled down a book. It was Harry Price's *Fifty Years of Psychical Research*. "There's a picture of Kluski's glove in this," she said.

Cryder sniffed, "If he's in the racket he'll know that one."

"That's just why," his daughter concluded. "That's all there is. There isn't any more. Let me handle him."

There had been no problem connected with making the date when father and daughter returned with the volume, a book with which Hero was familiar, and the news that there was nothing that gave any hint as to how a wax cast of the hand, complete with fingerprints, of a dead person might be produced under seance conditions.

Hero had known from the time the Cryders had disappeared together that this would be the case. He was aware that he had excited the suspicion and hostility of Paul Cryder, and wondered whether the antagonism he seemed to have aroused included the daughter. He said, "I don't think it can be done myself and actually don't believe it has. A client of mine in London heard from a source that a medium was supposed to have produced a materialisation and asked me to check. But you know what those second- and thirdhand reports are."

Was it true? Had there suddenly come a lightening to the unhappy, flabby countenance of Paul Cryder? At any rate he went to the cellarette, poured himself a drink neat, and said, raising his glass, "Your health. Down the hatch!" and put it away. "Sorry we can't help you. You here for long?"

"Holiday," Hero said briefly and then looked to Tina Cryder who was standing over by the grand piano, close by the large cabinet photo of herself with the Great Scarlett, watching him. Hero wondered just how deliberate was the juxtaposition. She was clad in a loose beige wool spring suit with a short jacket concealing the actual lines and curves of her figure; but there, just beside her, they were exposed by the classic costume of the magician's female assistant, close-fitting leotard with the ridiculously abbreviated spangled skirt that displayed the shining limbs.

"Are you working now?" Hero asked her.

"Not at the moment."

"I wonder," Hero said, "whether upon such short acquaintance if it would be considered an impertinence for me to ask whether you would be willing to show me something of New York one evening?"

There was an unmistakable look exchanged between father and daughter. Hero caught it and Tina knew he had. She laughed deliciously and said, "That's the way the British do it, Father. I'll probably receive a formal note confirming it in the morning."

Hero said, "Other country, other customs. Do you like to dance?"

"I love it!"

"I don't twist," Hero warned.

Tina laughed again, "That's only for middle-aged people."

"Tonight?"

Tina looked thoughtful, doubtful, and regretful—"I'm not sure that I can."

Cryder who was pouring himself another drink, turned half-way around to stare at his daughter with the most absurd expression of anxiety. She avoided his gaze.

"Do you think you might try? I'd like to take you dancing," Hero persisted.

"Would you really? Perhaps I'll cancel my date then."

Paul Cryder found his speech again, "Sure, sure! That's a good idea." Then to Hero, "You take Tina out. She'll show you the town. You'll enjoy yourself."

Hero thought to himself, *How heavy-handed can you get?* Aloud he asked, "Do we dress?"

The girl's expression turned comically mocking. "Don't the British always?"

"Shall I call for you, say, at eight o'clock?"

Tina replied, "It's a long way to come. Wouldn't you like me to meet you uptown somewhere?"

Hero said, "I'm old-fashioned. I'll come for you." His words were cool, but his look was not. The under-cover message he was sending said, *"It will be that much longer that we can be together."*

Tina Cryder said, "That would be nice."

On the way back, Hero irritably considered the situation. He had, of course, been dwelling in a fool's paradise to have even hoped the problem could have been solved so simply, merely by his asking an American magic-shop proprietor to provide him with the secret of the hand. But there was more to his feeling of discomfort than that. He had been manoeuvred, pushed around. He had gone there seeking intelligence. It seemed perhaps that he had given more information than he had come away with and had been set up for further revelations.

Had he wasted time when he might have been doing something more promising? There was the over-all anxiety of moments lost. How much more of that precious commodity was there left to their account? How much longer before Constable would react to the increasing pressure upon him to do so? How far had his preparations already proceeded? What if at the next seance Mary Constable were not to appear? Might it not trigger Constable into immediate action—flight or contact with the Russians? Why the devil hadn't they called him in before, when there would have been still time to explore all avenues?

The train clattered into Grand Central Station. It was still not too late in the afternoon for some research. Instead of returning to his hotel he walked over to the library to examine the American bibliography of the subject of fingerprints.

The catalogue and reading rooms of the New York Public Library were even more impressive than those of the British Museum. There must have been more than a hundred cards on fingerprints alone, plus as many more by cross reference. Hero selected eight and, presenting his slips at the desk of the main reading room, was given a cipher, and sat watching the red numbers flash up on two huge boards, as though some gigantic computer were operating. When his appeared he collected the books and retired to one of the reading tables to study them.

He achieved little illumination beyond details of a method by which criminals had been able to transfer the fingerprints of someone other than themselves to substances such as glass, or wood, thus establishing a fake alibi and implicating innocent parties. He learned a lot about the obliteration and alteration of fingerprints upon the living but nothing about the return of the dead. He closed the books and sat contemplating them gloomily and wondering in what kind of failure and humiliation his first American assignment would end.

He had a sudden impulse to send for the text of the tablets of King Shamshi-Adad, Ferguson had mentioned. He went to the card index file, looked under Von Schweringen, found it listed, wrote it on a ticket, and presented it. He had a fifteen-minute wait before his number blinked up on the board. The attendant handed him a slender volume, bound in a neutral cover. Hero took it to his table. As had been suggested, it was indeed something. On a series of tablets, some three thousand years before, someone had listed the concubines of the king, along with the pertinent details of his activities with them. It made modern pornography seem like nursery tales.

A voice at his elbow whispered, "Lush, isn't it?" Startled, Hero looked up to see Dr. Ferguson sitting beside him. "Don't let me disturb you. It gets better after the old fellow warms up a bit." And then he added innocently, "Was it me or Shamshi you were looking for?"

Hero suppressed a smile. Actually he had not thought Ferguson would be working late on a Saturday afternoon. At the same time, he was glad to see him. He was content, however, that evidence of his research was at hand and that Dr. Ferguson was eyeing speculatively the volumes he had taken out on the subject of fingerprints.

Ferguson nodded in the direction of these books and said, in the accepted reading-room *sotto voce,* "It is precisely the fingerprints which puts one off the idea of any genuine breakthrough, doesn't it? But of course, you will have thought of that. Fingerprints do call for epidermal cells, somehow. One *will* keep pretending that it's the body which is immortal and it's the one thing that is not." Then he added, "I hear from Wiener that you have had a visit with my friend Constable."

Hero nodded, but did not choose to follow the lead. Instead he asked, "Do you know a man called Paul Cryder?"

Dr. Ferguson took hold of the glasses hanging around his neck by their black ribbon, set them on his nose, and regarded Hero through them, almost as though he had been an interesting specimen of some kind. "The magician's supplier." Apparently there was no subject upon which Dr. Ferguson did not have some information, or knowledge. "My dear boy, how very clever of you to have thought of him. It should have occurred to me long ago. I believe—I have heard—that he has a daughter who is quite a dish."

"I think he knows how to make the wax glove," Hero said.

Dr. Ferguson breathed a great sigh, "Ah! That simplifies the problem then."

"It doesn't," Hero countered, "he isn't telling."

"You've seen him?"

"Yes. He doesn't trust me. He isn't talking." Then he added, "He's like a lot of those chaps: they let go with just so much but there are some professional secrets you can't pry out of them for love or money."

Dr. Ferguson was now regarding Hero with some perturbation. "My dear fellow, you simply must."

"I mean to."

"How?"

Willy-nilly, Hero's eyes were drawn to a purple passage in the open book before him, and as willy and nilly his mind turned to Tina Cryder and he felt ashamed and irritated with himself, as though he had been caught scribbling something on a privy wall. But he remembered then the exquisite sophistication of the man next to him and his own sense of humour rose to the rescue. "The dish!" he replied.

Dr. Ferguson murmured, "Even unto the supreme sacrifice . . ." and a reader near by went, "Shhh!"

Of all the places to feel presentiment or foreboding the reading room of the New York Public Library, vast, vivid, and normal with its expanse of oak tables and chairs and green lamp shades, would be the last. Yet Hero experienced a sudden sense of desolation and portentousness and he whispered, half to himself, "Someone is going to get hurt before this is over."

"You think so?" said Dr. Ferguson and by his tone accepted the finality of Hero's statement. "Precognition? A genuine case of premonition? Are you clairvoyant?"

Hero thought, *So you too have your small, undisclosed corners of doubts and beliefs.* He answered irritably, "How should I know? The evidence is unreliable. But if a dog can entertain forewarning of disaster, are we any better?"

Ferguson said gloomily, "Not much. By and large, not much." And then added, "You must keep your nerve, my boy," as though he himself had had a glimpse into the future. "We shall all have need of it, undoubtedly, before this is over. But time! There is so little time. You must hurry. And remember, Constable is my friend." He arose and went away, his shoulders a little more stooped. Hero continued to sit, his chin sunk onto his chest, his eyes no longer taking in the peculiarities of King Shamshi-Adad. His mind was flickering like heat lightning around the gloomy area of the stockroom behind the magic shop on Cedar Street, the reluctant proprietor and the girl whose ambition, as her father had put it, was to be a regular actress.

CHAPTER XI

Professor Constable Packs a Bag

Tina Cryder walked west on Twenty-ninth Street towards Twelfth Avenue. Her expression was concerned and her brow lined with worry, but her steps were firm and unhesitant. There was no indecision as to where she was going and what she must do. She was on the expensive payroll of a powerful secret organisation for a substantial sum in weekly payments. Those payments she now felt to be menaced and in need of protection. That the organisation and its aims might be threatened was no direct concern of hers.

She was quite intelligent enough to know very well who they were, the source of their funds, and the aim of the conspiracy. She had simply and deliberately closed her mind to these, to the point where they had ceased to exist. She was looking after Tina Cryder who had had the misfortune to be born into a world not of her own making, a world which was a violently predatory jungle. And she also lived in times which had seen the profession and fortunes of her family at lowest ebb, so that Tina had not been able to obtain the things she craved and which so many others less deserving and less endowed by nature seemed to have.

Tina Cryder was a true "have not," and she was neither intellectual nor political. She was beautiful and ambitious. She wanted money and a stage career. She was extraordinarily greedy. Ever since she could remember, when she craved something she wanted it with an uncontrollable fury; her desires, her wishes knew no bounds or curbs.

Where it came to talent and ability she just missed it. She had achieved a few small parts on the stage and in one or two pictures, but had not been able to go any further, for all of her looks, since she had never had the patience to work hard and train. Her natural beauty and grace, coupled with a certain laziness, had spoiled her for this, and somehow across the footlights or through the camera lens she simply failed to project. Casting directors either caught this at auditions or shortly after rehearsals had begun, and she would find herself replaced.

Her small nose registered displeasure as, walking westwards across Eleventh Avenue towards Twelfth and the river that same Saturday afternoon, the neighbourhood became even tattier and more redolent of refuse, chemicals, and gas works. It was from these surroundings that she had been struggling for so long to free herself and had reached the conclusion that money was the only solution. The social opportunities of the daughter of a purveyor of stink bombs, itching powder, and the water-into-wine trick were not exactly brilliant.

Twelfth Avenue at Twenty-ninth Street was a shabby, rundown waterfront section, paralleling the North River, and its piers in that section were devoted to banana boats and small coastal steamship companies. Overhead the West Side elevated highway blotted out the sky; below were motor trucks and drays, and on the west of the street, opposite the docks, were shabby, hundred-year-old brick buildings, used as lofts for storage, produce houses and in some cases garment sweatshops and small factories.

The southwest corner was taken up by one of the few remaining livery stables left in New York, since horse-drawn vehicles had all but completely disappeared from the streets. A few drays and small vans still used horses, and one famous firm of chocolatiers as well, for its snob value.

The entrance to the stables and storage quarters was on Twelfth Avenue, but the office of the Rafferty Brothers was on the corner, dingy and grimy from coal smoke and dust like all the shops in that neighbourhood, the windows and doors of half-frosted glass and the lettering thereon, RAFFERTY BROTHERS, LIVERY STABLES, almost eroded.

Tina felt nervous. She had gone there before upon several occasions, but each time it was she who had been summoned. This was the first visit on her own initiative, and she was not at all sure of her reception. Her instructions had always been: "Don't try to get in touch with us; when we want you we'll send for you."

She went in. The man she knew only as Mike was sitting at his desk behind a wooden railing with a swinging section in it. The desk was littered with papers but he was reading a paperback novel with a lurid cover. On the walls hung fly-specked calendars of steamers in gaudy colours, issued by the shipping companies. He was stringy and unkempt and wore a bowler hat on the back of his head, a shirt without a collar, a waistcoat unbuttoned, and a pencil tucked behind one ear.

He looked up at her with hostility and suspicious eyes as she closed the door behind her, but gave no sign of recognition.

Tina said, "Is Mr. Kelly here?"

"No, he ain't."

"Will he be here?"

"I wouldn't know."

"I want to—I've got to see Mr. Kelly."

"Is that so?"

Being crossed and frustrated in her desires always brought fire and colour to Tina and an edge to her temper. She said, "I've got to see him. Tell him it's important."

Mike echoed, "You've got to see him!" and then said, "Keep your hair on, sister! Go take a walk. Come back in an hour, maybe he'll be around."

It was a long hour of wandering about the noisy waterfront street, looking into the windows of ship's chandlers, cafes, and offices of obscure trading and forwarding companies. It all seemed to her so childish, these precautions, yet she supposed the people for whom she was working knew what they were doing and, among other things, wished to be certain that she had not been followed to the rendezvous. At the end of an hour, with an extra two or three minutes for good measure, she returned to the office. Mr. Kelly was there.

He might have been named Bajdingian, or Tewfik, Marasoupolous, or Cadagno but certainly not Kelly. He was a swarthy, narrow-faced little man with nervous, tobacco-stained fingers, piercingly brilliant eyes, and a bitter mouth. He was well dressed, except for a white silk scarf that he wore inside the collar of his coat. He could have been a Jew, an Armenian, a Turk or an Italian.

He was attending to his fingernails with a penknife when Tina entered and continued to do so for a few moments before looking up and jerking with his head in the direction of the door leading out from the back of the office. Tina went through the swinging section of the railing and out into the stables, where the atmosphere was heavy with the smell of hay, urine, manure, and horses. Half a dozen of the animals were stabled there and beyond, at the rear of the building, some disused delivery vans were parked, their shafts resting on the ground.

A minute or so later Mr. Kelly emerged from the door. He went to one of the vans and climbed into the driver's seat. Tina got in beside him.

Kelly said, "What the hell's the idea? You were told never to contact us. You could get into trouble."

Mr. Kelly as a figure of menace only made Tina wish to giggle. His sideburns were too long and his complexion too pasty. He didn't look as though he could hurt a fly. At any rate she wasn't afraid of him. She said, "Something's happened. I thought I'd better tell you about it."

Mr. Kelly said, "Okay, spill it." He talked with an accent of some kind.

"The Bessmers," she began, "they took on a new sitter last night, an Englishman who had lost his girl. I mean she died. They got me to play this girl. His name was Peter Fairweather. He was supposed to be some kind of a professor in an English university. They got me to kiss him and pretend I was his girl come back."

Mr. Kelly's dark eyes were burning.

"What did they shake him down for?"

"Twenty-five hundred. He's going for another thousand next Monday night."

Mr. Kelly said, "The sons of bitches! Don't we pay them enough to keep their noses clean? So what about him?"

"That isn't his real name. He came down to the shop today to see father." She reached into her bag and produced a card which she handed to Mr. Kelly. "This is his right name, Alexander Hero. Father looked him up later on, he's some kind of investigator. He works for the British Society for Psychical Research."

"What's that?"

"They investigate mediums and seances and things like that. There's one over here too."

"Go on," said Mr. Kelly.

"He was asking about a wax hand," Tina said.

Mr. Kelly's contribution was a single four-letter obscenity. Tina said nothing. She had heard it before.

Kelly asked, "How did you know him if all you did was smooch in the dark?"

"I had a look at him before the lights went out," Tina explained. "The Bessmers said they had a real sucker lined up and told me a lot about him and his fiancée and the job had to be done right. I wanted to see what I was up against, what kind of guy, how to act. I recognised him as soon as I came into the shop."

Mr. Kelly asked sharply, "Did he know you?"

"Certainly not! How could he? He never saw me in the cabinet. It was dark."

Kelly spat out of the window of the cab of the van and repeated, "The sons of bitches! Who was he working for? Who did you say he was? Where does he hang out?"

"I don't know. But I thought you ought to hear about him, in case . . ."

"You did what was correct," said Mr. Kelly, for the only time falling into the jargon of his affiliations. "Can you get any more dope on him?"

"Yes, I think so. I've got a date with him for tonight."

"Why?"

"To find out more about him. Father's scared."

"Oh yeah? Or maybe if he's handing out with that kind of dough to have a bite off it yourself? Don't you cross us, sister. You can run into awful trouble."

The little, vain man and his threats!

Tina cried, "Don't be stupid! Why do you think I came and told you? I want to find out." But she was not telling Mr. Kelly of all it was that she wanted to know further about Fairweather-Hero; about how much strength and satisfaction for her could lie within his embrace. But if something went wrong, she had already informed upon him. In the world of today both ends against the middle was the only safe way to play.

"Do you figure you're smart enough?"

"I'm a woman."

Mr. Kelly sniggered unpleasantly. He asked, "When are you supposed to give him the business again?"

"Monday night, at the next seance."

Mr. Kelly reflected for a moment, then he said, "Okay, see if you can pump him. Unless you hear from us come in about ten-thirty on Monday morning and report. You've got your instructions on the other business. Okay, beat it! Go out through the stable entrance, walk down Twelfth Avenue to Twenty-seventh Street, go east and get a cab on Eleventh. One of us will be watching to see that no one's tailing you."

Tina jumped out of the van and shut the door behind her. Through the window she could see the glitter of Mr. Kelly's eyes. They were bright and hard. She turned away and for the first time she felt a little afraid of him and wished that she had not come, that she had first kept her rendezvous with the Englishman.

As she reached the door the sibilant, accented whisper followed her, "And keep your goddam nose clean. We're watching you."

Jane Constable looked into her husband's study on her way to an evening of dinner and theatre with friends. It was nearing six o'clock. She was a tall woman of elegance and breeding, still handsome, with a broad, intelligent brow, good features, and fine, calm eyes. Of late she had both resigned and adapted herself to the role of science widow, as her husband, with the excuse of his work and the project, had neglected the social life they had both so enjoyed together and which with their similar cultural tastes had kept them so close.

Yet Jane Constable was uneasy, for she was well aware that work was not the whole story and that since the death of their daughter her husband had been more and more withdrawn from her. Instead of their bereavement bringing them closer together, it was almost as though the spectre of their dead child had risen to separate them. Jane Constable had always given in to her husband, his work, his way of life; she had known that he would dominate when she had married him and was satisfied to have it so, but on this one great point of contention, which had grown up between them, she was not prepared to yield. Something within her, that last, intimate, closely guarded bit of self that must never be surrendered, forbade it.

She paused in the doorway of the study. "Still working, Sam?"

He did not hear her, and she saw then that he was standing by the glass case, looking down upon the wax hand she so hated, his expression concentrated, rapt, wholly engrossed.

As always she was swept with the feeling of revulsion and protest which, curiously, this time evolved into the form of a sentence in her mind, though she seemed more to hear it as a voice in her ears, *Thou shalt not make unto thee any graven image.*

Constable broke out of the reverie and saw his wife. He looked across the gulf that separated them. She was stately in evening dress and furs, her hair hardly touched with grey, her inner calmness so visible through her demeanour. All his misery, doubts, and anguish of soul boiled into sudden anger against her. His lion's head came up, his strong chin thrust forward and a glare came into his eyes. He said harshly, "Jane! I want to talk to you!"

His wife came into the study but somehow found herself unable to cross the invisible line of demarcation which would have put her at his side, and thus, instead, the hand in the glass case remained a barrier. "Is something wrong, Sam?"

"I want you to do something for me, Jane. I insist upon it."

She knew what was coming—dreaded it.

"Monday night I want you to come with me—to see our daughter."

"Sam, please don't ask me. You know I won't want to—I can't."

"Why not? Would it hurt you for once to crack that cold, calm, stubborn façade and go to your child, even though it tore your heart out?"

"Sam, please! Must we go through all this again?"

His glare if anything had become more savage. "Why, why, why? Why not? Why won't you go when I tell you she's there? Don't you want to hear her voice again, feel her presence, the touch of her hand, her laugh, her breath upon your face?"

"Sam!" cried Jane Constable, and if he wished the façade cracked he had his way for in her voice was mingled outrage and the deep anguish of a mother. "How can you? I hear her voice! I hear it every waking moment. I feel her touch! I bore her, Sam. I have never forgotten a gesture, a movement of her body or a caress. Isn't that enough?"

"Does it fill your arms?" Constable said harshly. "It doesn't mine. Is imagination enough for you, or looking at a photograph when you can have her back the way she was? I tell you she's there, her voice, her laugh; her lips have touched my cheek; the things she knows. I couldn't be mistaken . . ."

"Sam, Sam, I beg of you! I have made my peace with death, can't you . . . ?"

PROFESSOR CONSTABLE PACKS A BAG   139

He brushed her words aside, cut her off. "Do you remember that night when she was a baby, the summer we were in the Adirondacks and we came into her room and there was a spider on the pillow of her crib an inch from her face? And I knew it for what it was, a Black Widow and deadly to her? And I willed *her* not to move and I willed *it* not to move with everything I had and I took the thing in my fingers and crushed it? Only you and I knew about this, no one else, not even Mary, for she was too young, or so it seemed. We never mentioned it to anyone because we were so frightened we didn't even wish to think about it . . ."

The glare in Constable's eyes had turned now to fervour. "But *she* knew," he said, "Mary knew. She felt my will all about her, protecting her. She obeyed me and remained motionless. She told me so herself."

Jane asked, "When?" and already knew what the answer would be.

"One night last week. She whispered it to me."

Jane said nothing, looking at him silently and miserably.

"Don't you believe me?" Constable cried. "How could they have known? How could anyone have known?"

Was there any use in saying to him that in later life he or she could have told the story and then forgotten that they had, or that somehow even he might himself have told or hinted it to these people in that house to which she would not go?

Constable lost his temper. "Don't you believe in anything?" he bawled.

And because he was so angry, Jane Constable felt that she must think before she spoke, and she reflected long and deeply within herself trying to uncover, to know beyond any peradventure of a doubt just what it was she did believe. Then she replied slowly and carefully, "I believe in a Higher Power we call God; that we come from Him and at our end return to Him and become a part of Him. I believe that that is what and where Mary is now. And that is where I want her to be. Her memory is alive within me. What further proof is needed that . . ."

Constable broke in upon her again with a gesture pointing to the waxen hand and gave her a hard and challenging look. "That," he said. "There it is. She's come back. There's no getting around that."

As always when he referred to the hand, she did not know what to say. For indeed, there it was, visible, tangible, unexplainable, the young fingers curled beseechingly, with all their tracery of lines and markings as they had been in life. Yet never once since it had been there, from the very first time she had seen it, had it reached to her heart. On the contrary. In the mellow glow of the study lamps it appeared to her now to glitter monstrously as though it were shedding light of its own and somehow wickedly and impiously as well. It went against the grain of everything she felt or was.

Constable discerned the revulsion which, as always, the hand seemed to stir within her, and had he been less of an egotist might have heeded it as an instinctive and trustworthy protest arising from a sincere woman. This time he controlled the anger it always aroused in him and said almost humbly, "Jane, please! If I asked you—if I begged of you to come with me just this once . . . I need you to come."

Her intelligence took note of the swift change of tactic but her heart was moved to know there was more behind this than just stubbornness and the necessity of the assertive male to have his way. Behind it might lie some kind of crisis. Was this a genuine cry for help from this self-sufficient man?

"Oh, Sam, why? Why do you want me to do this? Tell me."

"You'd *know* if she was there!" It was a groan, the truth forced agonizedly from him, the one truth he had not meant to speak.

And thereby he defeated himself, and Operation Foxglove once more fell into deadly jeopardy.

For she had been on the point of yielding. Only womanlike she had asked that last question, demanded that final explanation before bridging the gulf that had separated them for so long by going to him and consenting to accompany him. Instead, his

reply startled her and released trains of thought so near her subconscious that she was hardly aware of them. The words "You'd
know!" were echoing within her. She had no wish to know other
than what she already knew, what she had told him were her beliefs and the compromise she had been able to arrive at with the
inevitable. But what if something were to take place there, something heard, something seen, something felt, a ghost touch bringing alive once again all the painful reality? Her beliefs were
important to her.

Her mind, with its human weakness unable to confess the
truth, provided her with cover. If he still had his doubts let him
resolve them for himself. She could not help him. The wax hand
coruscating wickedly rearoused in all her the antagonism and disgust she had felt when first her husband had told her of the seance room and what transpired there. It was against nature. She
could not bring herself to do it. She said—"I'm sorry, Sam. I don't
want to. I can't."

Constable regarded her silently for a moment yet somehow no
longer with antagonism. The fire seemed to have gone out of
him. "All right, Jane. Skip it. I'll go it alone."

She felt suddenly chilled by his last remark, for if there had
been masculine self-pity in it her sensitive ear would have caught
it. But it had been a simple matter-of-fact statement without
emotion, and she had the feeling of the closing of a door. It
was too late to knock upon it now. He would not open it.

"Have a good time, Jane. I may be working late."

He waited until he heard the front door close and a car drive
off. Then he went to a wall safe which he opened. From it he
removed a number of black loose-leafed notebooks and several
folded blueprints. These he put into a small, rectangular, leather
despatch case. He rummaged through a drawer of his desk from
which he took several other documents. Returning to the safe he
reached to the back of it and produced a small article of glass
and metal, about the size of an egg, which he regarded with a
curious smile before he put it with the other things in the case.

He shut it. It was too big to go into the wall safe, so he closed that and looked about the room for a place to conceal the bag he had packed. There was a cupboard at the far side. He went to it and, almost like a child, hid it at the bottom behind boxes and the folds of a coat. On the way to the door he paused for a moment at the glass case, his fingers drumming upon it. Then he put out the lights and went upstairs.

CHAPTER XII

Time Out for Tina

It was a bad beginning, the stimulation and excitement Hero
was already experiencing on this trip downtown to collect Tina
Cryder. He had gone by taxi in order to have one to take them
back and as the vehicle whipped down the West Side elevated
highway, he realised that he was not as coolly objective and prepared for the evening as he might have been.

He was well aware how easy it was to build up whole series
of false hypotheses stemming from one error in judgement. It
might have been his own libido or male vanity which had given
him the impression that Tina Cryder was in any way as interested in him as he in her. As for his conviction that Paul Cryder
knew something he was not telling about the wax hand, it was
based only upon his observation of Cryder's behaviour when the
subject was introduced, not a particle of which could be put forward as evidence. He knew that given a set of circumstances a
man with toothache, upset stomach, or domestic worries or who
had just had a shock or a disappointment might react entirely
differently than he would otherwise. Wishful thinking was the
investigator's most dangerous catalyst. Because he wanted Cryder to have the secret of the hand, all the latter's reactions, his
hesitations, his repetitions could have coloured Hero's judgement. Cryder might very well not know any more than the rest
of them.

As for what had seemed such an obvious understanding between father and daughter to make the date with Hero, nothing
had actually transpired which could not be justified by ordinary

hospitality extended to a visitor from overseas recommended by a business colleague.

It was with such reasoning and doubts that Hero attempted to put his judgement back into the saddle. Yet as the cab passed the comparative flatlands between midtown and downtown New York and the great mountain ranges of the skyscrapers of lower Manhattan loomed ahead of them, a curious, singing excitement in his breast would not be downed. He wondered what she would be wearing.

As his taxi swung down off the ramp and began to negotiate the maze of one-way streets that led to its destination, Hero had all but composed himself. Whatever happened during the evening it would have to be played by ear and he had better keep his wits about him.

The New York financial district after dark was as dead as the City of London. Drays and lorries rumbled along the river front, but here, close to Broadway, there were only empty streets and darkened windows, except where dim lights burned in shops in accordance with police regulations. This end of Broadway had an occasional pedestrian and a thin stream of traffic but the side passage of Cedar Street at nine o'clock on a Saturday night, was left empty and deserted.

As the cab drew up before No. 43a, Hero saw that the gloomy shop front was dark except for a single naked bulb illuminating the arid counter, but there was a light burning behind the curtains of the room above. Telling the driver to hold his flag, Hero got out wondering how to go about it and what the approach to the dwelling part of the shop would be at this time of night. Then he found that the door had been left open for him.

He went inside with the jangling bell to announce him, traversed the length of the shop to the curtained partition and when he drew it aside there was light on the stairs leading to the upper floor and Tina's voice came floating down. "Sorry, almost ready. Do come up."

Hero went upstairs to the drawing-room part of the old house.

Of Paul Cryder there was no sign and no way of knowing whether he was in or out. The door to what must have been his apartment was shut, but that leading to Tina Cryder's bedroom was ajar and behind it he could see the reflection of her movements before a mirror in the change of light and shadow. She did not speak again and while he waited uncontrollably, the excitement returned to Hero once more.

And then she opened the door and stood in the entrance between the two rooms with a curious innocence of presentation, like a little girl in her first party dress, hoping wistfully for approval.

Immediately and irrevocably the magic was there, the attraction and the desire.

She was wearing an expensively simple light blue dinner frock. The material was wild silk, lustrous and whispering, the skirt short and full, the front severe, the neckline straight across and high. Behind her, through the open door, there was a full-length mirror, and he could see the back of the frock was bare, in one daring sweep almost to the waist. Over her shoulder Hero glimpsed more, the foot of a large, frilly bed on which lay a white mink jacket and white gloves. The colour of the dress had been chosen for her eyes. She wore her hair upswept in a huge burnished coil at the top of her head. It gave her height. It also made Hero feel that it was so artfully and cunningly contrived that if a single pin was removed the whole would come tumbling down in one glorious, shining cascade.

They were almost lost in that first instant of appraisal of one another. So powerful was the feeling of rediscovery that seized them both, that they were nearly swept into one another's arms then and there. They were saved by the knowledge that whatever, this was how the evening would end. All this in no more than a few seconds, without exchange of a word.

Now that they knew, now that it was certain, the urgency was no longer there, their ardour controlled by the desire to postpone the climax, to enjoy the step-by-step approach to intimacy, to sharpen sensation by suspense, to increase enjoyment by delay.

And thus the moment having passed, they spoke almost stiffly and formally to one another.

"I've kept the cab," Hero said.

"Oh, good. They're difficult to get down here this time of night. Do you like my frock?"

"You look charming. Where shall we go?"

"Are you feeling very rich?"

"I've broken into my piggy bank."

"There's a restaurant called The Four Seasons. It's an experience, if you've never been there before."

"The food?" Hero queried.

"Yes. And the size of the check—even for New York."

Her concern with money might have impressed itself upon Hero had he not been too captivated with her presence, the compactness, neatness, and shining radiance of her and the fragrance that surrounded her, a Paris scent with which he was familiar.

"Can one dance there?"

"No. Afterwards, if you like, we can go on to El Morocco."

"You see," Hero said, "what would I do without you?"

She laughed at this and turned to get her wrap. In doing so she opened wider the door to her room. The long pier mirror, reflecting the bed now revealed a pale blue nightdress lying across the counterpane, its message clear and unmistakable, and once more Hero was filled with the thrill of promised conquest. He wished that at that moment he had not had a sudden mental flash of Dr. Ferguson sitting next to him in the reading room of the Public Library, gazing at him quizzically and murmuring, "Even unto the supreme sacrifice . . ." It did serve momentarily, however, to make him smile inwardly and remember that he was there on business as well as pleasure.

All the way uptown in the cab they kept apart, sitting and chatting primly like two adolescents on their first date, and Hero found the paradox delicious.

The taxi burst from the bowels of the Pan American building straddling Park Avenue into the canyon of brilliantly illuminated towers and office structures and dropped them before the burnished copper mass of the Seagram edifice at Fifty-second Street, where The Four Seasons was located.

The maître d'hôtel said, "Have you a reservation, sir?" but his wise eyes were estimating and judging them.

Hero said, "No, I'm sorry but—" The tint of a ten-dollar-bill showed from the corner of his hand.

"I think we can take care of you, sir."

Tina smiled with warmth and satisfaction and gave Hero's arm a small squeeze as they followed the head waiter past the pool, one of the features of the décor, to a discreet table. Hero knew that it was a good one and not in those outer Siberias reserved for tourists or the nonelect. It was a satisfactory beginning.

Tina was as avid as a child and they ordered Sevruga caviar and vodka. She was steeping herself in the elegance of the restaurant and drawing it about her shoulders, inhaling its odour of wealth and sophistication. The place was a kind of cathedral of eating with Picasso décor instead of stained-glass windows. The waiters trod like acolytes. Every woman there was fresh from the hairdresser; every man just emerged from the attentions of the barbershop. If such a thing were possible, Hero thought, here one could be suffocated by luxury. The aquamarine fires of Tina's eyes reflected her delight. She received overt glances from men at other tables.

The head waiter recommended baby spring lamb on a spit from the grill. A trolley of fresh, uncooked vegetables arranged like gigantic bouquets of flowers was presented, and they chose them with all the excitement of children confronted with a novelty. The wine Hero ordered was a Richbourg '47, the champagne an Irroy '53. While waiting for the arrival of the caviar they drank small glasses of the iced Polish vodka.

Hero said, "You Americans know how to live."

Tina said, "So do you British," and when Hero raised an enquiring eyebrow she gestured with a look about the room and said, "This is fun for an evening, but I prefer the quiet elegance of London. I used to love to go to the Savoy Grill after the show."

"With Will Scarletto?" Hero asked.

Tina affected not to notice that the question was pointed and merely replied, "Not always. I've a number of friends in London."

"I might have been one of them," Hero said. "Except that I was off in Norfolk dehaunting someone's ancestral home during the time of the Great Scarlett's engagement. If I had been in London I should most certainly have gone to see his act and then I would have asked you for a date. That was about three years ago, wasn't it?"

Tina nodded without speaking, but she was thinking: *And I would have made one with you and who knows what would have happened, if we had caught fire the same way and I could have held you. And I might have stayed on forever and wouldn't be here mired and frightened, a traitoress and in trouble because of the presence of this man I am going to love tonight.*

Aloud she murmured, "Dehaunting houses? Is that what you do?"

"Sometimes."

"And what else?"

"Catch nasty little brats who think it's funny to play poltergeist and tan their bottoms for them."

Tina smiled, "I thought you were a magician?"

"Strictly amateur. Second-class sleight-of-hand. You'd turn up your lovely nose, but I need it for my business. Do you remember that line from the song in *Annie Get Your Gun,* 'Anything you can do I can do better?' I sing that to my friends the mediums. My job is to duplicate all of their rotten tricks." He suddenly found himself humming the line of Irving Berlin's music.

"Except make a wax glove?" Tina suggested.

Hero laughed, "Oh," he scoffed, "you know very well that Harry Houdini and Joe Rinn exposed that years ago."

Tina was regarding him curiously and with a tiny smile that

was half mocking. "All except the fingerprints you were asking about," she said.

Hero shrugged it off. "There's probably a way of doing that too."

"And if there weren't?"

Hero regarded the girl frankly and engagingly. He said, "That's just the difference between your work and mine. You know every time. There's always the gimmick. I never do." He let his glance rest upon the white arms of the girl, the thick coil of shining hair, and finally let his eyes become entangled in her own level gaze.

"And if there was no way to reproduce the fingerprints of the dead, except by the dead themselves . . ." Hero was half musing, "then all those with their hands hovering over the buttons of the engines of death would have to think again, for they would know that there would be a judgement and that those who first named heaven and hell were neither dreamers nor liars. And I should know that I need never worry about losing you, for I would be certain of finding you in paradise."

Tina Cryder thought to herself: *You smooth, lying bastard! All you want is what I want and after you've had it, you won't care whether I am alive or dead, in paradise or in purgatory. But who knows what I will feel? And if you knew what I knew, Mr. Peter Fairweather, you wouldn't be sitting there so sure of yourself.* To mask any expression her thoughts might have reflected she took refuge in mockery. "And for this people pay money?" she asked.

Hero picked up her tone. "Thriving business," he said. "Spooks have a way of knocking down property values or when someone's rich, old aunt is being milked by some bag of a medium with a moustache and bad breath, the worried heirs engage me to get Auntie out of her clutches."

Tina laughed softly. "Is that what you are over here for now?" she asked.

"Good heavens, no! I wouldn't suppose anyone here would be troubled with such nonsense. We are still backward when it comes to that sort of thing. I've come over for a rest and a holiday. Sometimes my work gets a little strenuous." He pushed his cuff away from his right wrist, revealing the still purple scars where wire had cut into his flesh during an encounter with a charlatan, which had almost cost him his hand. Tina regarded these for a moment before she picked up his hand and impulsively but softly pressed her lips to them, and her fine eyes were suddenly filled with query and sympathy. But she was thinking: *Liar! Liar! Liar! You're here because of Constable and the Bessmers and Father and me, but I'm in love, and I'm going to have you, and after that Mr. Kelly can deal with it.*

The touch of her lips sent a little shudder through Hero. For a fleeting instant he thought of the Judas kiss, but other thoughts less Biblical took over.

The caviar arrived, large grey pearls exquisitely presented in a block of ice carved to represent a sturgeon. The waiter spooned it out.

Hero said lightly, "Foreign exchange for the Russ, I suppose?"

Tina Cryder said, "Don't be silly! Why spoil it?"

And later Hero asked, "And you? Where else have you been?"

"Oh, everywhere, I suppose," Tina replied. "Stockholm, Rome, Athens, Cairo, Istanbul. And to South America too. Karl Boehmer took me all over with him, as long as engagements lasted. Then suddenly people didn't seem to care any more about seeing the lady vanishing." Tina felt Hero's eyes appraising her and added, "I was younger then. And besides, I was trained as a contortionist."

"A contortionist?"

Once more they glanced at one another and became entangled, unable to look away. Each read the other's thoughts so that they both suddenly burst into laughter that now, for the first time, was tinged with intimacy. They had moved closer together and as they bit with gusto into caviar spread upon toast, their lips were still wreathed in leftover smiles.

Dishes came and went. They ate and talked of the worlds and places they both knew, while the wines warmed them. Hero wanted to ask once more about the hand but dared not. Instinct told him that she was waiting for him to do so. But she steered clear of the subject and there was nothing he could do. He learned only, or rather confirmed what was already obvious, the collapse of the magic house of Cryder and the daughter out of work because there was no longer a demand for the old-style magician.

One thing developed which was both odd and unexpected. Tina Cryder did not try to bluff him about her theatrical career. Something impelled her to tell the truth, that she had tried the stage and failed. And this confession had the effect of touching Hero's heart, which was perhaps why it had been made, though he did not stop to think of this at the moment, or that for some women sex must be linked to a genuine emotion of some sort.

When they emerged onto Park Avenue it was midnight. The Avenue was still a swift flowing river of light, traffic, cars and cabs, but the air was cool and fresh, and through the gap made by the tops of the buildings they could see a few pale silver stars trying to compete with the man-made galaxies of electricity.

"It's only a few blocks," Tina said. "Shall we walk?"

They set out for East Fifty-fourth Street. She had taken his arm lightly, but a moment later his hand had found hers. It was a restless little thing that would not lie there in his palm to be clutched but kept moving as though in response to thoughts and impulses in her. And this movement became a stimulant so powerful that he did not dare to look at her, nor did she turn to regard him, and so they walked the few streets in silence with only the fluttering of the little fingers sending out their signals of desire.

They were shocked for a moment, when they entered the blare, smoke, and clatter of the night club. El Morocco was jammed, as always on a Saturday night, with would-be patrons waiting behind ropes, and here the lack of reservation might have foiled them, for not even the show of money made an impression, had not the man at the barrier remembered Tina Cryder. It was probably her eyes that he recalled, but also the once or twice she had been there with a film director. It was his job to know such things. He spoke a few words out of the side of his mouth to one of the head waiters. Tina and Hero were passed through into the main room where they occupied one of the zebra-type benches, pushed shoulder to shoulder and thigh to thigh.

"How do you do it?" Tina asked. "And you a stranger in town."

"It was you," Hero said. "I saw it happen." He ordered champagne but had a curious feeling that they would not be drinking much of it.

The room was rocking with music, drums, and people. Past midnight the smartness, the tidiness, the groomed look had left the girls and the men who were there. Faces were flushed, eyes were glistening with drink and physical excitement, strands of hair were awry, expensive dresses crumpled. The faces of the men were red and showed the shine of sweat; they danced with their mouths pressed to the cheeks or ears of their partners. The drum rhythms were savage and soon began to beat into Hero's brain.

The waiter placed a silver bucket on the table before them and uncorked the wine. Tina Cryder and Alexander Hero lifted their glasses to one another in a silent toast and sipped, regarding one another over the rims.

Hero asked, "Shall we?" and arose. As he did so he was aware that his legs were trembling slightly. She came around from the other side of the table and slipped into his arms, and then they were moving on the jam-packed floor, pushed, bumped, prodded by all the bodies gyrating about them where, seemingly, there was not an inch of space to move. Because she was so tiny, Hero had to bend down, and then his lips came only to the thick, soft, fragrant hair. He inhaled it as though to draw all of her within himself.

Yet the effect was curious and desexing and both were aware of it. External forces were thrusting them at each other, nudging, plucking or spinning them about, in that kind of floor-crush dance sought by those who needed stimulation. They had wished to dance, to test their rhythms with one another. Here was only heat and noise and alcoholic gregariousness of which they had no need. They were friends and companions now who wanted one another and were prepared to acknowledge their impatience. They had waited long enough. They edged and struggled their way back to their table, and when they had sat down Hero said, "I don't think I can take this. Can you?"

She shook her head.

"Shall we go home?"

"Yes." Hero called for his bill, and they went out and into a waiting taxi.

Thereafter neither of them was able to think, or plan, or judge, or pretend. The cab had hardly drawn away from the canopy of the nightclub and headed downtown when they were in one another's arms. There was no drifting towards the vortex; they were plunging downwards, drowning in passion, dizzying one another, lost to everything but the physical contact no longer to be postponed. Sometimes they would break apart from the embrace in which they had been locked, to regard one another, astonished at the depth and power of the attraction that had them in its grip. They would pause as if to see whether it was true, what they were experiencing in this first embrace, only to be swept even closer together again. The instruments of their bodies were keyed to still higher pitch by this violent physical union, furious, tender, demanding, aggressive, and yielding, leaving them breathless and speechless.

The cab had stopped some several seconds at the shop at Cedar Street before they realised they were there, and they sprang apart, looking at one another once more with that astonishment that had never left them, but at this time tinged with impatience and eagerness. They spoke no word. Hero handed the driver a crumpled five-dollar bill and waved him away. Tina Cryder took the key to the shop from her handbag and inserted it into the lock. Her hand was trembling. They went in and she led the way through the partition and up the stairs, switching on the light from below. They still did not speak, only moved together as though in a dream.

She entered her bedroom, drawing him in her wake and the silence that had grown between them built up the tensions until they were well nigh unbearable. The subtle message of the blue nightdress on the fresh white counterpane was now a clamour. Tina threw her wrap across the chair and turned to face Hero and the lovely eyes into which he looked down were now cloudy and swimming. Her lips were parted hungrily for contact.

Alexander Hero spoke the first words since they had left the club, but in a voice he hardly recognised as his, hoarse and strained. He said, "Your hair," and reached for it. But she was before him to give him his desire and reaching up swiftly loosened the knot, shook her head and, as he had known it would, the hair came cascading down about her face and shoulders.

It was after five o'clock in the morning, shortly before dawn, that Tina Cryder let Hero out of the shop and they parted with a final kiss that began with soft, clinging tenderness and then yet again threatened to fan the glow of leftover passion into flame, but Tina broke away and whispered, "No. Father wakes up early."

There had been no sign or sound from the apartment of Paul Cryder. Whether he had slept through their return, or had chosen to ignore what, otherwise, he might have suspected, there was no way of knowing.

"When shall I see you again?" Hero asked.

Tina Cryder did not know how she could deny him, for she was still lost in love and filled with echoes of their encounter. She whispered, "I don't know. Call me."

"I want to kiss you again," Hero said.

"No. No more."

But she did, on her tiptoes, her arms about his neck, and her body pressed to his. When finally they made the effort to part, she opened the door and half thrust him out. He wanted still to remain and say something more, though he did not know what, when the door was shut and the light in the shop was extinquished for it was no longer dark.

Now Hero walked the few steps over to Broadway and caught an early-bird cruising cab and rode northwards to his hotel. And as he sat back in the seat of the car and listened to the whine of the tyres as it wheeled through the empty city, with all his will power he kept himself tightly wrapped in the memories of the experience through which he had just passed. It was as though he had encrusted himself, with a kind of mental armour which had let him lie with Tina Cryder, proof against the whisperings of conscience, memories, fears and reason.

Above all—above everything—he did not wish to contemplate at that moment the fact that Ruth Lesley and Tina Cryder were probably one and the same person.

CHAPTER XIII

Mr. O'Brien Issues Instructions

Alexander Hero awoke in his hotel room well after midday to a sense of profound depression and discomfort. He had left a message to take care of the eight o'clock FBI call and now was struggling not only with that sense of lost time and space from having slept the morning away, but also with all of the alarms and revelations of the night before plus the feeling of shame for an indulgence that might very well have let the side down.

It was pouring outside; rain and wind from low-hanging grey clouds had already swallowed the spire of the Chrysler building and threatened to descend to his own sixteenth-storey window. He reflected gloomily upon the consequences of his visit to the magic shop and in particular his impulsive, passionate affair with the proprietor's daughter. For if it was true, as now in calm retrospect he was convinced it was, that Tina Cryder was not only the materialisation of Ruth Lesley, but the voice and figure of Mary Constable as well, then it would also follow that she would know that Alexander Hero and Peter Fairweather were also one and the same person. His cover would be broken and his usefulness to Ferguson, Wiener, and Operation Foxglove at an end.

For a moment the sinking feeling in the pit of his stomach engendered by these thoughts led him to a pitch of such despondency that he was on the verge of telephoning Wiener to tell him, and indeed had removed the instrument from its cradle, when his mind, in a moment of recovery and perhaps self-defence, flashed ahead to the dialogue that must ensue, after he had confessed to Wiener the first embrace of the girl in the cabinet who purported to be Ruth Lesley.

Wiener: "What makes you think Ruth Lesley is this girl Tina Cryder?"

Hero: "The first time I kissed her in the taxi I suspected it, but by then it was too late. After I had been to bed with her I was certain."

The utter ridiculousness of this struck Hero in time, and he replaced the telephone before the operator had had a chance to answer. It would be simply impossible to say this to a man of Wiener's calibre, to insist that he, Alexander Hero, could identify a woman kissed in the dark by the unique, sexual stimulation of her mouth.

Hero rang Room Service for coffee and brunch, showered while waiting for it to appear, and tried to bring some order into his way of reasoning. He remained confirmed in his feeling that there simply was not enough to go on. Wiener could hardly be expected to take seriously the extracurricular dalliances of a British psychical researcher whom he did not like anyway. Or, take it another way, supposing Wiener did credit Hero's story and convictions and panicked to the point of taking steps which would put Operation Foxglove on the rocks and all because he, Alexander Hero, had not been able to keep his trousers buttoned, and had become involved with a sharp little bit. Furious with himself as he was, Hero still smiled suddenly at the thought of sex and spies. Whenever was there time for the worming-out or exchange of secrets?

Hero's practice of independent psychical investigator came to his rescue to bolster his decision not to call Wiener. Personal conviction, no matter how strong, was not evidence. All through his career he had had to struggle against that very thing, the personal conviction of witnesses that what they had thought they had seen, heard, or felt was gospel. There was actually not an iota of proof or tangible evidence that the girl in the cabinet or the Constable child was Tina Cryder. Appearances were circumstantial. She was tiny enough for Mary Constable with her long hair let down. She was an actress and probably an excellent mimic. And as for the tall girl he had held to himself in the cabinet, this could have been one of the oldest tricks and illusions furthered by darkness.

Surmise! Good guesses! Probably very close to the truth but no proof. Why not wait and see what developed at the promised seance the next night? Would Ruth Lesley appear once more in the cabinet and yield to him in an embrace? Would Mary Constable be there? Would he be barred from the house on West Ninety-first Street? Would anything be different from what it had been before? If so, that would constitute evidence and the beginning of proof. If, on the other hand, Ruth Lesley again materialised, and particularly if he managed to look at her and she proved to be someone totally different, then his cover would not be broken and he would be saved from making more of an ass of himself than already he had.

Hero remembered then that he had promised Wiener to try to arrange to take him to the seance. Time enough to open up to the FBI man after Wiener had had the opportunity of independent observation and corroboration.

On an impulse he picked up the phone and gave the number of the Cryder shop, for Tina had said, "Call me," and it was probably politic to do so. And then there was the off chance that some remark, some inflection of her voice, might furnish a clue as to the actual state of things between them. Whether or not his cover was broken he must, for the time being, behave and act as though it was not.

He listened to the ringing signal unanswered for a full minute before he hung up, half relieved, half disturbed. He thought then to call Bessmer for an appointment but decided against it. If Tina Cryder had warned Bessmer of the double role that Hero was playing, the spiritualist would probably refuse to see him. Better to present himself on his doorstep as a *fait accompli* and play it by ear from there. When his meal came he ate it in a slightly better frame of mind, finished dressing, and took a cab up to the house on West Ninety-first Street.

Hero tugged at the old-fashioned wire bellpull and listened to the clangor inside the house. The blinds to the front parlour were drawn, although it was still early in the afternoon, shortly after three o'clock. As he waited, Hero thought with some irony that it would not be long before Wiener knew about this visit. The FBI men would be shooting with their telescopic lens from one of the rooms in a similar brownstone house opposite. Hero wondered whether he would be able to spot the camera they used at nighttime and how it had been concealed. He looked upward to the ceiling of the portico where he was standing but saw nothing except at one end where there appeared to be a discoloration of the moulding and two small ends of wire hung loose.

No one came to answer the door, and when he went outside for another pull at the bell, he had the impression that someone had nipped a look at him from behind the blind. He rang again, and as he passed once more through the first glass doors the inner one was opened, not this time by Pratt, but by Bessmer himself.

"Friend Fairweather," he boomed, "an unexpected visitor, but always a pleasure. I hope it isn't distress which brings you to our doorstep on this day of rest and prayer? Come in, come in."

Hero thought: *Rest and prayer are good!* Bessmer's face was flushed and he smelled of whisky. The man was also both nervous and distracted. Hero felt that his greeting was almost mechanical and lacked unction.

Bessmer preceded him and Hero was about to go into the parlour immediately to the right of the hall, as he had done before, when Bessmer hurriedly stopped him saying, "No, no. Not in there. Mother is resting. Come, we will go into the other room," and he led the way down the hall.

It was an odd place for Mother to be resting, Hero thought. Besides which, he had caught a glimpse of her and Pratt at the table, bending over what seemed to be a small black object about the size of a matchbox.

The door at the end of the corridor opened into what had been the seance room but which was merely fitted out as a kind of second parlour with heavy Mission furniture; a large breakfront bookcase at one side and the big gramophone unit on the other.

"Here," Bessmer said, "you sit here for a second while I look to see if Mother's all right, and I'll be with you."

Hero wondered what was up. The man was thoroughly uncomfortable and not because of Hero's visit. His attack of nerves was from something more long-standing, and he had in all probability been drinking because of it or, Hero smiled to himself, it was possible that he had just caught him and Ma at their Sunday afternoon booze-up.

He sat down in one of the heavy leather armchairs as Bessmer's footsteps diminished down the passage and heard him go into the front room followed by the low murmur of voices raised only once by what Hero judged was an angry remark or comment from Mother. At no time did Hero stir from the chair, yet by the time Bessmer returned he had the room cased, eye-measured, and analysed and was fairly certain of the entrance and exit from the cabinet.

There was a rectangle of steel curtain rail screwed into the ceiling. There were no telltale signs of a trap door there, such as ridges or cracks in the plaster or discolorations. The cabinet area itself gave upon the rear window of the room, looking out over the typical New York backyard area, crisscrossed by fences, the home of one or two desultory acacia trees and a number of cats. Nothing so crude as ingress by the windows would be attempted. The breakfront bookcase was suspicious, and Hero had known of partitions that swung open to admit characters from the adjoining room, but this one was too far, actually, from the cabinet, and its purpose was probably to prove by its own integrity the honesty of the operation. There then remained the floor area. The part where the cabinet had been was covered by several small Turkish rugs, while the bulk of the room was covered with a large red oriental carpet. But where the floor showed, it was of parquet. That, of course, would be it. The rug flipped back, the trap door opened, the small figure of a girl who had once been a contortionist whipped through it with lightning speed, and later, if anyone were curious enough to look beneath the rug, there would be only the grooving of the boards of the parquet floor to be seen. So much for that.

Bessmer entered the room. He seemed to have taken the trouble to compose himself and was once more in command, though he could not keep the liquor he had taken from glistening in his eyes.

"Now, Fairweather, in what manner can we serve you?"

Hero had to exercise the mental muscle that turned him into Peter Fairweather, and he struggled to recall his characteristics.

"I have a friend," he began tentatively.

"Any friend of yours is a friend of ours," intoned Bessmer.

"I should like your permission to bring him with me to the seance tomorrow night."

To Hero's surprise Bessmer was not regarding him as sharply as he would have expected but instead rather benignly. He asked, "Is he one of us? Has he suffered a bereavement? Is he a believer? What does he seek at the Fountain of the Holy Ozone?"

In spite of Bessmer's unusual air of affability these were the sixty-four-dollar questions—who and why? Hero had the choice of a number of cards he could play and on impulse selected the Joker.

"None of these," he replied. "To tell the truth it's a lawyer I've known for some years. He often comes to England. Last night he managed to irritate me beyond endurance. I had occasion to tell him of my extraordinary experience through your generosity. He laughed at me."

"They scoffed at The Man," Bessmer said sepulchrally.

Hero felt that he was on the right track; he said, "I'd give"—he hesitated—"well, quite something to make a convert of him." For an instant the flare of greed joined the shine of alcohol in Bessmer's eyes, and his small mouth made a sucking noise. "—As a contribution to the Church," Hero concluded.

"Your friend will be welcome in our circle," Bessmer said.

Hero said, "Thank you. I shall appreciate that," and then added, "By the way, he is a Jew. Do you mind?"

Bessmer said unctuously, "Jesus was a Jew. The Church of His Breath, the Holy Ozone, is non-sectarian and bars no race, creed or colour. Perhaps if I might have his name and address?"

Hero replied, "His name is Saul Roth. He is a tax lawyer living at 229 East Fifty-sixth Street." The name and the address was one that Wiener used occasionally as a cover and which he had given Hero should he need it some time.

No telltale expression crossed Bessmer's face as he noted this down, and they discussed the matter a while longer, at the conclusion of which, as Hero prepared to leave, Bessmer stopped him, saying, "Friend Fairweather, perhaps you will answer a few questions of interest to me and Mother, having lately come here from the other side of the pond. Though you have never before experienced communication with the hereafter, what would you say our reception would be if we decided to visit your country?"

The question so startled both Alexander Hero and Peter Fairweather that neither replied immediately, and Hero, recovering from his astonishment, thought: *I'll be blowed! The nervousness, the drink, the affability, the little black box and the busted wires, are you and Mum getting ready to do a bunk?*

"Why, yes," stammered Peter Fairweather, finally. "Of course —I'm sure . . ."

"There must be as many folks in distress over there as here that we could help with our simple Gospel and the power that comes to Mother. There was a time when England was a happy place for people of our faith, then—ah—I believe the climate deteriorated for some years, but perhaps by now . . ."

"Oh, I'm certain they'd love you," Peter Fairweather said, almost in an excess of heat. "I mean there are a number of spiritualist churches—one reads notices here and there of meetings. You would be very welcome, I'm sure."

Bessmer went all creamy and smooth. "We were wondering, Mother and I, whether perhaps in the light of your successful contact you might not care to sponsor us and spread the word amongst your friends and acquaintances?"

Hero thought: *That would be the day!* But aloud he said, "Of course, I'd be glad—do anything I can to help—I mean, it would be wonderful for me if you and Mrs. Bessmer came over there—for Ruth and me."

"Then shall we take it as read?" Bessmer said with a satisfied air. "And shall we say nothing further about this to anyone and let it come as a complete surprise, should we decide to visit your shores?"

As Hero took up his hat to go, Bessmer wrote upon a card and handed it to him. "For your lawyer friend," he said. "I hope we shall be able to have a little demonstration for him." They walked to the front door. Hero was able to keep his eyes from the two small cut wires in the roof of the vestibule, but Bessmer was unable to refrain from darting a quick glance upwards.

On Monday morning Tina Cryder once more sat in the van at the back of the Rafferty Brothers livery stables with Mr. Kelly and another, a Mr. O'Brien, who kept out of what little light there was and spoke mostly in monosyllables from the interior of the delivery van, addressing himself to the backs of Mr. Kelly and Tina. And if the kind of Irishman Mr. Kelly was could be considered indeterminate, though mainly Mediterranean, there was no such problem concerning Mr. O'Brien. He looked as though, swaddled now in civilian clothes, he had descended from one of those group photographs of the Kremlin balcony on Review Day. He was built four-square, with a head like a cube, short, bristling hair, little pig's eyes, and broad nostrils flaring like a pig's snout.

The man whose pseudonym was Mr. O'Brien was a professional killer whose concern was practical and political murder. At home in Russia he had a fat wife and three bouncing children with whom he was kindly and loving and even, sometimes, gay. But at work he was unsentimental. The man called Kelly was afraid of him. So was Tina Cryder.

While Mr. O'Brien lurked in the darkness of the van behind them in the shape of a bulky shadow whose heavy breathing made his presence known, Mr. Kelly interrogated Tina.

"Okay, what did you find out?"

The girl was nervous. "Well, he's some kind of a detective."

"What do you mean, some kind of a detective, is he or isn't he?"

"He said he was an investigator. That's the same thing, isn't it?"

"What, you mean he admitted it? What the hell kind of a detective is that?"

"Not just that way," Tina said. "He's an investigator for the Society of Psychical Research in London."

"What's that? What does he investigate?"

"Ghosts."

Kelly's mouth took a bitter turn. "Listen you," he said, "cut out the clowning or . . ."

He was interrupted by a thick voice from the gloom behind them both which said, "Shut up, Kelly! Let the girl talk."

"And spirit mediums," Tina said. "He's against them."

The man named O'Brien grunted and Kelly asked, "Who's he working for over here?"

Tina Cryder replied, "He said he was here on holiday."

Kelly asked, "Did you believe that?"

"No, he's a liar. Did you tell Mr. O'Brien about the cock-and-bull story of Peter Fairweather and the girl who was supposed to have died?"

Mr. O'Brien's voice was heard again, "Yes. He told me. What else have you found out?"

Tina Cryder said, "That's all," and looked back to speak to the shadow when the voice said, quietly, "Don't turn around. Please just sit as you are. Have you told the Bessmers about this man?"

"No."

"That is good. There is no need to do so. They are stupid."

And then he added, "Does this man suspect you have broken his cover?"

"No."

"You have slept with him."

Tina was not clear whether this was a question or a statement and she did not reply to it.

Mr. O'Brien now continued to interrogate. "He is coming again to the seance tonight?"

Tina replied, "He told the Bessmers that he would. He's paying a lot."

O'Brien said, "The Bessmers are not only stupid, they are greedy. They will be sorry, I think. And he will come into the cabinet again?"

"Yes. I'm sure he will—if only to maintain his cover."

"And what are your instructions from the Bessmers?"

A hard little suppressed laugh knotted itself inside of Tina Cryder. "To 'give him some more lovin'' is the way Bessmer put it."

Mr. O'Brien grunted again, this time with satisfaction. "So then. That is good. Now here, take this. No, no, do not turn round. Put your hand behind you."

When Tina Cryder did so a small object which, in the dark, felt like a ring and a cork, was thrust into her hand and when she brought it around to what dim light there was to look at it, it was exactly that, a small, gold band like a wedding ring, apparently attached to something which was embedded in the cork.

"Do not handle the ring. Do not touch the cork," warned the thick voice of Mr. O'Brien. "Put it in your handbag and listen to me carefully."

Tina Cryder was beginning to feel ill and frightened.

"Pay attention now." The accented voice of Mr. O'Brien took on a slow, meticulous pace. "When you go into the cabinet tonight, you will be wearing the ring on the third finger of your right hand. Do not remove the cork until this man approaches. Then pull it off. There is a needle attached to the ring. Be very, very careful not to prick yourself. Keep your hand open and the point of the needle away from you. When he enters the cabinet you will embrace him again, as you did the last time. In the normal position for such an embrace your right hand will rest at the base of his neck. Press the needle home. If you are quick he will barely feel it, if at all. But even though he should feel it, before he can react it will be too late. Replace the needle in the cork and leave the cabinet at once, and the house as well. The ring you will return to Mr. Kelly the following morning, after you have received the usual telephone call. Have you understood this?"

It was only then that the full implication of her instructions turned Tina Cryder's stomach topsy-turvy. For while he had been speaking, the quiet, careful, matter-of-fact voice of Mr. O'Brien had been like someone giving directions for the use of some new kind of tin-opener or household gadget. The object seemed to burn in her hand and she had a moment of sweaty fear when she thought that the needle might penetrate the cork. She cried, "What is it? It won't kill him, will it?"

From the darkness behind, Mr. O'Brien enquired without emotion, "What if it does?"

"I wouldn't do it," Tina cried. "Oh, my God! Take it back. I wouldn't touch it!" Panic made her limbs twitch, and as though he feared she might run out, Kelly, sitting beside her, seized her arm and held it. But Mr. O'Brien remained calm and unexcited. He said, "I am afraid that you have no choice in the matter. You are an intelligent girl, which is why your work for us has been satisfactory. It is not necessary for me to discuss the consequences of disobedience."

Tina Cryder felt herself sinking into a dark well of terror and wondered whether she was going to pass out. But through it all penetrated the quiet, relentless voice.

"However, you need not worry. It will only result in his feeling ill and losing consciousness. The Bessmers will naturally remove him to another room to recover, after which we will make our own arrangements. There will be no danger to yourself, unless you disobey. And, of course, we shall know."

"Oh, my God!" Tina Cryder said again. "Do you swear it won't hurt him?"

"It is not necessary to swear. I have told you. That is sufficient. Place the ring in your handbag and please repeat the instructions I have given you."

Tina felt impelled, caught up, half hypnotised. She dropped the ring into her bag, glad to get it out of her sweating palm, and tried to repeat the orders. Mr. O'Brien prompted her gently until he was satisfied. He then concluded, "You will remain sitting here until Mike comes to tell you it is all right for you to leave."

Tina heard heavy, scraping movements behind her, indicative of the departure of Mr. O'Brien. Kelly relaxed the grip he had taken of her wrist ever since he had thought she might be going to run. He said, "You better do what he told you to, sister, or else! I wouldn't monkey around if I were you." He climbed down from the front seat of the van and sauntered off in the direction of the office, leaving the girl sitting by herself in the semi-gloom of the stable, with only the stamping and munching of the horses and her thoughts to keep her company.

She was cold with fear. What had appeared to be a safe enough caper into which she had gone with her eyes open for the money that had been offered and which had seemed to be fairly secure from possible repercussions had suddenly developed into something deadly. She had no way of ascertaining if O'Brien was telling her the truth as to whether the dose of the ring-hypodermic was lethal or only knockout.

If the former, she would be a murderess. In cold blood she would have killed the man in whose arms she had taken pleasure the night before. And if the latter—temporary loss of consciousness while O'Brien and his people spirited him away? What were "their own arrangements," of which O'Brien had talked? In her mind Tina always used the name "O'Brien," for it helped to salve her conscience. She had, after all, she told herself, done no more than what she had already been doing for the Bessmers to lay her hands on some money, namely, "materialise" in various guises at seances to fool a crowd of saps. It was actually nothing worse, she further equivocated, than she had done on the stage, where she had assisted at illusions for people who had paid at the box office to be fooled.

And as for the Englishman and what would happen to him after his "faint," he would have to take his chances. That was his business. What was he doing, snooping around there and pretending to be someone he wasn't, if he hadn't been paid for it? Bad luck for him that he had wandered into her father's shop the other afternoon. Good luck for her.

Look out for number one! Take care of little Tina. You only had to read the papers to know what could happen to you: people disappearing, people being shot, important men or refugees suddenly found dead from a heart attack on staircases or in the streets. Would the stuff with which the ring was loaded produce a heart attack? Peter Fairweather, the visiting Englishman, dead in a medium's cabinet from too much emotion at encountering his lost fiancée. And on her waking and sleeping conscience— murder.

What would happen? Would he cry out, struggle, attempt to escape, or feel nothing and suddenly in the darkness slide to the floor, perhaps even dragging her down with him? If he were dead, she tried to convince herself, it would have been O'Brien who had done it, not she. But it wouldn't wash, and she pressed her hands to her temples and screwed her eyes shut in an attempt to shut out the horror. Someone touched her and she screamed and then choked off the cry. It was the sallow man with the bowler hat from the front office, who was known as Mike. He said, "Okay. You can beat it now. Use the side door, walk over to Ninth Avenue and take the bus down to Fourteenth Street, change to the crosstown one over to Third Avenue. If you get the all clear from our guy then, you can take a taxi."

He wandered back to the front office. Tina got out of the wagon and emerged from the side door and out of the corner of her eye saw the man who usually tailed her for protection saunter off after her. Her mind was numb from thinking and worrying. As she hurried along her handbag struck against her knee and a wave of nausea engulfed her as she remembered what it contained.

CHAPTER XIV

Saul Wiener Meets His Ancestor

"Exactly what is it I do?" Saul Wiener asked of Hero. They were on their way driving north together proceeding to the house of the Bessmers for the Monday night seance.

"Nervous?" Hero asked.

"Frankly, yes."

Hero warmed to him for his honesty. On the other hand, Saul Wiener's attitude towards him and his work had never been exactly flattering.

Hero said, "It's a sensible approach. I always am. It's a primitive atavism. It all takes place in the dark, and when I was a little boy I was afraid of the dark."

"I suppose I was too."

"You will be fitted into the chain of sitters," Hero said. "I don't know what your assigned position will be. At present I'm the fair-haired boy—on your cash—and sit at Bessmer's right, with Woodmanston next to me. You will probably be sitting next to Woodmanston. I shouldn't try to slip hands, if I were you. It wants practice."

"Slip hands?"

"Break the chain, so you can move about. But it takes an expert. The mediums do it all the time when they're in with the sitters. If the medium wants to free one hand, he or she simply holds two hands with the remaining one. If he wants to get out completely, he simply joins the two hands on his left and right. If a foot control is being attempted as well, by using heel and toe, it will give the impression of two feet where there is only one."

"Geezuzz!" said Wiener.

"But I don't want you moving about," Hero said, "or, for that matter, breaking the chain. You have promised not to grab. I want you to observe, and for that you will need your wits about you and all your powers of concentration."

Wiener said, "I'll try, coach." But there was just the faintest tinge of sarcasm and mockery in the statement. He had used the term coach, but Hero felt he would have preferred the more derogatory name of Buster, or even Junior.

"Look here," Hero said, "let me quote something to you. It's from a book entitled *The Secrets of Houdini,* by a man named Cannell, and I remember it because the man from whom I learned most of what I know in this business read it to me the first time he ever took me into a seance room. It goes roughly like this: 'There is no darkness like that of a seance room and no atmosphere which can compare with it. After an hour in dark and silence even a highly sceptical person often becomes susceptible and finds himself thinking that, after all, there may be something in it. The creation of such an atmosphere is part of the medium's business. Those taking part in the seance are, generally, at the lowest ebb of their powers of scrutiny and critical observation when the manifestations begin.' "

Wiener grinned and said, "You have been warned." Then he asked, "Are you still susceptible?"

"Invariably," Hero replied, "at least during a first visit and when I run up against something new."

"But this is your second visit . . ."

"Exactly," Hero assented. "So I shall be having a bit of a look round. Mother uses infra-red to keep from tripping over her sitters' feet when she is on the prowl." And he produced a small black tube from his pocket and said, "This is just a bit more modern. It's called black light. I think you chaps were using it on your sniperscopes in Korea. I'm going to have a look, I hope, at Ruth Lesley and Mary Constable."

"If there are a Ruth Lesley and a Mary Constable." Wiener's tone was still mocking, and Hero was almost pleased that it should be so.

"If there are a Ruth Lesley and a Mary Constable," he repeated carefully. Then he added, "Incidentally, I suppose you know the Bessmers have the wind up. They were making enquiries on the suitability of setting up shop in London. They've come across one of your little boxes."

Wiener was looking slightly sheepish and annoyed. "It was damn bad luck," he said, "and nothing else."

"Did they pick up a camera?" Hero asked. "I thought I saw . . ."

"No. Just the infra-red lamp. The camera's next door. But, of course, they'd know what the box was for. Do you know what happened? It wouldn't again in a million years. One of those goddam New York sparrows got itself trapped inside that first doorway and was raising a hell of a kerfuffle. Bessmer, the old woman and Pratt all came out to see what was up and free the birdie, and, of course, there it was. We'd had it pretty well concealed, but if you were messing about the ceiling there with a broom, trying to clear out an hysterical sparrow, you'd see it, naturally. We can show you the movies of it all, if you like."

Hero asked, "Wouldn't they reckon to be under surveillance anyway?"

Wiener replied, "Yes, but it's always a nasty shock when you have it verified like that." He then said with a lightness he did not feel, "Well, no more pretty night pictures. I so hoped to be able to present you with one of us arm-in-arming it into the Bessmers' house, for your memory book." He was irritated not only over the misfortune which had now alerted the Bessmers, but because somehow the Englishman had managed to find out and tax him with it. The cab drew up before No. 12A West Ninety-first Street, or rather behind another one that was discharging a passenger who paid off and then waited to have a look at who was arriving. Hero saw that it was Professor

Constable. He said to Wiener, "He doesn't know you, does he?"

"No, fortunately I've avoided meeting him."

Constable said, "Oh, Fairweather! Nice to see you again."

"Professor Constable, Saul Roth," Hero said. "Roth is a lawyer, a friend and—a sceptic."

Constable acknowledged this revelation with no more than a grunt and was on his way up the steps. Hero and Wiener followed. From within, as the front door opened, they could hear the booming voice of Bessmer, "Prepare yourselves, folks. Think right thoughts. Mother's resting. She feels the power on herself."

Hero left the envelope with the cash contribution with Pratt and turned to Wiener. "I'll introduce you to Bessmer and then turn you over to Woodmanston, who will do the rest of the job."

Bessmer came across to the door as they entered and greeted them, "Friend Fairweather! A real pleasure to see you and have you with us again," and Hero thought he noticed a deeper note of affability, as though all that had transpired between them the afternoon before had admitted Fairweather into closer and more intimate contact. "And this will be your friend, Mr. Roth. I have always been a great admirer of the legal mind. But I hope you will be able to experience something with us here tonight which will lead you upwards and onwards along another path."

Woodmanston came bustling up and Hero passed Wiener to him. The sitters were essentially the same as at the previous session. Only one of the Irish widows was absent.

When the partitioning doors were rolled back, the black draped cabinet and the circle of chairs were as they had been before. But the sitting arrangements turned out not quite as Hero had expected, for Wiener was placed between Bessmer and Woodmanston this time, the position that Hero had occupied originally, whilst he was put at Woodmanston's right with Weitzenkorn on the other side. Constable was slumped in his usual chair. This was probably the pattern, with Bessmer taking no chances on newcomers turning out to have propensities for wandering. Hero was relieved. He would not have been afraid to match his skill against Bessmer's, but it would have been more difficult. Evading Woodmanston and Weitzenkorn, should he feel the need to explore, presented no problem.

Mrs. Bessmer had not yet appeared and while they sat waiting Bessmer said to Woodmanston, "Mother will want you to tie her again, since we have a new sitter with us."

Woodmanston twittered, "Yes. Of course. Delighted."

Mrs. Bessmer came stumping into the room. Hero thought that she was looking grim, preoccupied, and bad-tempered.

Bessmer greeted her, "Ah, Mother. Here you are. Do you feel the power on you tonight?"

"I've got the power, all right," she replied. "Come, let's get on with it then."

Pratt was there to whip back the curtains of the cabinet, showing the same arrangement of paraphernalia on the table, to which had been added a long length of rope.

Woodmanston arose from his chair. Bessmer said to Wiener, "Might you like to accompany him, friend Roth, and observe that everything is hunky-dory—even tie a few knots yourself, if you like? That way you will be satisfied."

Wiener got up and followed Woodmanston to the cabinet, where the latter began to bind Mrs. Bessmer to her chair. Wiener was surprised at the thoroughness of the little man and the job he was doing, for he lashed each of the woman's fat legs to a rung of the chair, roped her hands behind her through the rungs, and finally trussed her neck and shoulders as well.

"Don't spare me, Mr. Woodmanston," Sarah Bessmer said. "We have a doubting Thomas in our midst. Are you satisfied, Mr. Roth?"

Wiener examined the lashings and the knots. He said to Woodmanston, "That rope is cutting into her flesh there."

Sarah Bessmer said, "If it'll get you into the Church, I won't have suffered in vain."

The two men returned to their seats. Bessmer called, "Join hands, friends. Pray. Open your minds. Prepare to receive communication." There was a rustle as they linked hands. The burly

Pratt stepped forward, closed the curtains of the cabinet, and then took up his position by the phonograph. Bessmer said, "Friend Roth, concentrate on someone you would like to hear from who has gone before." Then he cried, "Lights out, Pratt." The seance room was plunged into total darkness.

Peter Fairweather gripped the moist hands of the men on either side of him and felt that his palms were sweating too. The hunt was on in earnest now. Before long he would be summoned to the cabinet to meet his dead fiancée once more. When next he gathered her into his arms, he would definitely know.

In another part of the house on West Ninety-first Street, Tina Cryder waited for the signal to carry out her assignment. On the third finger of her right hand she wore the gold band and went over her instructions again, move by move, as she had so many times before. If fate so decided, she knew that she would carry them out to the letter, for she was lost, caught up, trapped, and no longer able to evade the consequences. There was no more that she could do than she had done, and if it suited fate to send the Englishman into the darkened cabinet with her, then she would press her hand and what it contained to his warm neck, and if he died from it, it were better he than Tina Cryder.

The darkness folded itself about the head and shoulders of Saul Wiener like a heavy cloak, and at once, remembering the words that the English investigator had quoted him, he set about manufacturing resistance to whatever kind of manifestation there would be, recalling all that Alexander Hero had said about seances and the people who created them. Yet he was not comfortable, for the heavy darkness was a fact and could not be imagined away, and he realised now that he did not like having his hands held. If something or someone were to emerge out of the pitch blackness and touch him, he could not defend himself or brush it off. He had a moment of clarity when he realised that this was perhaps exactly the state of mind they wished him in, uneasy, apprehensive, imaginative. The one thing he must not think of was something touching him in the dark. And so he continued to think about it.

Hero had described to him the conduct of the first seance, the music, singing, and the noises. There were none of these now. They simply sat in complete silence, waiting. The others were apparently accustomed to this kind of approach, for no one moved or spoke. Wiener heard the ticking of his wrist watch, the beating of his heart, and the muffled noises of the city from without. Once he had waited in a pitch-dark cellar for a killer to move and shoot it out with him. He had been neither nervous nor afraid but only coldly calculating how he would carry out his assignment and survive.

What was he waiting for here? Nasty pranks played upon stupid, innocent boobs. Childish spook stuff, sheets flapping, tambourines rattling, phosphorescent faces. He didn't believe in ghosts or spirits or the dead returning. What did he believe in, then? And did he believe in anything? He thought to himself that he was a Jew and therefore believed in God. But what was God and who and where was He? Was He there in the darkness with them or was He only an idea, an abstraction, a superstition? And if he thought this, how did he, Wiener, differ from any of the others, concealed there by the darkness, those who believed that the souls of the dead lived on?

He was straining his senses now, though he knew he should not—his eyes to catch any faint glimmer, his ear to pick up so much as a scratch of sound. Hero had asked him to observe, and Wiener knew very well that for observation there should be relaxation. For the first time he understood something of the nature of the work of Alexander Hero, as well as the man himself, and why he refused either to believe or disbelieve, and somehow through it all managed to keep an open mind.

A cold wind suddenly blew on Saul Wiener's face; something icy touched him. He cried out in spite of himself, "Jesus Christ!"

He was touched again, but this time it was soft, warm, unidentifiable, but caressing. His jangled nerves gave way and he began to struggle.

Bessmer held his hand tightly and whispered, "Shhh! Don't worry, there's nothing to hurt you. The spirits are all lovin'."

Wiener felt his gorge rise in irrational anger against the man, and then as he felt his fingers gripped tighter, he wanted to shout, "Let go of my hand, you crooked bastard!" but did not, because just in time he realised that he was off base and confused.

"Music, Pratt," Bessmer shouted. "All join in now, and help the power come into Mother."

The silence was shattered by the banging of church bells and the hymn "Onward Christian Soldiers," which the sitters in the room, now relieved from tension, took up and chorused with glee like children. And Wiener felt himself caught in the rhythm, his feet tapping in time to the music and the urge to let out his lungs and sing with them until anger at himself once more brought him around as he thought, *Hell's bells! What is this? What do they think they're doing? They can't get away with it!* But he knew he was no longer a calm, reasoning, objective observer.

To add to his confusion a most unholy row emanated from the area of the cabinet, topping the singing and the gramophone music, an overpowering clatter of tambourine, harmonica, trumpet blasts, thumps and bangs and bashings, groans and strangulated cries which then died away. A faint, reddish glow permeated and dispelled some of the darkness, and Wiener saw the curtains agitated violently, swelling, swaying and billowing outwards, as though some gigantic struggle were going on within.

He thought at once of the shaking tent of the Ojibwa Indians and the medicine man lying trussed within and what Alexander Hero told him of the strange and accurate prophecies that had issued from the tent, things that the man inside could not possibly have known.

"Hi there!" shouted Bessmer on his left suddenly. "The power is strong on Mother tonight. Don't anybody move." The light faded into darkness again, leaving green images on the retina of the eye. From the direction of the cabinet a voice spoke, "How! Me here, Big Chief Thundering-Cloud." From the sitters came the pathetically ridiculous answering cries of "How—how, Big Chief," and Wiener felt that he ought to be roaring with laughter, but somehow there was no laughter in him.

Bessmer intoned, "Welcome, Big Chief. What spirits are coming through tonight? Who are they asking for?"

"One spirit my own people. She very strong. She speak." Then silence and a soft voice, young and low half whispering, "A-to-tar-ho," and then twice repeated.

"What's that?" said Bessmer sharply. "What did you say? Who are you?"

Saul Wiener said, "My God! That's my Indian name," and did not know that he had spoken aloud.

"Is that for you, friend Roth?" came Bessmer's voice. "Hold fast then, don't break the chain. Say who you are, spirit."

Unintelligible words replied out of the darkness, the voice soft as the eye of a doe, *"Nene tentatsitsanekare kahnik tenkanietahkwe,"* unintelligible to all but Wiener, who was listening to someone say in the Mohawk language that she was the "First-Flower-That-Comes-After-the-Snow."

Confusion was mounting in Wiener. The Bessmers had never laid eyes on him before. There was not a chance in a million of their hitting upon a Mohawk great-great-great-great-grandmother by accident. His voice no more than a hoarse croak, he addressed a few words towards the dark patch whence the speech was coming.

The reply came drifting back, more faintly, in the same language, *"Onen ki wahi kwienah ne onkwanakeraserakon, aontaskwehtahkwe* [Good-bye, son of our tribe. Believe in us]." And then there was an end to it. The voice of Chief Thundering-Cloud added a valedictory, "First-Flower-That-Comes-After-the-Snow gone back to happy hunting ground." Saul Wiener felt cold and a little sick.

He was outraged, too, feeling that somehow he'd been had

and that in the darkness someone, the foul woman in the cabinet or the graceful young voice, or the man next to him, or all three for that matter, were laughing at him for his idiocy in spouting in Mohawk before all those assembled. His sharp intellect was even able to stand aside and observe his own confused state of mind, and for the first time he was able to appreciate how Samuel Hale Constable had come to get himself so embroiled. And he was wondering whether, perhaps, this was why Hero had been so amenable to having him accompany him to the seance, and, if so, one up to the Englishman.

What shook him so was that waiting there in the dark, he *had* been thinking of his Indian ancestress almost as a challenge to these fakers. The communication had been a shock. There was no earthly or unearthly reason why his long defunct, aborigine forebear should wish to communicate with him, but if there were such a thing as an afterlife, there was also no reason why she should not. But again, with humiliation and anger he realised that one result of all this hocus-pocus had been to let the little word "if" creep in.

With quite different ears now, he listened to the nonsense being retailed by Big Chief Thundering-Cloud, followed by the simperings of little Devi, the Indian princess, and even while he marvelled how grown people could stomach such trash, he found himself weighing the messages and wondering what secret germs of truth were contained in them and the comfort they seemed to bring to the sitters at whom they were directed.

Wiener's state of mind was such that when suddenly little Devi, with a jingling of bangles and rattling of the tambourine, announced the presence of the spirit fiancée of Peter Fair-weather, and the first soft, pleading, seductive call of that name issued from the direction of the cabinet, he momentarily forgot the plot and Hero's cover. He accepted Ruth Lesley as the personification of someone real until, with a further rush of irritation, he remembered that of everything that had taken place in the seance room up to then, this one was the palpable and

incontrovertible fraud. There never had been a Peter Fairweather or a Ruth Lesley and the person hidden in the cabinet,
to whom Alexander Hero was now going, aided by the faint,
reddish glow which revealed the details of gently moving curtains, was flesh and blood.

"Peter, I'm here. Dear Peter!"

Wiener felt Woodmanston on his right shift as Hero broke
the chain of hands and heard Hero's chair scrape as he stood up
in the guise of Peter Fairweather. He heard Hero/Fairweather
say, "Ruth! Oh, dear God! Ruth! Do you know what day this is,
Ruth?"

From the direction of the cabinet came the reply, "The day
we met, Peter, a year ago. Oh, Peter, come to me!"

Wiener heard the Englishman utter a half sob and move in
the direction of the cabinet. The voices, the acting on the part
of both was superb and he had once more to force himself to the
contemplation of the trap that was ready to be sprung. In a few
seconds, using his special equipment, Hero would be able to
"see" the person who was speaking, identify her, or commit her
features to memory, and somehow perhaps use it as a key to
unlock the problem. Later, much much later, Wiener was to
wonder that in those moments he had had not the slightest premonition, inkling, or psychic warning that, moving through the
darkness, the British investigator was walking towards his death.

The cabinet and the room had now fallen into silence. One
hardly heard the breathing of the sitters, rapt in their witnessing
of this occult love story, the evidence of their ears that the barriers
indeed had been broken down and the living and the dead were
to be united.

The faint illumination of the dim red light that emanated
from some corner of the seance room was such that they and
Wiener could just make out the dark patch denoting the area of
the cabinet and the vaguest hint of the outline of the tall man
proceeding thither, the shape of head and shoulders.

The figure became even less distinguishable as it moved slowly into the area of the curtains, yet Wiener, straining his eyes, managed to preserve its outline. It paused there for an instant.

"Ruth! Ruth! Are you there?"

"Oh, Peter! Peter!"

This was the love cry of a woman, wrung from her throat before the moment when she would melt into the arms of her man, and every person who had ever loved recognised and thrilled to it and in the darkness waited as expectedly as though the scene were being unrolled before them on a screen, like a film.

There was silence again, and then a thud as though a body had tumbled to the ground.

But the Indian in Wiener's blood was in his eyes too, and enabled him somehow to pierce the gloom and catch a hint of a new outline for Alexander Hero, who appeared to have fallen to his knees before the cabinet and, from the incline of his head and the hunch of his shoulders, had buried his face in his hands and now emitted a groan as of a tortured animal. Wiener heard him say, "I can't! No more, no more!"

What the devil! Wiener thought to himself. *Is he funking it?*

The soft voice called, "Peter, my dearest, why don't you come to me?"

"Ruth, no! It's more than flesh and blood can stand. I had no right to call you back. We must leave one another in peace."

The hair at the nape of Wiener's neck was standing up, and his nerves were tingling like alarm bells at the mystery of the double drama, the play within the play, which seemed to be going on before him, and now he was conscious of a danger which he did not understand, some kind of deadly duel being fought out under cover of the thick gloom.

"Go back, Ruth, until we meet again. Some day I'll come to you."

"Won't you say good-bye, Peter?"

"Good-bye, Ruth!"

Wiener saw that the outline of Hero on his knees before the cabinet had not altered. He was not going to enter. Something had gone wrong. He was aware that his left hand was being strongly crushed. It was the one held by Arnold Bessmer, and his grip was not only powerful but icy cold, as though all the heat had suddenly fled from the man.

Softer and more distant came the voice of Ruth Lesley, "Good-bye then, Peter. Good-bye."

The tambourine rattled faintly once, succeeded by silence which was suddenly and terrifyingly broken by strangulated grunts and moans, mewlings and choking cries from the direction of the cabinet, followed by the hoarse voice of Arnold Bessmer shouting, "Are you all right, Mother? What's up, Mother?"

As though in reply the tambourine banged, the accordion wheezed a snatch of melody, thumps and raps came in swift succession. Wiener felt the tension of Bessmer's grip relax some-what and at the same time saw the outline of Hero's figure at its full height. It was shambling back through the darkness to the circle of chairs. He took his seat and the hands of those on either side of him, and the chain was complete once more.

Why had Hero not entered the cabinet to spy on the person there? What had been the meaning of the corny and idiotic drama of abnegation and farewell, enacted for the benefit of whom? Before Wiener's intensely alerted mind could explore further, the tinkling of wrist and ankle bells heralding the presence of Princess Devi was heard again, followed by the moronic baby-talk voice, hardly improved by being spoken through the open end of a tin trumpet. She lisped, "Pwofessor Constable, Pwofessor Constable, are you there?"

"Yes, I'm here." Constable's voice, which contained a mixture half of disgust, half of eagerness, almost like a pupil in a class-room who has waited too long to be called upon, came from Wiener's left. The FBI man shifted to try to look in its direction, but there was no longer any light in the seance room. Whoever was in charge, in all probability Pratt, had received some cue to extinguish the glow of the red bulb and the place was now once more smothered in impenetrable blackness.

"Mary's not coming tonight." There was a curious kind of petulant arrogance in the baby-talk voice, almost a kind of satisfaction as she made the announcement.

"What's that? Why isn't she coming? Where is she?" Constable demanded.

"She's gone far, far away. Maybe she won't ever be coming back again. Ooh, poor Mary, it's cold and dark where she is."

"What's that?" Constable asked again. "Goddam it, you go get her! I want her here." It was as though he and that idiot voice were alone in the room.

To Wiener, the dialogue and its implications had taken on the quality of an abysmal nightmare, made all the more horrible and sinister by the idiotic words and voice in which was cloaked the threat that Constable had lost his daughter for the second time.

"I know where Mary is," said little Devi, "but she's too far away. She can't come. She's crying."

The jerk of Bessmer's body and the noise of the chair told Wiener that Constable had risen to his feet. He bawled into the darkness, "Get out, you imbecile! Mrs. Bessmer, get Mary! You've got the power. You bring her here!"

Saul Wiener felt as though his emotions could take no more battering from the horrible, undignified exposure of a human soul—Samuel Hale Constable pleading with that dreadful woman for a ghost.

The tambourine rattled, the bells jingled. "Perhaps some day," sang little Devi. "Perhaps never. Good-bye, good-bye."

Something white and luminous appeared in the direction of the cabinet for a moment and waved uncertainly. The voice of Chief Thundering-Cloud was heard once more, muttering, but what he said was not distinguishable. The clatter of special noises began again, but diminishing in decibels and receding as though the whole company of spooks, bag and baggage, were taking their departure. Mrs. Bessmer began to gag and choke again and her husband shouted, "Lights, Pratt! That's all! She's suffering."

The blaze of electric bulbs from the chandelier smote all of their retinas, dazzling and half blinding Wiener, but he could still make out, as the black curtained cabinet fell to the ground, Mother Bessmer, purple-faced, straining and struggling against her bonds. Wiener, glancing swiftly to his right, saw that Alexander Hero was sitting, his hands still in the clasp of the chain, his head sunk onto his chest, his eyes unseeing as one lost in deep thought.

CHAPTER XV

"Give Me Twenty-four Hours."

They escaped from the ghastly after-seance collation more quickly than they had expected. It was of much shorter duration than the first. There was no fire or enthusiasm to it. Mrs. Bessmer pleaded fatigue and vanished, and it was obvious that her husband would be glad to see them go as well, though not before he had had a word with both Wiener and Hero/Fairweather. To the former, he said, "I hope you're satisfied, Mr. Roth. I didn't catch the language that was being spoken. Is there someone in your family of Indian blood?"

"Possibly," Wiener replied curtly.

Bessmer turned to the other man. "You disappointed me, friend Fairweather. We don't like Mother using up the power for nothing. Does that mean we shan't be seeing any more of you during your stay, or," and he paused significantly, "else-where?"

Wiener thought he understood now the reason for Bessmer's agitation when Hero refused to enter the cabinet and had, in effect, parted from his sweetheart. He stood to lose a succulent sucker.

Fairweather said, "No, no, no! I just can't say. I shan't forget my promise. I suppose I made an exhibition of myself. I was upset."

Bessmer turned away. He was far from his old, easy, smarmy self and had not much to say when the company broke up and left, Wiener and Fairweather the first to escape.

The two men walked east to Central Park West and hailed a taxi.

Hero said, "I think, perhaps, we'd better have a drink."

Wiener replied, "You bet!" and said to the driver, "Lindy's."

The driver nodded and spun them thither, catching the green of the progressive traffic lights with virtuosity.

Lindy's restaurant at Broadway and Fifty-first Street had the window packed with smoked ham, sausages, and every kind of German delicatessen. Within was a bedlam of crashing crockery and conversation. The large room was divided into aisles of low, partitioned booths. It smelled of beer, onions, liverwurst, and sauerkraut. The waiters wore black jackets and white aprons and stiff, starched shirt fronts. Hero smiled at Wiener's choice of place and acknowledged to himself that it was clever. Ensconced in one of those booths in the middle of the room, there was no more chance of their being overheard against that din than if they had been on a desert island.

When the waiter came and Wiener looked to Hero to make his choice, the latter said, "Bourbon, I like the taste and it's strong."

"Mine too," said Wiener. "Double, on the rocks, I. W. Harper."

The drinks arrived, two wide tumblers of the rich, amber-coloured fluid with floating, curiously shaped, cylindrical pieces of ice with holes through them and twists of lemon peel. Both men took solid pulls at their glasses, sending down large, dynamite-powered jolts to their middles. They felt they needed them.

After the dust of the explosion had settled and relaxation had begun to set in, Hero asked, "Well, how did you like it?"

Wiener replied simply, "I didn't." Then, with a sudden burst of frankness, released by the blockbuster he had just swallowed, he said, "I wish to Christ I hadn't gone!"

Hero threw him a half mischievous sidelong glance and said, "You fell for it, didn't you? The shaking tent of the Ojibwas still works. Ugh! How!"

Wiener reacted with a kind of controlled fury. "You're so

damned smart! Where would the Bessmers have got the information about my ancestor? Or the knowledge of the Mohawk language?"

Hero could see that the FBI man was genuinely angry and disturbed. Well, he was going to be still more so.

"I told them."

"What?"

"How else? When I arranged with Bessmer to accept you for the seance without an interview, I leaked information about the 'First-Flower-That-Comes-After-the-Snow.' Bessmer is clever, even though limited. A couple of hours in the public library would yield enough phrases in any language required to bamboozle you after you'd had a seance-in-darkness treatment. I warned you, didn't I?" And he began to quote once more, "There is no darkness like that of a seance room and no atmosphere which can compare with it."

Wiener interrupted him, burning, "*You* told him! Why you son-of-a-bitch!" And then in a voice of deep disgust, he added, "Why, hell, there was no trick to it at all."

Hero had another slug of the bourbon, which he swallowed along with his satisfaction. He said equably, "That's what they all say when the gimmick is explained. Did you ever hear of a magician's confederate? Harry Houdini sometimes had a half dozen. He wouldn't have been able to effect a single escape without the aid of one."

Wiener was still glaring at him, but some of the fire was dying from his gaze. Hero said, "But if I hadn't told you, from then on you'd always have had some kind of doubt, or worries about the hereafter, wouldn't you?"

The anger had all died in Wiener and had been replaced by a kind of frank interest. "Like our friend Constable?" he suggested.

"Like our friend Constable."

Wiener said, "You went to a lot of trouble to set up that object lesson for me, didn't you? I suppose I asked for it."

"As a matter of fact," Hero conceded, "it was one way of getting you into the place without too much questioning and suspicion. I was glad to have you there. What was your impression?"

"That most of it was corny as hell," Wiener said, "and behind the corn there was something very nasty. What was it? Why didn't you go into the cabinet to meet your girl friend? I thought you were dying to have a look."

"I was," Hero said, "until the mail was delivered." He reached into his inside pocket and produced a handkerchief, flat and carefully folded and handed it to Wiener. Within it was a small sheet of paper, block size, torn from a "Don't Forget" pad. Over the top in red print was the square lettering, DON'T FORGET and then in a scrawled message: *"Don't go into the cabinet tonight. No matter what happens, don't go in. Your life is in danger. For God's sake don't ignore this warning."* And then incongruously, as though the writer had not known what else to say or how to conclude it, it ended with the same phrase which was printed in red at the top, *"Don't Forget."*

Wiener said incredulously, after he had read it, "You got that?"

"Delivered in the dark," Hero replied. "It was stuffed into my breast pocket."

"Did you see . . . ?"

"No, I didn't. There was no opportunity to slip hands. It was over very quickly, and I suppose if I had been able to take a look, there would have been only a figure shrouded in black. That's the sensible way to move about a seance room if you think you're likely to be spotted and don't want to be."

Wiener bent over the note and read it again carefully and just as carefully refrained from touching it in deference to Hero's care in preserving any fingerprints that might be on it. Then the FBI man looked up into Hero's face and said, in a voice that was curiously flat, "And *that* kept you from going into the cabinet?"

Hero felt the cutting contempt beneath the statement but he held his temper. To a man of Wiener's profession and icy temperament the warning would have been a challenge. He thought he would let Wiener's sentence cool off a little before he answered it, so he produced a pipe and pouch, filled up, fired, and sent a chaser of bourbon down after the first drag of smoke before he replied. "Don't let my name put you off, Wiener. I'm not particularly brave, and I told you before that I am no police-man. I'm an investigator. Alive, I hope to be able to help you. You wouldn't be very pleased with a dead one on your hands."

Wiener experienced a moment of contrition, but he was not yet ready to let Hero know. Hero's war record was a part of the dossier he had had upon the Englishman, before he had accepted him from Ferguson, and he was certain that the British were not in the habit of awarding a DSO and bar for non-bravery. On his own part, although he had marched into the tommy-gun fire of a midwestern kidnap gang, he was aware that he would not have got up out of his seat at that seance and walked into that cabinet in the dark for a million dollars.

Hero had had some moments of doubt and indecision himself, moments literally, for the time left to him to make up his mind had been practically nil, and it had to be decided during that brief exchange with the seductive voice calling to him from behind the curtains.

The note had been placed on him swiftly and efficiently. Behind him he had felt the momentary passage, or rather wafting of air upon his neck, someone had reached over his shoulder, for the sensitive skin of his ear had detected the close approach of another physical body; then he had felt the introduction of something into the breast pocket of his coat and heard just the faintest whisper of paper. This had occurred early in the seance, before the manifestation organised for Wiener.

Rather than risk disturbing the chair, Hero had decided to wait, for he would need both hands free to read the message. Once he was up, and on his way to the cabinet, he had put the note to the scrutiny of the special eyeglass lens he had palmed. As he had expected, the vicinity of the cabinet was bathed in infra-red rays, and he absorbed the faint, reddish glow of the message: *Don't go into the cabinet tonight. No matter what*

*happens, don't go in. Your life is in danger. For God's sake don't
ignore this warning.*

Two possibilities presented themselves. The note was either
genuine, designed to keep him from some real and potent danger
which threatened him within the cabinet, or there was no danger
and the intention was to keep him from carrying out his plan to
scrutinise the face of Ruth Lesley and if possible, as he expected,
identify her with Tina Cryder.

Who had planted the note upon his person? Tina Cryder?
Someone unknown? Wouldn't Tina have written, 'Don't *come*
into the cabinet tonight,' if it was she who was warning him?
The note read like messages sent to fiction detectives. But life
often followed fiction. And the line, *"For God's sake don't ignore
this warning"* had the ring of a genuine cry of anguish.

All these thoughts and questions were darting through Hero's
mind like camera exposures of a thousandth of a second.

And there were more. If they were trying to frighten him off
it was his duty to go in and carry out his plan. But it was also his
duty to stay alive. Both Ferguson and Wiener had made it plain
that for the moment he was all that stood between them and the
collapse of Operation Foxglove or worse, the defection or high
treason of Constable.

Alexander Hero had but one fear of death and that was by
negligence or idiocy. To die quixotically and uselessly seemed to
him the nadir of human folly.

And in those few seconds granted him, there had been time
also to remember that if Tina Cryder was Ruth Lesley and Mary
Constable, his cover had been broken and if she had informed
those behind her, the game might be taking a very serious turn
indeed. One last, lightninglike weighing of contingencies: the
case did not hinge on whether Tina Cryder was Ruth Lesley,
but on the hand of Mary Constable. There were other means of
identifying the person in the cabinet.

Anger, pride, the competitive instinct and the desire not to
appear a coward before the American agent urged Hero to go in.

Common sense, reasoning, intelligence and his insistence that he was indeed not a policeman had said, "Stay out!"

His final decision came about through a most realistic premonition, a warning conveyed to his nerves through the pores of his skin, that if he went in he would die and probably very quickly.

Alexander Hero rewrapped the note in the clean handkerchief. "Would you put your young man onto that, please?" he said. "Of course, my prints will be on it, but there ought to be another, or others as well."

Wiener stowed it away carefully. "Whose, do you think?"

For a moment Hero was on the verge of telling him, of confessing to the night on Cedar Street and sending Wiener and his men down there to collect not only Tina Cryder but her father too. They could then search through what must be absolute warrens behind as well as, probably, beneath the place to look for a hidden laboratory or some hitherto unknown equipment for the transfer of the fingerprints of the dead to the hand of someone living.

Yet what if there was nothing there, if all they picked up was a stupefied, down-at-the-heels magic merchant, his stock of outmoded tricks, and a pretty daughter whose only crime was that she was a bad actress? Valuable time would have been lost, the raid would unquestionably have press repercussions which would alert the Russians that the hunt was on. It wouldn't do. The Cryders were his pigeons. He, Alexander Hero, had the entrée there now, a double one, thanks to his intimacy with the daughter. It was up to him to pursue the investigation in that area.

Therefore, he resisted the impulse and said, "I don't know, but my hunch is that before long they'll match up."

They both then lapsed into a moody silence, sipping their drinks, glancing about at the Broadway after-theatre types filling the restaurant, and listening to the clatter, and between them lay the subject which up to then they had avoided, but whose presence in both their minds was again building up tension.

Their glances finally met and held, and Wiener said, "Well, I suppose we'd better get onto it."

"Yes."

"You hear the last message to Constable?"

"I did."

Wiener was looking at Hero levelly now, and coldly. "It said, 'You go and sing to the Russians, or you'll never see your kid again in this life or any other.' The Bessmers must have spilled that we were photographing their house and so the trap has been sprung. Tomorrow we pick up Constable, Bessmer and Company, the lot, and put them under lock and key."

"And Operation Foxglove?"

Wiener nursed his drink and said with scorn in his voice, "How would *you* like to have to make the decision—whether nobody gets it and we're even Stephen again, or the Russ has it and we haven't? I've made mine."

Hero said, "Give me twenty-four hours."

Wiener simply laughed unpleasantly and said nothing.

"Give me twenty-four hours," Hero repeated. "If by then I haven't . . ."

Wiener said, "The Russian Consulate opens at nine o'clock in the morning. All Constable has to do is drive up in a cab, give his name at the door, and the reception committee will be waiting for him."

"If I can put him on ice for you . . ."

For the first time Wiener showed a sign of wavering. He asked, "What do you mean, 'put him on ice'?"

"Keep him from defecting for another day, if that's what's on his mind; sow doubt; put him off his balance. He's in a state now. Remember, to him I'm a man in the same boat as he is. He'll listen to me."

Wiener was thinking hard.

Hero continued, "You've got a watch on his house—if it doesn't work, well then . . ."

Wiener was studying Hero carefully now. He said, "You know something, don't you? And you're not telling."

"I'm not sure," Hero said.

Wiener pointed a long, bony finger at him and exploded, "Goddam it to hell! If you're keeping something from me and this thing blows up, I'll have your ass in a sling too. This isn't any kiss-the-pillow cricket game with a by-your-leave and time-out-for-tea."

Hero drained his glass and put it down. "That's that then. I thought you chaps had a reputation for being bloody certain before you pulled the trigger. All right, you know your business."

"Wait a minute," Wiener suddenly temporised. "What are you going to do then?"

"Notify Dr. Ferguson that whatever usefulness I might have had here is at an end."

Hero saw the change of light that came into Wiener's eyes and had the momentary impression that for some reason or other the FBI man was a little afraid of Ferguson. It was probably that he was simply overpowered by his urbanity and that having appealed to Ferguson, he was suddenly worried about taking matters in his own hand. "Are you sure that you can keep Constable cooled for twenty-four hours?" he asked.

Hero's equable temper was fraying a little. He snapped, "I said 'if.' You want everything cut-and-dried and in black-and-white. I also said if it didn't come off you could take him then. But I think I can, or I shouldn't have suggested it."

Wiener said, "I'd like to get to Washington and have a personal word with Ned Brickman, my immediate boss, and Walter Augstadt, as well as J. Edgar."

"And get the load off *your* shoulders?" Hero put in.

Wiener was suddenly human again. "Well, wouldn't you? But what will you do? Can I know that?"

Hero realised suddenly that Wiener was as frightened as he and staggering under the burden of responsibility. He replied, "Tell him I've had a message from his daughter, Mary, and if necessary produce another in his home for him."

"Ah," breathed Wiener, and a gleam of hope came into his eyes. He looked at his watch and said, "I can catch the one o'clock train for Washington. But you're agreed if Constable so much as sticks his nose out of the house, we take him?"

"Yes."

Wiener called for the bill. He said, "And if after twenty-four hours you haven't . . ." He left the sentence hanging in the air.

Hero left it there too. He had been seized by a premonition that he would solve the problem, but refrained from saying so, for he thought quite possibly this conviction might have been the result of the little victory scored over Wiener and hence not to be trusted.

The FBI man shrugged, excused himself, and left to make a telephone call. When he returned they went out into the street. It was twenty-five minutes to one. He said, "I've made arrangements. Constable's house will be covered. And a man will meet me at the station to pick up that note for Ferris to test for prints." He hailed a cab and directed, "Penn Station," to the driver. He stood for a moment with his foot on the running board contemplating Hero gloomily. "I wish you weren't so damn secretive. You'll keep in touch with my office? You can talk to Sullivan. He can reach me at any time of the day or night."

"Yes, I will."

They parted without shaking hands.

CHAPTER XVI

Would Not the Violated Spirit Have Protested?

The night operator at the Tuscany said, "Worth-two, one, three, ni-yen, seven doesn't answer, Mr. Hero. Do you want me to try again later?"

Hero replied, "What? No, thank you. I don't think so. Will you try this number instead, please?" He had the Manhattan telephone book open and checked the number once more against the name of Constable, Samuel Hale, 529 West 113th Street, "River-side-nine, zero, two, one, five."

He heard the clicks as the operator dialled and rapidly reviewed what he would say. He refused even to consider the contingency that Constable might not be there, that he might have the phone switched off, or that he could even have begun his defection that very night. For all anyone knew, Constable might some time ago already have arranged a tentative or initial contact with the Russians in case he wanted to use it. Hero willed it not to be so.

He heard the sound of the connection going home and then the long brrr of the American ringing signal, so different from the British double ring.

There were six long, torturous ones which could only be leading to a "Don't answer" and the complete collapse of his plans, when he heard the sound of the receiver being removed, though there was no voice reply at the other end.

Hero almost struck his teeth on the mouthpiece shouting, "Hallo! Hallo! Is Professor Constable there?"

There was a further wait and silence, and Hero again cried,

"Hallo! Professor Constable?" sweating that he might simply hang up.

"Well?" It was Constable's voice.

"This is Fairweather."

"Who?"

"Peter Fairweather. Do you remember? We were at the seance together."

Another wait and then, "Yes, Fairweather, what is it? What do you want?"

If there was recognition there was no warmth of desire to continue the acquaintance in the voice, certainly not that of the friendly person who had invited him in for a drink and a snack. Neither was it the voice of one who had been asleep. It belonged to a man who was very much awake and preoccupied.

It had to be Peter Fairweather speaking now—the weak, somewhat shy, confused Englishman. He had to hook Constable and yet at the same time not spoil the game by being too quick or saying the wrong thing. He began, "I've had a tremendous experience, sir. Something frightening, yet . . ." and here he hesitated to draw an answer.

It was a cold one. "Is it something that has to be discussed at half-past one in the morning, Fairweather?"

"I'm sorry, Professor Constable. I didn't realise how late . . . I couldn't wait. When I came home after the seance tonight I tried it. I tried to get through. Somehow I did."

"What? Tried to get through where?"

"To Ruth."

Hero heard Constable snort at the other end. "I thought you were all through with that."

"It's the Bessmers," Peter Fairweather said. "I can't stomach them. And when I thought I'd sent Ruth away, I couldn't bear it either, so I put the lights out and sat in the dark and tried. And then it happened."

There was again a moment's pause from the other end and then, "You say you succeeded?"

"Yes."

"I congratulate you. May I ask what this has to do with me?"

"Only this, sir. While I was trying to get Ruth . . . while she was there . . . or I felt she was, Mary . . . your daughter, came through!"

"*What?*" Professor Constable's shout buzzed and rattled the tympanum of the telephone speaker. "What's that you say? Come on man, speak up."

"Your daughter, she was there . . ."

"Physical?"

"Her voice. Her . . . her presence. Something of what she was like, or must have been like."

"Did she speak? Did she say anything?"

"Yes, something."

"Well?" The fierceness of Constable's query must have shaken the cables.

"She said, 'Tell Daddy . . .'"

"Yes, go on. What was it?"

Alexander Hero gave a demonstration of a man on the verge of hysterics of which the Cambridge Dramatic Society would have been proud. His voice rising almost to a feminine wail, he said, "I don't know. I couldn't hear. There was confusion. Ruth was there for a moment and then they were both gone. Nobody was there any longer. I felt ill. Maybe I even passed out for a while. I didn't know what time it was when I rang you. But I had to tell you about it, and say that maybe if I came and we tried together, she would . . ."

Professor Constable's voice now burned with eagerness. He said, "Yes, yes, of course. Don't waste time then, man. Get in a cab and come up here. I'll be waiting for you."

Peter Fairweather dissolved into a babble of incoherence. He seemed to be at the point of tears. He said, "I can't now. My nerves are gone. You don't know what it's like, unless you've been through it. It's frightening and it's sublime. I can't any more tonight. I shall go to pieces. Perhaps tomorrow."

"All right then, tomorrow. Come up tomorrow. In the morning?"

"All right, in the morning." Fairweather was letting himself be led.

"Say nine o'clock? Are you an early riser?"

"Nine o'clock. I'll be there."

Constable's voice was peremptory, "Sharp!" he commanded. As though hypnotised, Fairweather repeated, "Nine o'clock sharp, sir." And the connection was broken.

Hero wiped the sweat from his forehead. Whatever else, Professor Constable was on ice for that night.

Hero looked at his watch. He felt in need of a drink, picked up the phone, and asked for Room Service. The operator said, "Room Service is closed, Mr. Hero, but the boy could go out for something if you wanted."

"No, no, never mind."

"Do you want me to try your Worth number again?"

Hero glanced at the pad next to the telephone on which he had scrawled, Tina Cryder, Worth 2–1397. "All right," he said.

The number rang interminably without reply, and butterflies recommenced their work in Hero's stomach as the operator said, "Still no answer."

And Hero replied, "Thank you. We'll close down for the night, then. Put a DON'T DISTURB on until eight."

Why was there no reply? They might have been away all day on Sunday, but Cryder must have been in his shop on a working day. Surely the phone from the shop would be switched upstairs into one or both of their rooms? It was shortly before two o'clock in the morning. He had offered Wiener results in twenty-four hours.

Hero was still convinced that the answer lay with the Cryders. If that was the case, then that was where he ought to be. He searched in his bag for his skeleton keys, a duplicate of a set made for the late Harry Houdini, five which would open almost any standard, old-fashioned lock. He picked up his sniperscope, gloves, and a small electric torch, put on his jacket, and went out.

At that time of night a taxi downtown would have probably been as quick as the underground, but cabs meant drivers and they bore witness. He did not know what he might find at the shop of Paul Cryder, but if burglarised entry was necessary, he was prepared to risk it and hence not anxious to leave a trail behind him. He smiled to himself as he thought that Wiener would probably approve. He was beginning to act far too much like the policeman he was always saying he was not. He walked swiftly the three blocks up to Grand Central, plunged into the subway, and caught a downtown train.

The ancient dead slept quietly and peacefully in Trinity churchyard, Hero thought, for at that late hour all lower Broadway seemed like an extension of the territory. It was as empty as a stage set after the actors had departed and his footsteps seemed to ring hollowly on the pavement.

He walked the two blocks north and then turned left into Cedar Street, concentrating upon the bluff he would put up, provided the Cryders were there. He held enough cards in his hand, had collected sufficient knowledge, he thought, to make it stick—the secret of the hand in exchange for immunity and he would justify the deal to Wiener afterwards. He felt certain that the Americans were interested neither in punishment nor revenge. The overriding concern was Operation Foxglove and the decontamination, as it were, of Professor Constable.

Cedar Street was empty of pedestrians, though he could see farther down at its end, where it met West Street and the docks, there was movement and traffic and the noise therefrom would provide some cover. He reconnoitred the shop from the far side of the street, knowing that sometime during the night hours, perhaps more than once, a policeman would pass that way on patrol, trying the doors of the shops to make sure they were properly locked. There was a naked bulb burning inside the dusty window of Paul Cryder's magic shop. No light issued from behind the drawn curtains of Tina's room above. For an instant his mind replayed the scene: the bedroom, the white mink jacket and gloves carelessly thrown across the chair, the pale blue nightdress on the counterpane and the girl turning to him, arms upraised, exquisite eyes swimming, lips parted. He erased the picture by wondering what she would be like when he presented her and her father with an "either-or—tell or take your chances with the police and the FBI." Would she spit, scratch, and claw, or dissolve into tears? And how much would her sexuality which had so unstrung him, affect him then?

He crossed over, lingered a moment before the radio shop next door, casing the street for any approaching pedestrian or blue-coated patrolman. There was none. He drew on his gloves, moved to the Cryders' shop, and gently tried the handle of the door. It did not give. His skeleton keys would be of no avail against the Yale lock on the outside. However, there was another device which would deal with that, and the lock looked old and worn, with probably much of the resistance gone out of the spring. What worried him was that the door might be bolted from the inside as well. From his pocket he produced a thin, stiff piece of celluloid, forced it into the crack of the door where the catch would be and pressed. It yielded easily. Hero exhaled a sigh of relief. There was no inside bolt. Evidently the Cryders' merchandise was not of the kind to attract thieves.

He glanced once more up and down the empty street and then pushing the door open an inch at a time, he entered the shop, closed and locked it behind him. Even with the great care he had exercised, the spring bell suspended over the entrance, which jangled so loudly at the approach of any customer, had given out one faint "tonk" which, to his nervous ears, had sounded like Big Ben.

Hero was aware that he was now in the light of the bulb hanging over the counter, completely visible from the outside, and to anyone passing. Walking as silently as he could on boards that groaned and creaked at every step, he passed through the curtained partition into the darkness behind it, the gloom of which was lightened by the few rays penetrating the curtain from the front of the shop. Above stairs it was pitch black and not a sound was to be heard from there.

Hero now withdrew the small sniperscope from his pocket and with it familiarised himself thoroughly with the whereabouts of pieces of furniture and mapped out a safe pathway to the stairs, so that he would be able to negotiate it in total darkness. He was not yet prepared to risk the use of the electric torch.

He had taken off and pocketed his watch, so that the luminous dial would not show but he counted the ticks now, for two minutes, listening. Not so much as the faintest sound reached his ears. He thereupon crossed the area to the steps leading to the first floor, and testing each board and taking infinite pains, he mounted them.

On the landing there was more light, sufficient to show the shapes of the things with which he was already familiar, the piano, a large couch, chairs, and the cocktail cabinet. He waited to determine the source of the light and saw that it came from the street without, for the doors of both the front room of Tina Cryder and the back room of her father stood ajar. Some of the illumination must be penetrating the drawn curtains of the girl's room. Less came from the direction of Cryder's, since it must open upon a backyard and the rear of the house in the next block.

Hero listened again. He heard nothing but the muted rumbling of the traffic from West Street and wondered whether it was strong enough to cover the sound of the regular breathing of sleepers. Then, turning his back upon Tina's room, he crept over to the door leading to her father's for his business that night was with Paul Cryder. If there was an altercation and the girl woke, well, then one would cross that bridge when one came to it.

Carefully he pushed the door fully open and again the sniperscope showed him the shape of what was within; a dressing table, a small bureau, several chairs, a door leading to what might have been a bathroom and then, to the left, a large bed.

The outline of the form upon it was not of someone huddled down in sleep, but of a man sitting up and Hero experienced a moment of panic at the possibility that Paul Cryder was propped up in bed, a gun pointed, his finger on the trigger, waiting to squeeze when his own form should be outlined by the frame of the door.

He conquered himself and made his peace with his princi-
ples. This was a calculable risk. He pushed on the button of his
electric torch. The face and the upper half of the figure of Paul
Cryder leaped out of the darkness, his eyes staring into the light
and reflecting it curiously.

He was indeed sitting up in bed, leaning back against the
headboard, pillows behind his neck. He was wearing a pyjama
jacket of striped purple and white. There was no gun in his
fingers, but at his right hand and resting open upon the bed, a
book.

The circle of the torch, centred upon his face, revealed a look
of intense surprise. He did not speak or cry out. The expression
of surprise did not alter. Then Hero saw that he was staring at
nothing, would never look at anything again. The man was dead.

Hero remained standing in the doorway for a full minute, to
make absolutely certain, then he tiptoed carefully to the bedside,
looked into the pupils of the eyes, stripped the glove from his
right hand, and allowed his fingertips to rest for a moment upon
the inside of the man's wrist. There was no pulse. The flesh was
hardly cold, and *rigor mortis* had not yet set in. He had died only
a short time before. From what?

Thoroughly conscious now of the danger of his naked hand,
and the importance of touching nothing, Hero quickly replaced
his glove. There was a blueish tinge to the lips and a lividness
to the skin of Cryder's cheeks and forehead, indicative of the
lack of oxygen resulting from suffocation, or from certain forms
of heart attack. Had Paul Cryder after putting out the light simply succumbed to a thrombosis, death taking him with such swift-
ness and surprise that he was not able even to cry out to the girl
sleeping but two rooms removed?

The girl sleeping? Hero felt himself go cold and clammy, and
the sweat burst from every pore. It was that too silent silence,
the absence of so much as a sigh, or the creak of a bed as a body
shifted. He bent over the corpse of Paul Cryder and examined it
more closely. There was a discoloration, an oval patch of faint
stain on the breast, just below the chin. He leaned closer and

with great care sniffed at the mouth of the dead man. Bitter almonds, or imagination?

Hero straightened up and a great, long sigh was torn from him. He snapped off the torch and made his way out of the room, across the one that intervened, pausing only a moment at the door, before going into Tina's, to find what he was already certain must await him.

She lay dead of the same cause, stretched out in sleep on her back, her hair flowing, a dark stream across the pillow, in the circle of the torchlight, her childlike arms and tiny hands above the counterpane, her body slightly curved. But there was no blood, only the cyanosed lips and the flushed face. Thank God, her eyes had been closed, Hero thought, and he did not have to stare into those aquamarine pools. She had been killed in her sleep.

Hero now made his second swift examination. The same stain was on the sheet and the nightdress of the girl, the same lingering odour of bitter almonds, and this time it was not imagination.

The phrase, almost like a newspaper headline, "TWIN MURDERS," crept into Hero's mind, and then the word "murder" was expunged and "execution" substituted. He was remembering a man named Bogdan Stashinsky, a Soviet spy and hatchet man, who had been tried and imprisoned in West Germany several years before for the gas-pistol murder of two targets of Russian political vengeance.

The pistol had been double-barrelled, discharging a spray of cyanide of potassium. During his trial, Stashinsky had testified how he had encountered one of his victims on a stairway and had exploded the cartridge into his face, nose, and mouth. The sharp intake of his breath as he had gasped in surprise and fright had drawn the spray and gas into his lungs, and he had collapsed, in all probability dead before his body had touched the stairs.

As though he had been a spectator, Hero thought he saw the execution of the Cryders taking place. A man had let himself into the shop, perhaps as he himself had, and found his way upstairs to the room of Paul Cryder, who had been sitting up in bed, reading. Engrossed in his book, he would not have seen or heard

anything until it was too late, and before he could so much as
move or cry out, the man who had appeared in the doorway had
raised his arm, there had been a hiss and some liquid had taken
him full in the face. And after that, darkness. Tina Cryder had
not even been awakened. When the second barrel was discharged into her lungs death had come simply as a transition
from sleeping to never again awakening.

So they were killed! The cyanide signature on both the
corpses was Russian.

But why the death sentence? What had they done, they who
had served the Soviet "apparatus" in their plot to capture the
mind and the knowledge of Samuel Constable, to merit being
wiped off the face of the earth with no more compunction than
a couple of insects? No trial—simply execution!

And now, searching for the answer, Alexander Hero came
upon one so horrible that he could hardly bear to entertain it. It
stemmed from no more than a surmise, a hypothesis, but his
vivid, analytical mind seized on it immediately and embellished
it with fiendish, retributory gusto. The note thrust into his
pocket during the seance, warning him, entreating him not to
enter the cabinet! Had she traded her life for his? Had she known
of a plot to kill him in the dark of the cabinet; had she herself
been a part of the plot and an instrument of the killing? Had
that been the trap that the terrified girl had sought to avoid her
part in by the note? If he managed to read it and refrained from
entering the cabinet, she could maintain that it was not her
fault. Had he disregarded it and gone in, would she have killed
him?

The Russians then had known somehow that she had failed.
They had left arrangements and orders to kill. The orders had
been disobeyed. Tina Cryder was now a risk they no longer
could afford and her father as well, for he would know as much
as she.

Hero's conscience struggled against this reconstruction. She
might have died for many reasons. She might have endangered
the scheme in some other way, or they could have suspected her

of preparing to become a double agent. But he always returned to the heavy weight upon his conscience of his first premise.

And now, the man who was by profession a ghost hunter and a patient siever of evidence in the search for proof of life in the hereafter, looked down upon the shell that had harboured the mystery that was Tina Cryder. He thought, *If there are such things as ghosts of the foully murdered and restless spirits, violently ejected from their envelopes, wouldn't you be here now to tell me?*

He put out his torch and waited for a few moments in the darkness. There was not so much as a whisper, and he felt a wave of pity over the muteness of the thing on the bed. He switched on his lamp again and moved it about the room. There were her silken clothes upon a chair, her tiny slippers. The beam crossed her boudoir table with its load of bottles, pots, creams, lotions, astringents, and expensive crystal scent containers, and Hero reflected that it was probably for these pathetic feminine luxuries that she had sold herself to the enemies of her country.

His light picked up a bottle of extraordinary shape, black in colour, encrusted with silver moons and stars. Hero thought that this had not been there when he had spent the night with Tina Cryder.

He went over to the table, picked it up with his gloved hand and read the name thereon, "Music of the Stars," and the trademark of the Paris maker.

The felicitous name seemed to ring through him like a bell and conjured up thoughts of the vast and endless reaches of space, the novae, exploding stars, whirling in expanding galaxies, unleashing their radio waves down the long light years. He was reminded of Constable's vision of his child, forever lost beyond the furthermost reaches of those galaxies, and he thought of Ruth Lesley.

Hero unstoppered the bottle and sniffed, and in an instant he was carried back to the moment in the cabinet when he had held "Ruth Lesley" in his arms. And so that scent had been called "Music of the Stars"; Tina Cryder had worn it, perhaps half cynically, as Ruth, and it had lingered upon her as Mary Constable. She had, of course, concealed the bottle when she knew that he would be sleeping with her.

He replaced the container carefully, went over his movements in his mind to make certain he had disturbed nothing and left no traces of his visit. He turned then for a farewell glance at the face of the dead girl to say a kind of "thank-you" to her, if indeed she had managed to spare him, and at that moment was overcome with the horror of realisation which turned him cold and clammy.

She was dead and he was alive, but how long would he survive the order of execution that must have been issued for him as well? He saw then that if she had saved him, she had also betrayed him to the enemy, his cover was broken. If she knew that Alexander Hero and Peter Fairweather were one and the same person, so would her employers. The fact that he had escaped the fate of these two did not mean the hunt was off but only postponed. Standing there, with the torch in his hand, he could be a target at that very moment and he extinguished it swiftly and then strained his ears to listen for any eventual creak of board or rustle of clothing. He felt naked, vulnerable, and, for the first time during this investigation, thoroughly frightened.

But there still remained a task for him which he knew he must face or fail in the purpose of his dangerous visit. This was the search of the premises for some clue or bit of evidence that might shed light upon the hand of Mary Constable. Hero thought bitterly that these two upstairs with him would not object and what he might find, if anything, could no longer affect them. But what if the killer were still there, lurking somewhere in the silent, empty shadows of the house?

He would, Hero thought, his mission accomplished, wish to escape as quickly as possible. But supposing he had not been able to do so, hampered by passing footsteps or the time-consuming visit of the patrolman to the block, leisurely trying each doorway? Or even the arrival of Hero himself, which might have driven him away from the entrance to hide somewhere amongst the grotesque apparatus of the stockrooms.

Using only his sniperscope now, which was able to show him little more than outlines, Hero crept downstairs and forced himself to an examination of the premises behind the shop. He called upon all of his senses, straining eyes and ears and even the olfactory, in case beneath the all-pervading mustiness of old costumes and gear he might be able to scent a human body odour, and he knew that he himself must be giving off the smell of fear. He had hated night-fighting in the war and hunting in the dark.

His heart stopped and he felt that it might never resume its beat again when, at the entrance to a second storeroom, looking through the cylindrical tube, he picked up the shape of a figure, broad, bulky, motionless, standing at the side of the aisle. He froze into immobility, silently filling his lungs with all of the air he could gulp, so that should a deadly spray be discharged into his face he would be able to exhale and not draw death into his chest. He waited, holding it. He knew that skin-diving, he could contain his breath for two minutes under water. His now violently pounding heart would probably allow him little over a minute. The figure remained as motionless as he. Was it aware of his presence? Was it trying to wait him out, force the first move?

It was the dark which was no longer to be endured. His wire-taut nerves could tolerate no more and drove him into action, foolhardy or not—attack. He switched on his torch and flashed upon the yellow, hideously grinning visage of a Chinaman. But to Alexander Hero it appeared like the face of an angel from heaven because he recognised it immediately, particularly when the rays of his light revealed heavily brocaded and encrusted robes. It was an automaton, such as were popular in magic shows of the Victorian era, lifelike figures of wood which moved, answered questions, ate, drank, scored victories at chess or draughts. Nevertheless, he felt such a weakness in his knees that he sat down upon the floor for a moment and tried to laugh himself into some courage.

Thereafter, things went better, and he was able to get on with it and to his great disappointment found nothing. He spent some time in the vast magic library with books spilling over into another room, but there was little with which he was not familiar. There was no laboratory, secret chamber, or equipment of any kind to indicate that the hand of Mary Constable might have been devised or manufactured there.

He now pocketed his torch and sniperscope, made his way back to the curtain leading to the front of the shop and listened for footsteps on the pavement outside. He heard none and, slipping through, extinguished the single light. Again he waited, listening and looking, peering out through the grimy shop window. It was a bad moment, for if a patrolman were to pass by then and note the bulb no longer burning in the shop, he would be trapped. The street, however, remained empty and quiet, and carefully he opened the door, this time avoiding the nerve-jangling tonk of the spring bell above. He went out, pulled the door to, but not quite shut and walked swiftly away eastwards.

He did not continue towards the river though, but turned left on Greenwich Street and thence downtown as far as Rector and back to Broadway. He was feeling conspicuous in his British clothes and was sure that had he continued on to the active, milling river front he would stand out and somebody might remember. What he wished was to return to his hotel unnoticed and if possible in such a manner that no one would be able to place him in the vicinity of the shop in Cedar Street when the balloon went up.

During the time he had been searching the premises he had already mentally vetoed the idea of an anonymous call from a telephone box. Calls could be traced; his English voice and accent were almost impossible to disguise. But there were other ways of alerting the police, and he had hit upon what he felt was a certain one by extinguishing the light in the shop and leaving the door ajar. The next time a patrolman on the beat went by, he would notice that the window was dark, try the door, find it open, and then within minutes the New York Police Department would be at work.

He walked up Broadway once more, heading for the Wall Street subway station with which he was now familiar and wished that his footsteps would not ring so loudly on the deserted pavement, advertising his presence. An occasional yellow cab or heavily loaded lorry passed him, and Hero would turn his head away towards the buildings so that no passing driver could catch a glimpse of his face by a street lamp, and then there would again be silence but for his echoing footsteps.

Hero found himself at an entrance to the subway, but the southbound stairs instead of the ones which would lead him to trains northwards to Grand Central. He plunged down the steps, negotiated the change booth and the turnstiles, and, peering over the edge of the platform into the black tunnel, saw the two green eyes of an approaching train. He boarded the first car, consulted the map of the subway system he carried with him in his pocket, and saw where he was and whither bound. He went as far as Borough Hall in Brooklyn where he crossed over and caught a return train back to Manhattan.

In the car with him were sleepy-eyed workers in transit, either returning home from late jobs or setting out for early ones. Most of them were reading morning newspapers. His imagination began to work again. Any one of those behind the screen of the picture pages of the *Daily News* or *Mirror* could be his assigned executioner. He would never know him, not even see him until it was too late. He could pop out from anywhere, at any time; from a doorway or behind a pillar, or even in the corridor of his hotel. In fact surprise was an essential part of the attack, so that he would gasp and draw in his breath. Did they know where he lived? Ought he to change his hotel? Had he told Tina Cryder where he was staying? He could not even remember.

Hero realised that his nerves were in a shocking state and that if he let his fantasies play any further he would become valueless to the project upon which he was engaged. He persuaded himself that if the killer of Paul and Tina Cryder had all his buttons, he must by now have already begun his underground journey back to Moscow.

He disembarked at Grand Central Station, feeling calmer. It was then just past two-thirty. The teeming, early-morning life there restored his confidence. On reaching the hotel he went to his room and headed for the telephone. It was now, he knew, very much time to bring Saul Wiener into the picture.

But even as he lifted the instrument from its cradle, he realised that he had completely forgotten that Wiener was on a train somewhere between New York and Washington. Nevertheless, when the operator came on with a, "Still up, Mr. Hero?" he replied, "Can't sleep. I've got toothache," and gave the emergency number with which Wiener had provided him for an eventual night call.

After the first ring a voice replied, "FBI, Sullivan speaking." Hero knew him as the night man in charge.

"This is Alexander Hero. What are the chances of getting in touch with Mr. Wiener?"

Sullivan asked sharply, "Are you in trouble?"

Hero said, "No, but I'd like to get a message to him. I know he's on his way to Washington."

There was a momentary pause during which Hero heard a noise as though pages were being turned over. Sullivan said, "There's no radio-telephone on the one o'clock, only on the Congressional. Do you want him flagged down at Baltimore?"

Hero reflected swiftly and concluded that there was no point in a telephone talk with Wiener. He would need him there when the police pathologists came to the conclusion that the two corpses at No. 43a Cedar Street were dead not from natural causes but double homicide. Also, he wanted the prints of Tina Cryder's fingers and, above all, those of her palm, before the violent dissolution she had undergone should alter them. Aloud he said, "No, that won't be necessary. What time does he arrive in Washington?"

"Passengers get off at seven-thirty, but the train pulls in at six."

"Would you be so kind as to advise Mr. Wiener then that I called and suggest that if possible he return immediately."

"We'll do that," Sullivan said, and then, after a moment's hesitation, "You wouldn't care to tell us what this is all about? In case Mr. Wiener . . ."

Hero said, "Thank you, no. I prefer to wait until I can discuss it with him personally."

He hung up and turned away from the telephone to go to the bathroom when without warning, his lie to the operator about the toothache became an agonising, throbbing reality.

It staggered him as it had the night it hit when he was leaving the house of Professor Constable and sent him tottering to a chair where he collapsed, groaning and holding the side of his jaw. If anything it was even worse than the first attack and from the rhythmical pulsation of pain he knew that there was to be no miracle of cessation. This one wasn't going away.

He did not know what to do or where to turn. The excruciating pain was addling his mind, sending chills down his spine and causing him to break out in sweat. He could no longer think about anything but escape from the hot poker that was being thrust through his cheek at ten second intervals, and setting fire to every nerve in his body.

He got up and made his way to the bathroom, where he had a tube of aspirin and swallowed four, but with not much hope that they would do any more than muddle his brain still further. He half started to take off his clothes but desisted as he felt that there would be no sleep for him that night. Indeed, he realised, his problem was how to survive until morning when he could get to the dentist. This sent him scrabbling to his brief case for the address, as though holding in his hand "Felix Hofstetter, D.D.S., 239 West End Avenue," might prove an anodyne. It didn't. What Hero wanted was whisky. The combination of that and aspirin might do the trick. With Room Service suspended the thing to do was to go out and get sodden and then sit on the doorstep of Dr. Hofstetter until he appeared.

It was a solid idea to adhere to and clinging to it enabled Hero to endure the agony of making himself presentable for the dentist that morning, which consisted of shaving and changing his shirt. He put on his coat, went out, and rang for the lift.

The operator, a sallow, tired-looking young man with not much chin sighed as they descended and murmured to no one in particular, "Oh, brother," and, thinking he caught a look of interrogation from his passenger, said, "I'm bushed. My feet are killing me. Will I be glad when I'm relieved."

Hero was not interested in the lift boy's feet; he was fighting off another of those swelling onslaughts that was threatening to tear the roof off his head. He asked the boy, "Where would there be a bar open at this time of the morning?"

"O'Danahey's Bar and Grill. Corner of Thirty-eighth and Third Avenue."

Hero said, "Thanks." When they got to the ground floor the lobby was deserted, the desk clerk having disappeared momentarily. Hero didn't bother to drop his room key on the counter. His mind was on the oasis, and he walked east to Third Avenue and south one block to where the glow of the neon sign advertised the good news that O'Danahey's was open for business.

Within was a long, polished mahogany bar with the usual array of glassware and bottles behind it, tended by a fat Irish barman with oiled hair. There were a few tables at which night owls were sitting, and one or two stragglers perched at the bar.

Hero embraced the mahogany as though it had been his long lost brother and said, "Double bourbon."

The barman lifted an eyebrow, "I thought all you Limeys only drank scotch! Any particular brand?"

Hero groaned, "No, no, just bourbon."

The bartender's choice rested upon the orange-labelled bottle of Old Grandad, and he poured the double. Hero had it out of his fingers before it touched the bar and knocked it back.

The barman goggled. "Holy smokes!" he said. "Woman trouble?"

"Toothache," Hero gasped, his eyes watering.

The man clucked sympathetically. "You got the right medicine for it. You'd better have another. You got any painkiller?"

Hero held up the aspirin tube.

The barman shook his head. "That stuff's no good. Here, try a couple of these," and he produced some tablets from a box. Hero swallowed them and sipped the second double more slowly and waited for the whisky to set up a counteroffensive.

"What time your dentist open up?" the man asked.

"Nine o'clock, I hope," Hero replied and then gave vent to a groan, torn from the very depths of his being. "Oh, blimey!"

"Ain't he gonna be there?" the barman asked solicitously.

"No, no, it's something else." Hero had just remembered that at nine o'clock in the morning he was due at the home of Professor Constable to produce a message from his dead child. Constable's last, peremptory words, "Nine o'clock sharp!" rang through his aching head. Felix Hofstetter, D.D.S. receded once more into the distance. It would not have mattered if he had showed up drunk at the dentist, who would have understood, but he could not appear sozzled and produce any kind of convincing manifestation for Constable. Even the only known emergency treatment for the world's most gigantic toothache was to be denied to him.

He sighed, "I've just remembered. Got another appointment at nine o'clock in the morning. Can't afford to turn up there blotto."

"Brother," said the barman, "you're in a fix."

"If only I could take my mind off this bloody pain until morning, I might get away with being half sloshed."

"Why don't you go to the movies?" the barman asked.

"What? At this hour?"

"Sure," replied the barman. "One of them grind-houses over on West Forty-second Street. Twenty-four hours a day. *Dracula, The Slavering Beast, The Monster from Mars,* and all that kind of crap. If that don't take your mind off it, nothing will. You might even get to go to sleep for an hour or so."

Hero said, "Do you know, I think I might try that."

The pain was still authoritative but no longer to the point where it sent him reeling. If, somehow, he could manage to keep just that balance of not being too befuddled by either the agony or the drink, he could stand it. He thanked his friend and advisor, paid his bill, picked up a night-hawk driver, and rode over to West Forty-second Street where, for eighty-five cents, he bought a ticket to the West Side Theatre, admitting him to four uninterrupted hours of horror films.

CHAPTER XVII

The Hand Speaks

The barman had been right. The idiocy unreeling across the screen did somehow fix his attention. Furthermore, to the credit of that sage, Hero had even managed to achieve an hour's snooze in the darkened cinema, which, upon awakening, left him slightly refreshed and able to concentrate upon The Thing which, in clothes drenched with blood and his mask of sunken eyes, gaping jaws, and snaggle teeth, was creeping down the castle corridor, its destination the room of the virginal heroine.

He remembered suddenly what lay ahead, and in panic he slapped the sides of his jacket and trousers and was relieved to find that he had not removed the sniperscope or the skeleton keys. He still had not solved the problem of what kind of demonstration he would be able to put up for Constable, even granted that he had been in better shape.

The Thing invaded the virgin's room: her screams rang through the theatre; her protector arrived through the window, swinging on a rope like a monkey to give battle; and Hero realised that this was where he had come in. He looked at his watch and saw that it was eight o'clock in the morning. The night at least had been defeated.

He emerged from the theatre and stood blinking on Forty-second Street for several minutes, until the pupils of his eyes accustomed themselves to the bright daylight. At a cafeteria on Eighth Avenue he ordered some porridge, scrambled eggs, and relays of black coffee. The food would buttress him, and the coffee, he hoped, would serve the purpose of uniting with the tablets which the barman had given him. The tooth was still reporting regularly with hammer blows. He tried to keep his mind on the work that lay ahead, but his ever recurring dream was of sitting in Dr. Hofstetter's chair and enjoying the first jab of the novocaine needle.

What the devil was he going to do for Constable? He had an almost limitless bag of tricks used in demonstrations of the crookedness of mediums, but many of them called for preparation and besides were designed for halfwits. Constable was certainly no fool and had not fallen for the business until he had been offered "scientific proof."

At twenty minutes to nine Hero finished his breakfast, paid his check and went out, found the entrance to the uptown I. R. T. subway and descended. In three minutes he was whizzed to Seventy-second Street, in three more to Ninety-sixth, where he changed to the local which had just drawn into the opposite platform. The 103rd Street station was passed at ten minutes to nine. The next stop was his, but between 103rd and 110th streets the local, which had been swaying along at a good pace, suddenly slowed to a crawl and then stopped.

At first the fact that they had halted did not even impinge upon Hero's consciousness, for such slow-downs and waits were also a part of London's transportation system, a matter of safety signals or the station ahead not yet cleared. But when his watch told him it was one minute to nine and they were still standing in the darkened tunnel, he began to worry. The other passengers in the car sat patient as sheep, even when the lights flickered and went out, but in a few moments came on again. Then the unmistakable smell of smoke drifted through one of the open windows of the train.

The sliding doors between the carriages were jerked open and the guard appeared. He said, "Nothing to worry about, folks. There's been a short-circuit on the downtown side. They're going to cut the current off for about fifteen minutes. There's nothing to worry about. Take it easy." He went through to spread his message to the other cars. The lights went out again and stayed out. Two dim emergency bulbs came on.

Hero fretted helplessly about what Professor Constable might do when he was not there at nine sharp. And such was his frustration, trapped underground, that he almost forgot his aching tooth. What if Constable had tired of waiting for him, figured he wasn't coming, lost faith and headed for the Russian Consulate? Wiener's men would jump him. He sweated the minutes out in an agony of tension, passing up to the head of the train, questioning the guards whose only consolation was, "Can't go without the juice, mister. When they give us back the juice, we'll go."

At half-past nine the lights suddenly came on again and the car began to vibrate. Slowly the train crawled into the 110th Street station.

Upon regaining the street, Hero was too agitated to call a cab. It seemed to him that the hailing of it, the giving of the address, the hold-up at a traffic light would take longer than to go there on foot, and besides, he no longer trusted vehicles. He set off at a half run. By his watch it was twenty-five minutes to ten.

He was grateful for the downgrade towards the river when he turned the corner of 113th Street and sighted the white granite portico of Professor Constable's house in the middle of the block. As he did so he saw movement there, the opening of the door and Constable appearing. In one hand he carried a brief case that appeared to be heavy. A taxi drew away from the curb some distance below him, as though it had just discharged a passenger, its flag indicating that it was empty, and cruised slowly in the direction of the man standing in the entry way, looking for transportation.

For a moment Hero's limbs refused to function, and the scene, too, for an instant became fixed, as though a film had been stopped in mid-reel and all of the characters who had been moving through it became frozen.

A laundry van was parked across the street, a butcher boy was bicycling past, his basket balanced between the handlebars, a street cleaner was sweeping the gutter, a postman was delving into his bag of letters, a rag pedlar wheeled a hand cart, a man and a painter stood across the street looking at a house as though estimating the cost of a paint job.

And in that pregnant moment, Alexander Hero knew that none of them was what he seemed. All must be watchdogs of the FBI, converging on the man with the heavy brief case who had emerged from the house and who now hailed the cruising cab, the driver of which, in all probability, too, would be an agent of Wiener's counterespionage. If Constable said to him, "Russian Consulate, Third Avenue and Sixty-fifth Street," it would be all over with Operation Foxglove.

For this is exactly what a man of Constable's nature would do. There would be no slinking about after dark, no cloak-and-dagger or conspiratorial plans. In broad daylight he would drive up to the Soviet building, announce himself and say, "I have come to share my work with you and your scientists, for the sake of peace and the safety of the world."

"Professor Constable! Professor Constable!" Someone was shouting the name at almost an hysterical pitch, and then Hero realised that it was he himself who was calling and running down the hill.

"Professor Constable! Wait!"

The big man had one foot in the cab and was already leaning towards the driver as Hero rushed up to him, and he turned and looked but seemingly without recognition.

"Professor Constable—Peter Fairweather. I was delayed. There was an accident in the underground."

The man appeared to be in a daze, the kind engendered by living ahead of oneself, when the physical is hard put to catching up with the mental *fait accompli,* and for a moment Hero thought that Constable was not going to try and pull himself back.

"Yes, Fairweather. What is it?"

"The message. The message from Mary."

His expression changed and a different light came into his tawny eyes. He said, "You have a message from Mary?"

Hero spoke rapidly, endeavouring to pour his words into Constable's mind. "We were going to try. This morning. We were going to try for a contact. I phoned you last night. I told you that I'd tried by myself and had managed to get through to my fiancée, and that somehow your daughter was there too."

Constable looked at his watch, which stood at a quarter to ten. "I said nine o'clock sharp. When you didn't turn up I thought it was just a hoax of some kind. Are you certain you made contact?"

"Yes."

Constable jerked his head to the cab driver to go on. "Sorry, I won't be needing you."

The cabby said, "Okay, brother, suit yourself." He drove off.

A wave of nausea passed over Hero, but he could not tell whether it was from relief, or because of the prodigious wallop his tooth had just handed him again.

And the static street scene also dissolved. As though there had never been a pause, the butcher boy wheeled on his way; the rag man continued towards Riverside Drive; the painter and the client marched up the street arguing, with figures on a sheet of paper; the postman drew some letters from his sack and moved on; the street cleaner busily broomed the refuse in the gutter towards the opening of the sewer.

Constable led the way back into the house, and Hero reflected that now that the agents had seen him return and Hero enter with him, the heat would be off, at least temporarily. He followed Constable up the stairs and into his study.

"I think here—" the scientist said. He went to a cupboard, opened it, deposited the brief case there, and shut it again. He turned to Hero, scrutinised him through narrow lids, and said, "You don't look well. I know it's early in the day, but would you like a drink?"

It took every bit of intestinal fortitude that Hero could summon to reply, "N-no . . . no thank you. It might interfere with the power . . . I don't know, maybe I'd better not."

"You won't mind if I have one?"

Hero said, "No, no. Of course," and thought: *My God, if you've been pulled back from what I think you have, you need it more than I do.*

Constable went to a small cabinet, produced a bottle of scotch and a shot glass, filled it, tossed it off neat, refilled it, and disposed of the second in the same manner. "You're sure you won't change your mind? No, maybe you're right. Though sometimes I've had half a notion that Mother has been a bit stinko. Well, what do you suggest? How do you want it? Darkness? Music?" He was looking at Hero almost anxiously.

As it was wont to do in times of emergency, Hero's brain cleared and, denying the pain that still swept through him, gave a reassuring picture that it was he who held nearly all the cards. Constable would accept his conditions and go along with anything he suggested. The man was desperate to regain contact with his child. He was no longer Constable, the reasoning intellectual. He was that same bereaved father Hero had seen kneeling before the cabinet, babbling unashamedly before a group of sitters.

"Yes, in the dark, I think." He set a chair with its back to the glass and ebony cabinet containing the wax hand on its stand and motioned to the leather couch on the other side of the room. "Perhaps you'd like to sit over there?" He looked at the chair musingly for a moment and said, "I want to be tied. Have you got some rope?"

Constable replied, "What the devil for, man? Don't you think I trust you?"

Hero moved the chair away from its proximity to the cabinet, more into the centre of the room. He said, "I'm going to try to en-trance—that's how it seemed to work. If I'm in a trance I won't know what I'm doing. But if I'm confined, whatever happens I'll know it wasn't me." Left unsaid was, *and so will you.*

Constable nodded. "Whatever you say." He went out of the room and back along the passage towards the kitchen. Hero heard him shout upstairs, "Jane, I'm back. I don't want to be disturbed," and a woman's voice reply, "Oh, Sam! I thought you'd gone to the lab," and his answer, "I may not go." When he returned he was carrying a length of clothesline. "Will this do?"

Hero was grateful. He had been afraid that Constable might have produced a ball of thin string. "That's fine. Will you tie me?" He sat himself in the chair.

Constable approached diffidently. He said, "I'm not much good at this. Still, I've seen Aunty Woodmanston truss up Mother, so I suppose I can manage something similar." He went about it in a fairly workmanlike manner.

"I haven't cut off your circulation?"

"No."

"Music?"

"If possible."

Constable went and switched on a small portable radio and fiddled with the dial. There was a burst of music. "WQXR," he said. "The only station worth listening to. Music and not too much chatter. Hmmmph, Vivaldi's *Four Seasons*. Can you bear it?"

"I like it. I won't be able to get the third movement melody out of my mind for two days. That's fine."

"Lights?"

"Yes, please."

Constable went over to the switch by the door and clicked off the illumination. With the door shut, the blinds down and curtains drawn, it was pitch dark. Hero heard Constable feel his way back to the couch and settle there. He said to him, "Please, under no circumstances switch on the lights until I tell you. Also, I must ask you to remain sitting where you are and not move. Remember, I'm a novice at this. I don't know what is likely to happen, or on what dangerous ground I may be treading, nor do you. I shall do as I did last night, concentrate for contact with Ruth, for that was how it was that Mary came. Very well, I'm ready to begin. Don't be impatient, for it takes a while—or even if at first we have no results."

Constable spoke from the sofa, "You said you had the power."

"Quiet," said Hero.

The silence remained unbroken through the first two elegant movements of Vivaldi. Then it was broken by a series of sharp raps and taps that appeared to emanate first from one side of the room and then the other, accompanied by a curiously high-pitched moan, and for an instant there was a faint, pinkish glow near the ceiling, over by the door, which faded. From the vicinity of the man tied to the chair came heavy breathing, groans, and mutterings, at first unintelligible, later identifiable as the name "Ruth" repeated again and again. Then a period of silence, complete stillness for a moment, and as the third movement of the concerto came to an end and before the last could begin, there was heard in a penetrating whisper, twice repeated, the name "Peter."

Now the man in the chair began to cry out as though under great strain. "Ruth! Ruth! Are you there? Ruth, believe me, I never sent you away."

Then puzzlement came into the voice and question. "Mary? No, no, Ruth! Is that you again, Mary? Where is Ruth? She was here only a moment ago. Will she come back?"

He was speaking now, almost continuously, pausing only as though to listen to the replies to his questions. "Yes, I know you, Mary. I know who you are. Are you always together with Ruth now? Is that why you come when I ask for her? Oh, you want to see your father. He's here with me now. Yes, in the same room. He loves you very dearly, Mary. You do too? Yes, he knows this. He was sad when you said you couldn't come any more. What's that? They told a fib? Who told a fib? Yes, but who are They? They were the wrong ones, you say? They were bad? The others are good? Are They there now? Will They let you come to your father?"

Another cry pierced the darkness, from the other side of the room. "Mary! Mary!"

The voice of Fairweather rose again. "What's that? Wait, wait, I can't hear. Who, Ralph? I don't know you, Ralph. Don't interfere. I was talking to someone else. Who? My brother's son? Oh, Ralph, Ralph, not now! Another time. I was talking to Mary and Ruth. Are they there? Mary, your voice is fainter, will you come back? Yes, I understand—later. Will you leave a message for your father before you go? Yes, a message. You've left it, Mary? What is it? What was it? Where is it, Mary? You say we'll find it? Mary, where are you?"

Silence again. The music came to an end and the voice of the announcer identified it and introduced the next record, Mozart's Clarinet Concerto, played by Benny Goodman. In the interim, before it began the whisper was heard again, "Peter! Dear Peter!"

With the first bars of the concerto, Fairweather began to cry out and groan, plunging and tossing, so that the chair legs beat a tattoo on the floor. For a moment, from the sounds, he appeared in imminent danger of strangulation from which the words "Help" and "Lights" emerged.

Constable leaped from the couch and over to the door and switched on the lights, then turned to the man Fairweather, who was half unconscious against his bonds, his head rolling, the whites of his eyes showing, his face flushed and sweating, as crimson as Constable's was pale.

The scientist took the lolling head and held it to his chest, uncapped the nearby bottle, held it to the bared lips, forcing some of the liquid down. He never knew how welcome it was.

Gasping, Fairweather ceased to struggle and became more normal, his eyes focussing again. For a moment he looked at Constable as though he had never seen him in his life before. Then, slowly, he let recognition dawn in his eyes. He murmured, "Professor Constable, are you all right? Did anything happen? I thought Ruth . . . Your daughter Mary . . . My brother's son Ralph, was killed in a skiing accident when he was twelve. Why did he come?" He struggled for a moment and said in surprise, "Why am I bound? Oh, yes of course . . ."

Constable loosened the knots and freed Fairweather. He

said, "Man, you've done it! You've got the power! Mary was here, I heard her voice."

Alexander Hero stood up and shook the loose bonds from his shoulders and hips. He had been almost sure that in the welter of questions and answers Constable would imagine he had heard his daughter reply. He looked around the room now, as though still uncertain of his surroundings. Constable was regarding him with awe, and as though he had found his soul again. Hero was feeling dreadful, morally as well as physically.

Constable seemed to remember something and said, "There was to be a message. She said she would leave me a message. What was it? Do you know?"

Hero shook his head. "I don't know. I don't remember . . . How long have I been . . . ?"

Constable persisted, "She said we'd find it. That she was leaving it somewhere—it must be somewhere in this room."

Hero went through some motions of searching, looking over in the direction of the bookcase and lifting his eyes towards the ceiling cornices until the hoarse cry from Constable told him that the discovery had been made.

"Fairweather! Great God, Fairweather, look here!" He was standing over the cabinet that housed the wax hand, eyes starting from his head, his face livid with excitement. "There! The hand! Is that the message?"

It had been moved. Originally it had been posed on its back, the palm upturned to show the curled, beseeching fingers, and had lain from left to right. Now it had been turned from right to left, with the palm downwards, and with the curious effect that the hand no longer seemed to beseech, but rather to have something protective about it.

Constable almost hurled himself upon the case and tested the cover and then with hands trembling, produced the key and inserted it. There was a click. The case was still locked.

Hero now too stared down at the hand. He said, "It's been moved. But the case was locked, wasn't it?"

The scientist was jubilant. "Proof! Proof!" he cried. "They

keep asking me for proof and here it is. But what does it mean?"

Hero stared long and carefully at the hand. "I don't know," he said, "and can't be sure. It was the other way around when we came in, wasn't it? It was, the night I was here. No one is allowed to touch it . . . ?"

"No, no. No one. I swear no one in the house has moved it."

"It's a reversal, isn't it?" Hero said. "A change, an opposite, a complete turn around as it were, might one not say? I don't understand it, but if you . . ."

"I do, by God! I think I do! Man, what you've done for me!" Constable suddenly laid his hand on Hero's arm, and his eyes were as pleading as those of a dog. "Can you bring her to me? Will you bring her back to me physically, so that I can touch her again as I used to? You've got the power. Can you? Will you try?"

Hero put his fingers to the bridge of his nose and covered his eyes for an instant and said, "I can't now. I feel as weak as a kitten."

"Later? Can we try again this afternoon, or this evening?"

Hero shook his head like a punched prize fighter, as though to get rid of dizziness. He said, "If I feel I can, I will."

Constable asked, "How will I know?"

Hero replied, "May I telephone you? Perhaps later on in the day, when I've had some rest."

Constable said, "You're a good fellow, Fairweather. I'll be here. I'll be awaiting your call." And then he added, "I'm very shaken and very happy."

Twenty minutes later Alexander Hero was ensconced in the dental chair of Dr. Felix Hofstetter.

CHAPTER XVIII

Dr. Hofstetter Sings an Aria

Dr. Felix Hofstetter, Hero discovered very quickly, was that abomination of the fraternity, a cheerful, singing dentist who ministrated to descriptive ad lib musical accompaniment, borrowed from operas, cantatas, and oratorios.

Upon quitting Constable's house, Hero had hastened to the nearest drug store where there had been a telephone box and dialled the number of the dentist. When the nurse put him through he heard from him the miraculous and welcome news that he was lucky. Hofstetter had just received a cancellation and would be able to see Hero within ten minutes. The address in West End Avenue was only a dozen blocks or so from where Hero was calling, and in no time at all his dream became a reality. The stab of the novocaine needle was followed by blessed surcease from pain.

There was, however, no escape, from the bathroom baritone of Dr. Hofstetter. He was a kindly, beaming, round-faced little man with alert, interested eyes peering from gold-rimmed spectacles. He had fine, strong hands that he kept washing, and it was obvious to Hero, after a minute or so, that he was a first-class dental surgeon, quick, sure and practised in his movements. But he would sing.

After the first insertion of the little mirror, he took the theme, "Wha-at have we here?" and carried it through a half a dozen modulations and variations, until in turn he picked up the melodic reply, "A very nasty too-hooth," and warbled his way from major to minor and back to major again as he arranged picks, probes, and drills. He improvised upon "Rinse, please" and rendered an aria on, "We shall have to do a little dri-hilling" before, during, and after, until Hero thought he would go out of his mind. Dr. Hofstetter was no respecter of keys and furthermore appeared not to have much of an ear.

In self-defence Hero put on an interest he really did not feel in Hofstetter's procedure in the hope of getting spoken replies to his questions—anything to keep him from his maddening carolling. To some extent it worked, and Hero got a dissertation on American technological advances and the somewhat old-fashioned method which had been applied to the injured molar in London. The filling apparently presented a problem since so much of the tooth had been lost or damaged. It demanded not only stoppage but an anchor to its neighbour and some very delicate dental engineering of which it was obvious Dr. Hofstetter was perfectly capable. This, unfortunately, brought on another madrigal based upon the need for taking far more accurate impressions than would ordinarily be supplied by dental wax, one solid and the other of the hollow of the cavity.

"But we have the stu-huff for it here," sang Dr. Hofstetter. "We've got the stu-huff." He took from a cabinet a container with a fine nozzle, in which was a liquid of some kind under pressure.

On the container Hero read the trade name, "Instantoplast."

Hofstetter pulled on a pair of thin, surgical rubber gloves and since his patient had shown such interest in his work, he accompanied his subsequent operation with a recitativo. "First, we prepare the surface—now the Instantoplast." Hero heard a slight hissing as pressure on a button released a spray. "In she goes—out she comes. Just like magic." He went soaring away on the last phrase. "Just like magic. Just like ma-hagic."

It was, too, for in what had seemed barely an instant he had removed the inner and outer moulds and held them in his fingers. No more of that interminable waiting with gauze bits stuffed into his cheeks while cold water was run over wax to harden it.

"Rinse, please."

Hero leaned forward, took a sip of mouth wash, sloshed it

about, and spat out. Dr. Hofstetter had put something resembling a watchmaker's instrument into his eye and was examining the surface of the moulds, occasionally exploring them with a sharp, pointed steel tool. Hero asked, "Why do you have to wear rubber gloves?"

Hofstetter yodelled him the reply: so as not to get the stuff on his fingers, where it would stick and take the hairs off the back, unless the skin surface had been previously prepared, as he had the tooth.

"It gets as hard as rock," Hofstetter explained. "It's a new compound. Here, I'll show you," and then proceeded to demonstrate, first greasing the glove. Holding up his right hand away from him he sprayed his index finger, around which a smooth white coating appeared almost instantaneously. He waved his hand in the air for a moment and carefully pulled the hand from inside the glove, then withdrew the rubber from the white coating and showed Hero a paper-thin, perfectly formed cast of the shape of his finger. He established how hard it was by scratching on the tip with one of his instruments. "Wonderful stuff," he exclaimed, "you can do anything you like with it, cut it, drill it, channel it—"

Alexander Hero was now sitting bolt upright in the dentist's chair, watching Hofstetter, as with his case-hardened dental tool he drew several lines across the end of the cast finger. There was no crumbling, flaking or pitting as there would have been with plaster.

"Let me see that!" Hero had not realised how sharply he had spoken until he saw the surprise mirrored on the face of the mild-mannered dentist. "And the glove, please." Looking even more startled, Dr. Hofstetter passed both to Hero.

Hero tested the finger. Its tensile strength seemed to be enormous. "May I have your eyepiece!" Dr. Hofstetter, suspecting that he was dealing with someone very odd, relinquished it. Hero put it to his eye and examined the surface of the cast. Then without even asking the dentist's permission, took a steel probe from the tray and made several marks himself. His hands trembling slightly, he thrust the hardened cast into the rubber glove and pushed it home to the end of the finger. The marks and scratches showed through, as had the lines on the hand of Dr. Hofstetter.

Hero said, "Oh, my God! Liquid latex! One could spray it on."

Dr. Hofstetter hoped he knew to what his strange patient was referring and smiling tentatively nodded and said, "Make 'em yourself, if you like. Put the Goodyear Company out of business."

"I've got to get out of here!" exclaimed Hero and he started pulling at the dental bib which had been fastened about his neck.

He had managed to frighten the music out of Dr. Hofstetter who had become convinced that he was dealing with someone deranged. He said soothingly, "You'd better let me put something temporary into that cavity."

"I haven't got time. I've got to be somewhere."

"Perhaps," said Dr. Hofstetter, "but when you get there you won't be much good. When that novocaine wears off you'll wish you were dead."

The word applied more heat to Hero's train of thought: two people dead already, probably another if he was right, half the world threatened and the minutes of the twenty-four hours he had been allotted ticking away inexorably.

"Just you sit back and I'll fix you up in a jiffy," said Dr. Hofstetter. "It won't take a moment. Otherwise you wouldn't be able to stand the pain."

Hero let himself be pushed back into the chair and the bib readjusted. With what he thought he knew now, he would want his full wits about him for every second thereafter. And thus, while swiftly and efficiently Hofstetter supplied the temporary filling, Hero in his mind went over step by careful step, the manufacture and materialisation of the long-dead hand of Mary Constable.

Concentrating upon his work Hofstetter momentarily forgot his patient's earlier strange behaviour and sang, "All done, neat and tidy, until I see you again."

Hero was up out of the chair and headed for the door, but he caught himself in mid-dash, picked up the finger cast, the rubber glove, and the container of Instantoplast and said, "Can I take these? Do forgive me. Please send the bill to the Tuscany." Then, feeling that somehow he must say something more to convey the magnitude of his gratitude for what had happened, he shook the hand of the little dentist. "You don't know what you've done. You just don't know," he said and added, "Some day they could jolly well be putting up a statue to you." He had a wicked, semi-hysterical moment of feeling impelled to add, "with a lyre in your hand," but controlled himself and fled out of the door, leaving Dr. Hofstetter shaking his head, songless.

All the way in the cab downtown he was filled with the excitement of his discovery. Twenty-four hours he had asked for, twelve of them had not yet passed and the solution of the problem was within his grasp. Down Broadway, across Central Park by the Sixty-sixth Street transverse and southward once more in the great traffic stream of Park Avenue, he was working on the details of the process, weighing up, rejecting, refining, creating obstacles and then overcoming them, until he was satisfied that not a single loophole remained. Given what was necessary, he would be able to re-create the hand of Mary Constable under seance conditions. And what was more, another idea came to him that made him exclaim aloud and drive his fist into the palm of his hand with the excitement of it, something that would be a hammer-blow to shatter the last illusion that Professor Constable might still entertain after the demonstration. He wondered what Wiener would say when he told him and rather basked in anticipation. He would have to admit that the British might have their own methods, but they got there. He was grinning at the chauvinism as the cab drew up before the Tuscany and thus was wholly unprepared for the reception awaiting him.

A policeman had been stationed on the pavement beneath the canopy and took down the number of Hero's cab before it drove off. Another policeman was inside the lobby standing with two burly men, obviously plain-clothes detectives. As he stopped at the desk to ask for mail or messages the manager came out, stared at him, white-faced, and said, "My God, Mr. Hero! They've been looking for you. You'd better go up to your room right away."

There were more men on the eighteenth floor landing and in his room. Some were dusting for fingerprints. Saul Wiener came out of the bathroom, stared at Hero and said, "Where in the god-dam hell have you been?"

Out of his bewilderment Hero replied, "Having a tooth looked after."

"What, at half-past four in the morning?"

"Not exactly then. I was at the flicks."

"The flicks?"

A tall, heavy-set man with a florid face who stood near the FBI man interpreted, "He means the movies."

Wiener said bitterly, "Oh, brother! You're a beaut! You put the wind up Sullivan here," indicating the big man, obviously the one with whom Hero had talked on the telephone. "Why the devil didn't you check in as we'd agreed? I got your message from Sully at the station this morning at six. I phoned you, but they said there was no reply from your room. The Army flew me back. Sully said there was still no answer from your room at eight. We came over on the double. They said you'd come in around three. Sully logged your phone call at that time, and the operator confirmed that it was made from here. But nobody saw you go out."

Hero said, "What about the lift boy?"

Wiener said, "What?"

Sullivan explained again, "He means the elevator operator."

"His day off," Wiener snapped. "No telephone. He's gone fishing on a party boat. We've been trying to get hold of him."

"I don't understand," Hero said. "All these . . ." and he indicated the men in the room.

Wiener's reply was heavy with sarcasm. "Oh, nothing," he said. "Nothing at all! Except that sometime after you got out of here to go to the movies, somebody got in," he paused for effect and then made it, "with intent to kill."

"What?"

Wiener looked over to a group standing near the door and motioned to an old man with white hair and moustaches, who wore a kind of bandolier strap across shoulder and breast, terminating in a disc-shaped contraption at his hip. "Tell him, Joe."

The old man shuffled forward, and as he did so his hand went to the side of his jaw for a moment. He said, "I'm the night watchman here, Mr. Hero. I was on my four o'clock round, but I didn't get to your floor until about four twenty-five, or thereabouts. Just as I came to your door it clicked shut like someone had gone in. You know how our doors are. They close automatic. It's police regulations-like."

"Yes—" Hero said. He was conscious of a sick feeling in his stomach.

"Well, you see, there hadn't been nobody in the hall since I'd been checking the other doors."

The unhappy sensation in Hero's stomach was increasing.

"So it could have been maybe someone nipped in quick-like from the service stairs just before I got there. I rung down the lobby. They said you'd checked in at three and nobody had just gone up in the elevator. So I took it my duty to investigate like I been instructed. I opened the door. There wasn't any light inside. I switched on my flash and went in. There was somebody there. He came rushing out. He had a gun in his hand."

"Did you see him?"

"Just for a second, before he hit me." The old man suddenly looked foolish and apologetic. He said, "I'm still pretty spry, but I wasn't expecting anything, see?"

"What was he like?"

"Sort of square, but heavy-set with a hat pulled down over his eyes. It was only a second, maybe, and then he hit me. I guess, maybe, I must have been out for a couple of minutes, for when I come to I was on the floor and my flashlight was smashed. I went to the phone and told the operator to give the alarm. You wasn't in your room and the bed hadn't been slept in. She called the cops but they didn't find anyone."

Hero asked, "Was there anything peculiar about the gun? Did you get a look at it?"

The old man said, "Come to think of it, now that you say it, there was something funny. You know, when you look at a gun in an intruder's hand in the dark, you don't do a lot of thinking. But it was sort of funny—I mean, different-like. Not like an automatic, or a police .38, for instance."

Alexander Hero thought he might be sick and wondered whether he should make for the bathroom. He was seeing Cryder propped up in bed and the girl lying dead too, the blue about their lips. So then it was true. He likewise had been marked for execution. The man with the gas gun had not given up.

"There wasn't nothing taken. Nothing seemed to be disturbed," the old man continued.

"Okay, Joe," Wiener cut him off and turned to Hero. "Well," he said, "you look as though you'd seen one of those ghosts you're always looking for. I don't know why the hell you go to the movies at four-thirty in the morning, but if you hadn't you wouldn't be around here now. You keep saying you're not a detective, why the devil do you keep making like one? Why didn't you tell Sully what you'd found out that was putting the wind up you? Why don't you come clean?"

From where he was standing Hero was able to look into his bedroom and his bed with his pyjamas stretched across it, as he had left it the night before, and his horrid imagination supplied his own corpse lying there and Wiener and his cohorts standing about it debating the cause of death. He said, "He's killed twice already, maybe three times—I'd have been the fourth."

"What? Who?" Wiener cried. "Killed whom? What are you talking about?"

"Mary Constable and her father," and then as he caught the look of consternation on Wiener's face and realised what he had said, "No, no! I'm sorry, I mean the girl who played her and Ruth Lesley: Tina Cryder and her father, Paul—they were killed last night—early this morning. You'd better phone the Police Department and check whether the bodies have been found."

"What bodies? Who the hell are Tina and Paul Cryder?"

"They owned a magic shop at 43a Cedar Street. But they're dead now. And there might have been a third homicide."

"What, in the same place? Are you serious?"

"No, not in the same place, but probably not far from there; somebody who would have been an engraver at some time, possibly an old lag."

Sullivan supplied the interpretation without waiting to be asked, muttering, "Ex-con."

Wiener said sourly, "You astonish me, my dear Holmes." Nevertheless, he nodded his head at Sullivan who went to the telephone. To Hero he said almost soothingly, "Maybe you'd better sit down, old man. It's understandable that you've had a shock. So have we, for that matter, and I'm damned glad to see you. From now on we don't let you out of our sight for an instant. We'll clear out this mob, and perhaps you could begin at the beginning and tell us what all this is about."

Wiener's patronising restored Hero's control, and he was almost pleased to have another jolt for him. "Not yet—it will have to wait. We'd better get on up to the Bessmers'—if they're still alive . . ."

Wiener stared at him. "The Bessmers . . ."

They'd be next on the list, wouldn't they? Have you got a car?"

"Je-*suss!*" Wiener said feelingly.

Sullivan hung up the telephone into which he had been speaking softly, his hand masking his mouth. He said, "I've been on to Homicide. Patrolman Snyder reported two stiffs over a magic shop at 43a Cedar Street at five-thirty this morning. Owner and daughter, name of Cryder. The autopsy is on now. Homicide by cyanide poisoning suspected. A similar case reported at seven this morning. Unidentified man found dead in a cheap room on Forsythe Street by the landlady. But Fingerprints was just coming through while I was phoning. Fellow by the name of Polianski, alias William Pole, an engraver. His speciality was engraving twenty-dollar bills. He did fifteen years at Leavenworth."

Saul Wiener looked at Hero as though it was the first time ever he had seen him and there was a certain amount of wonder in his face. "Well, I'll be a son-of-a-bitch! Come on, you can tell me about it going up in the car. We'd better not waste any more time."

Hero said, "Before we go, can Mr. Sullivan phone back and get them to take the palm prints of the girl?"

"The palm prints! They'll have taken her fingerprints already."

"Yes, I'm sure they will," Hero said. "I think you'll find that they match up with those on that note of warning I gave you. But it's her palm prints I need now."

There was still amazement in Wiener's voice when he said to his assistant, "Do as the man asks, Sully. We'll be down in the car."

Hero had all but completed his story of the early morning's happenings when, with the police sirens going, they roared up to the house at Ninety-first Street. Wiener said grimly, "You know, if these two birds are dead you'll have a lot on your conscience. The Cryders, Polianski . . . If you'd only opened your mouth."

"Come off it, Wiener!" Hero said succinctly. "And don't you try to unload on me. You people are supposed to be the spy-catchers. You were convinced from Woodmanston's reports that there was hanky-panky going on in the seance room. That sort of thing calls for equipment, doesn't it? Why didn't you begin by checking on all possible sources of such gear? Conscience, my foot!"

Wiener didn't reply, but only looked at Hero curiously again. They slammed out of the car and up the steps of the house.

The birds, however, were not dead but only flown.

When there was no reply to the jangling of the bellpull, Sullivan produced the necessary skeletons to gain them entrance. The house was empty not only of the Bessmers but of the servants too. The bedrooms showed every evidence of a hasty, almost panicky departure. Anyone with half an eye could reconstruct from the pulled-out drawers, open cupboard doors, things spilled or left lying behind, the packing that had been done in frantic haste.

From the back of a drawer in a small bureau Hero's searching hands pulled forth a pair of extraordinary looking spectacles, somewhat like the compact, opera-glass type with side arms to fit over the ears, such as were sold for viewing sporting events, except that they were heavier; more like the frames used by occulists for testing eyes and they were equipped with double lenses, one of them tinted.

"Hello," Hero said. "Here we are. Mother left her spectacles behind. She *must* have been in a tizzy. Something new. You chaps are ahead of us in this kind of thing over here. We have a device like this: a scope in our laboratory in London for seeing in the dark, but this is the first I've seen to wear. It must have cost her a pretty packet." He dropped them into his pocket.

Wiener swore, "Damn! We could have collected those two."

"What would you have done with them?" Hero asked.

Wiener said morosely, "I suppose you're right," and then added, "Do you think Constable is safe?"

Hero said, "Yes. They want him alive, not dead. It's the basement here I want to look at."

They trooped down the stairs from the forsaken bedrooms to the ground floor where Hero, followed by Wiener and Sullivan reinspected the seance room as well as the front parlour. In the former, Hero kicked away the rugs, revealing the smooth parquet floor, merely commenting, "Enter ghosts, but it will have to be worked from below." He pointed up to the moulding that ran around the wall just below the ceiling. It was an unusual design, an oak-leaf frieze with acorns, all stained in the same dark mahogany as the walls.

"It's hard, even now," Hero said, "to see that some of the acorns are just holes. When you take that down you'll find some of your kind of toys behind it. Infra-red." He fished the curious, almost Martian-like, eyes-on-stalks contraption from his pocket and said, deprecatingly, "Mother's going to have to get new specs if they set up shop elsewhere. That's how she used to get about."

When they moved on to the room where Bessmer used to interview prospective clients, Hero said, "There'll be a microphone somewhere about, but you can turn that up later. It'll lead to the room below."

The basement floor consisted of a dining room at the front of the house entered by a long passage which led from the grilled servants' entrance to the kitchen at the back of the house. There was a pantry between kitchen and dining room and behind the kitchen, and opening directly onto the backyard a small utility room used for washing and ironing. There was a tall stepladder standing in one corner. Hero moved it to the window, climbed it, and pushed upon the ceiling. The trap door gave easily, smoothly, and noiselessly. There were two side flanges which hooked to keep it from closing.

"What about the cook?" Wiener asked.

Hero replied, "The seances never began until after nine. The estimable Pratt saw that she was out of the basement by that time and stayed out. Terrified her, no doubt. The refreshments were prepared in advance. It was Pratt who served them."

There were two other doors in the room one of which was a locked cupboard. Hero produced his skeleton keys and opened it. Wiener watched him silently with only the faintest shaking of his head. There were costumes of various kinds hanging up as well as sheets, lengths of cheese cloth, masks, make-up and several tubes of phosphorescent paint.

"Ghost Hall," Hero said. He pointed to a sailor suit—"Son lost at sea," and then an army uniform, "Son killed in the war. You name it, they had it!" He shut the cupboard and opened the other door. There were stairs leading down to a cellar.

Wiener put his hand on Hero's arm. Something had been worrying and nagging at him ever since Hero's narrative concerning the Cryders coming up in the car. He said, "Look here—as I get it, you went into the cabinet and there was this Ruth Lesley who gave you a hot reception, and she was tall and all that. And then you met this Cryder girl, who you say was knee-high to a bee, and went out on the town with her for an evening.

What the hell led you to connect the two, or even suspect . . . ?"

Hero paused on the top step, about to descend, turned and looked at the FBI man. "Oh, come on Saul," he said.

Wiener gasped, "My God! The first night! I thought you Limeys were supposed to be shy. And now she's dead and the guy got clean away."

Anger, which so rarely flared in Hero, exploded, "Goddam it!" he cried, "Do you think *I* like it? Don't you think I'd want to lay him by the heels, going about snuffing out lives as though they were candles? She was a human being. She was . . ." He did not finish the sentence, for his mind had carried him back to the bedroom over the shop on Cedar Street and those moments when they had discarded their outside personalities, jobs, vocations, and ambitions until nothing was left but a man and a woman caught in the web of desire and the things they said to and did for one another.

Wiener said, "Okay, Alex, I'm sorry. I've got as much tact as an elephant. But when you said she was a small girl . . ."

Hero nodded acknowledgement of the apology and, without a word, turned from the door and went back to the cupboard at the bottom of which was a small, empty, wooden box with the brand name of tinned pears stencilled on it. Hero now turned it on its side, so that the opening was towards him. "Tall girl," he said. "She stood on it. Remember how your senses deceived you up there in the dark the other night."

Wiener muttered an obscenity. Hero flipped the light switch at the head of the cellar steps and led the way down.

There was a large bin immediately beneath the front of the house, designed to take coal delivered through a chute from the sidewalk, then a boiler room containing a furnace for heating the house and hot water and the usual tangle of pipes and plumbing on the ceiling. There were two storage rooms for trunks and unwanted furniture and a larder for tinned food as well.

"What are you looking for?" Wiener asked.

Hero said, "Another room."

They came to it finally, at the back of the house, concealed behind an upturned table with some broken chairs piled up on top. When they moved these away they found a heavy padlock on the door. Hero said, "We'll want to get in here."

Sullivan went back to the coal bin, returned with an iron shovel and attacked the hasp of the padlock until it sprang open and they went inside. A single unshaded electric light hung on a cord from the ceiling, and when Hero turned it on it illuminated a workbench on which was scattered a variety of tools. Some shelves held a number of bottles and containers of liquid spray but the labels had been removed from them. At one end of the bench there stood a small electric cooker, a box type with only one element on top and an oven inside.

While Wiener and Sullivan watched him silently and sceptically, Hero smelled the nozzles of the various bottles, then opened the door of the oven and sniffed there too. He picked up a two-inch roll of adhesive tape from the shelf and examined it with apparent satisfaction. It was not the usual rough, surgical kind, but instead it was thin and the surface of smooth silk where a flat dressing was required which would not show beneath clothing. He rummaged beneath the bench and picked up off the floor a shrivelled, dark bit of rubber which he stretched until it became lighter in colour before tossing it back.

"By the way," he said carelessly, for he felt he could not resist throwing it away, "this morning I found out how to duplicate the hand of Mary Constable."

Wiener jumped as though something had stung him. "The hell, you say," he cried. "How? Where?"

"At the dentist's," Hero replied and then added, "and this is where they cooked it up."

Hero waited for Wiener to explode, but he didn't. Instead he drew a packet of cigarettes from his pocket, extricated one, lit it and went and stood in the doorway, his back three-quarters to the other two in the room, smoking. When he turned, his lean features were composed and all of the mockery had gone out of his dark eyes.

"Okay, Alex," he said quietly. "We go along with you. This has been a crazy case from the beginning, and maybe it calls for crazy ways. No, I'm not going to apologise to you again. I'm sick and tired of saying 'Excuse me.' You know damn well when they first brought you into this thing, I was against it and didn't think you knew your ass from your elbow." He broke into a sudden, boyish, friendly grin, "I'm still not entirely convinced that you do, but if you can make that hand, maybe we're in. So I'm saying, what do we do now, coach? And this time I'm not being sarcastic." After that, Hero told him.

He told him at considerable length, supplying lists of things and people he required and diagrams sketched on the back of several envelopes. And when he had finished Wiener whistled and said, "Why don't you ask for the moon?"

Hero said, "I would, if I thought we needed it, and if I did, you'd get it for me." He looked at his watch, the hands of which stood at a quarter to twelve. "We've got nine hours until seance time. It isn't much, but you've got a big organisation. I'll call Constable and alert Ferguson. They won't try anything with Constable, because they don't know yet what he's going to do, but when he comes to the seance tonight he ought to be well covered."

Wiener said suddenly, "How do I know that after this stunt of yours, even if it comes off, Constable won't fold up and pull out of Operation Foxglove?"

Hero looked at him. "You Americans do want everything cut and dried, black and white, don't you? I just don't know the answer to that one—yet."

CHAPTER XIX

None So Blind As Those Who Cannot See

Alexander Hero, soon to become Peter Fairweather, he hoped for the last time, stood in the hallway outside the seance room of the house at Ninety-first Street feeling like an actor in the wings. The stage was set and the other *dramatis personae* already there, playing their parts, introducing the plot of the play, as it were. He was only awaiting his cue to come on and initiate the dramatic action.

The cabinet was ready, the black curtains drawn aside to show the table with its same freight of apparatus, bell, accordion, trumpet, and musical instruments, but in addition there was now a second table directly in front of the cabinet, on which stood the equipment for the creation of a spirit hand. It consisted of a small electric plate at very low heat, on which was set a pot of liquid wax, kept at the temperature where it would neither solidify nor be too hot. There was also a large pail of cold water and several napkins. This was the equipment the Bessmers had used the night they had produced the spirit hand of Mary Constable. And, over on a side table, still in its case of glass and ebony was the very hand she had supposedly left and which Constable had been persuaded to bring along to the seance for purposes of comparison, should Fairweather be successful in his experiment.

Constable was present in the seance room, slightly irritable, nervous, and ill at ease. He had seemed more comfortable and at home with the heterogeneous collection of clients who were now absent, since this was a Tuesday night when there was no regular sitting and both Hero and Wiener had vetoed the idea of calling them in.

Instead, there were Dr. Ferguson and Saul Wiener, the latter of whom Constable knew only as Saul Roth, the sceptical lawyer friend of Fairweather who had been introduced at the last seance and had jabbered with some Indian or other. Over by the big automatic gramophone and the light switches was a large man with a florid, reddish face whom Constable had never seen before.

He was still confused and trying to orientate. He said, "Why did I have to come here? Fairweather was getting results at my house. What's become of the Bessmers?"

Dr. Frank Ferguson had one thumb hooked through the armhole of a fawn-coloured waistcoat, and the other hand was toying as usual with his pince-nez at the end of its long black ribbon. He now waved the glasses in the direction of Constable and said, with one of those lapses into slang which he so enjoyed, "The Bessmers, I'm afraid, my dear Sam, have taken a powder."

Constable thrust out his jaw in the direction of his friend and said, "What's that you say?"

"They have decamped," explained Dr. Ferguson mildly. "I believe, just a few steps ahead of the police."

The word "police" caused Constable to look about him with the greatest suspicion. "Why? The woman had the power."

Ferguson said, "I don't doubt that, but unfortunately they couldn't resist some rather unwholesome shenanigans for gain. Someone complained to the authorities. I would have headed them off, if I could, but it was too late. I should think the atmosphere might be better for our friend Fairweather because of their departure."

Constable half grunted in acknowledgement of this but then reiterated, "Why here? I feel as though we were trespassing."

Ferguson said thoughtfully, "I have been able to arrange it. One of the things of which every member of our Society is aware is that if you want results you must defer to the wishes of the mediums, since only through them can occurrences of any kind be obtained. Of course, if you wish to hold a seance under test conditions, that's something else again, if the medium will agree. It was Mr. Fairweather's idea that he make the attempt in exactly the same circumstances that produced for Mrs. Bessmer." And he concluded mildly, "The child, you know, is used to coming here. She apparently has had difficulty getting through elsewhere."

The argument seemed to satisfy Constable, who now said impatiently, "Well, what are we waiting for?"

"For Mr. Fairweather to compose himself," Ferguson replied. "You may not be aware of it, but what he is about to expose himself to is an ordeal." Turning in the direction of Wiener he continued, to Constable, "I believe you have already met Mr. Fairweather's friend, Mr. Saul Roth, who has asked permission to be present at this experiment? Mr. Roth is, shall I say, a semi-sceptic. I understand he had rather an unusual contact last night."

Mr. Roth said feelingly, "Brother, you can say that again."

Ferguson indicated the man at the side of the room, and said, "That is Mr. Sullivan, who will act in the place of Pratt, who is also no longer with us. Mr. Sullivan is a member of the Society and hence his presence will not be inharmonious."

Peter Fairweather walked into the room. All those present looked up startled, for he was so changed, though in just what way they could not have described accurately, except that he seemed thinner and paler and somehow withdrawn, as though he had already achieved some kind of contact with things beyond.

He took no notice of any of them but walked straight to the cabinet and inspected the chair, the length of clothesline on the table, the instruments and then the apparatus on the second table for the making of the hand.

The three men had now fallen silent and were sitting watching him. Fairweather came around the table and half leaning against it spoke in a voice so low that those in the room had to strain forward in order to hear him. He said, "Gentlemen, if you are ready to begin, I think I am. I have promised Professor Constable that I will attempt a physical manifestation of his daughter, but I think you should know that my primary purpose in this seance is to establish contact with my fiancée, Ruth Lesley. The last two times that I tried on my own, and under different conditions, to make this contact, Mary Constable, or someone or something very like her presence from previous seances, was there trying to communicate with her father. If this should occur again tonight, and so that we may have proof of her existence as she has heretofore supplied through the Bessmers, I have prepared the same kind of equipment as was used before, and which I found here in the house. If she leaves behind a duplicate of that hand," and he nodded in the direction of the glass case, "then we shall know."

He paused for a moment, looking over their heads seemingly into space, and concluded, "I am going to ask you to be very quiet during this experiment and not to leave your seats and under no circumstances to enter the cabinet, no matter what you hear from there, not even if you believe me to be in distress. It is my intention to go all out in this matter and the risks shall be mine. Is that understood?"

All three men nodded solemnly, and Wiener, to his chagrin, realised that he had already forgotten himself and was taking Fairweather and his words for what he purported to be, such was the hypnotic power of that damned place.

Fairweather nodded his head, "Very well then. I shall manage to let you know when I consider the seance at an end. I am ready. Professor Constable, would you tie me, please?"

When Alexander Hero was a boy, he had been given a walloping great magic set one Christmas and used to present shows for his mother, his stepsister Meg, and his stepfather, the Earl of Heth, performances that took an enormous amount of preparation behind makeshift curtains strung across the room and many nervous qualms as to whether he had practised his sleight-of-hand and rehearsed each trick sufficiently to be able to produce it effectively.

Absurdly now, bound hand, foot, and neck to his chair in Mother Bessmer's cabinet, Hero remembered those days, because his feelings were somewhat similar. He was about to present a magic show for stakes which were too high for one man alone. It was a game of winner take all, and the playing of it was now entirely in his hands and called for not only all his skill in prestidigitation but judgement as well. He had made a promise to Dr. Frank Ferguson and he was going to break it, because he felt he must. And his mind turned back to the noisy cafe on Broadway with Wiener sitting opposite him, looking at him scornfully over the rim of his glass and saying, "How would you like to have to make the decision whether nobody gets it and we're even again, or the Russ has it and we haven't." Well, he was now having to make that decision. As in so many things in life, it was a wager. The bet was on what kind of man Constable really was.

For Hero had agreed to the presence of the other men in that house, in addition to young Ferris, the fingerprint expert. Wiener had expressed the wish that his superior, Ned Brickman, assistant director of the FBI in Washington, be there for the showdown, as well as General Augstadt, and Hero had acquiesced. When they met earlier in the evening for the final planning, General Augstadt had been as hostile as ever. Brickman evidently had been thoroughly briefed on events by Wiener and displayed a cold but open mind. Physically, he was extraordinarily undistinguished, with a bland, smooth countenance, thin-lipped mouth, and sparse, sandy hair. He looked more like a schoolmaster or a lawyer than a policeman, but then Hero remembered that nearly all of those connected with the FBI had either been lawyers, or had legal training. They were also crack shots with pistol, rifle, or tommy gun, and fearless. There was no mistaking Brickman's grimness of purpose, however, and Hero felt how nervous Wiener was and hoped, for his sake, that he would be able to pull it off.

At the moment he was not in a hurry, for it was in Hero's mind to let Constable stew in the dark for a bit, to prepare him for the presentation; and he thought of the noises he would contribute, the absurd bangs on the tambourine, and the ridiculous things he would do with the lazy-tongs thrust out from behind the curtains of the cabinet to "float" objects about. The gramophone blared forth the first of the series of noise-covering hymns with which they had loaded it, and from without he heard Dr. Ferguson shout, "Sing!" and then the discordant voices of the three men, jarring against the chorale from the machine.

Hero relaxed against his bonds, before the exertion of releasing himself from them, as his thoughts turned back to the frantic nine hours through which they had just passed; the tension and tempo increasing as the minutes had ticked away. There had been the search for the necessary people, the telephone calls between Washington, New York, and Akron, the preparations, the tries and the first failures, then success followed by last-minute rehearsals to achieve the split-second timing which would be necessary. And now that the drama was under way, Hero was conscious of a lassitude, a fatigue binding his limbs, from which he knew he must rouse himself to play his part. Somehow it seemed almost pleasant to sit there in the total dark doing nothing.

His life therefore was saved by an itch. He might have remained thus tied for another ten minutes, before it was time to begin the manifestations, when he was attacked by a tickling between his shoulder blades that he couldn't scratch. He very much wanted his hands free. He tested the tension of the rope at the points where he had applied pressure during the binding and found that they gave easily enough, though he had to work at one knot with his teeth. He slipped first one hand, then the other, enjoyed a delicious killing of the irritation, then loosened the rope about his feet, leaving the strands slack in his lap. He was grateful that he had not been compelled to memorise the manner in which he had been tied, in order that at the end of the seance he would appear bound to his chair as he had been left. This time it would not be necessary.

He reached into his pocket and took out Mother Bessmer's extraordinary spectacles with their double lenses protruding from their heavy, steel frames which would enable him to see in the dark. The small boxes which disseminated the invisible light from behind the ceiling mouldings had been activated earlier in the evening from a control switch they had found.

Hero slipped the glasses onto his nose, fastening the wire arms behind his ears, and his heart stood still. There was someone else in the cabinet: a man.

So sickening was the shock of the discovery that Hero's heart missed beat after beat. For the intruder was standing just inside the curtains with his back to the room, motionless and staring at him, no more than four feet away.

Even in panic the mind often attempts to deny the worst, and for a thousandth of a second, Hero thought it might be Wiener or one of the others come into the cabinet to communicate with him, because of some unexpected emergency. But the hope died. Although the device, of course, did not show up detail to the extent of ordinary, faint illumination and threw no shadows, Mrs. Bessmer's equipment was very good and he could see the shape of the man and even something of the expression on the square, coarse face.

He was short, broad-shouldered, thickset, with heavy features and flaring nostrils, like the description of the intruder given by the Tuscany's night watchman.

This was the killer. Somehow he had managed to conceal himself inside the house and under cover of darkness and the racket from without, had succeeded in getting into the cabinet.

Frozen with horror, Hero waited for the hand to come up out of his pocket with the gas gun. No one would hear the sneeze of the pistol discharging the deadly spray into his mouth and nose. A cry for help was stifled in his throat. He had warned those outside under no circumstances to enter the cabinet, and besides, it would be too late. He could do nothing but sit there staring back at his executioner. Why wasn't the man moving? Why didn't he finish the job?

And in that instant's respite, Hero's brain commenced to tick over again. The man's curious stare and immobility! The expres-

sion so strangely blank! It came to Hero in a moment of revelation. The intruder was listening, not looking. He was blind—
blind in the sense that he could not see in the dark. What was
obvious was that he was unfamiliar with the practices of mediums and wholly unaware that he was illuminated by infra-red
and under observation. The knowledge of his advantage restored
Hero's courage and initiative. He would be able to dodge out of
the line of fire.

He tensed his muscles to do so as the man's right hand slowly
came up out of the pocket, but there was no gun in it. Instead,
he saw him open his fingers. Something appeared to be in the
palm of his hand, a cork which he now pulled away, and the
soft, shadowless light for an instant touched on something that
looked like a ring and a needle.

And then, in one of those flashes of intuition in which the
mind works like a computer at faster-than-lightning speed to de-
liver the answer, Hero knew that this was another weapon and in
the confines of the cabinet more deadly to him than even the gas
gun, and that this was the one which had been supplied to Tina
Cryder, who, as Ruth Lesley, would have put her arms about his
neck and quietly and efficiently pricked him to death.

The heavy face with the pig's snout and blank stare turned
from side to side. The man was not sure of Hero's actual location
within the cabinet. He would only be certain that his victim was
helpless, tied hand and foot to the chair. At the first sound that
gave away Hero's position he would hurl himself upon him, press
the needle through clothing into flesh—anywhere would do,
Hero had no doubt—and that would be the end.

Obligingly, Hero coughed and scraped his chair. He saw the
moonface turn to him, now no longer blank, saw the figure of
the man swell as he drew in breath and then both arms outstretched towards the sound he had heard. Like a great bear, he
swept forward as Hero leaped to one side away from the chair,
only to catch his foot in a strand of rope. The sweeping hand
missed him by a hair's breadth, but even as Hero went down

with the man on top of him he was able to seize the wrist with both of his hands and cling to it as they went to the floor grunting and threshing with the clatter of the overturned chair.

The three men without, sitting with their hands joined in the dark, sang:
"Mine eyes have seen the coming of the glory of the Lord,
"He is trampling out the vintage where the grapes of wrath
     are stored,"
and heard the groans, thumps, and heavy breathing from within the cabinet.

Saul Wiener was thinking: *Brother, that Limey can sure put it on when he wants to!*

Samuel Hale Constable: *The power's coming. He's got the power. If I only had the power, I could bring her back whenever I wanted.*

And Dr. Frank Ferguson: *They say the new tablets found at Abu Simbel are better than the Tel el-Amarna find. I wonder how I can secure a copy before that old fool, Foster, up at Yale gets his hands on them.*

Off in another part of the room General Walter Augstadt was saying to himself: *It's a lot of baloney,* because he was not feeling too happy. Next to him, Ned Brickman listened and if there had been light one would have seen no change of expression upon his smooth bland face, but he was thinking: *What the hell is this all about? If Saul Wiener louses this up, I'll nail his hide to the office door!*

Over by his post at the light switches and phonograph Dick Sullivan thought to himself: *Damn, if it doesn't sound like a hell of a fight going on. I wonder if I ought to go in there?* Then he remembered his orders and that he was still merely a cog in a great machine and decided to obey them.

From the cabinet came further heavy gasps, grunts, and threshings, then a jingle, then a rattle from the tambourine and a great sighlike squawk from the accordion.

Hero clung to the wrist. Somehow, in the melee, he had managed to get his foot free of the rope and now clamped a body scissors on the Russian. The man's free hand kept groping for Hero's face and eyes and pulling at the fingers enclosing his wrist to remind Hero what he kept forgetting, the advantage given him by Mother Bessmer's spectacles. The brute was still fighting in the dark.

Several times the broad palm with the ring and the needle passed before his eyes. He was scissoring the man with his legs, squeezing the breath out of him, and suddenly felt him weakening.

"Why," Hero said to himself in surprise, "he's flabby! There's nothing behind him." And then followed the thought: *Of course. He's only an executioner. He doesn't need strength. He uses a gas gun and the poison needle,* and even as he was thinking these thoughts he was bending the wrist and the hand inwards and downwards, until with a sudden thrust he jammed the palm with the needle against the thick neck rising from the tight, linen collar.

The man gave a great sigh, his body twitched twice, shuddered, and then went limp.

The man's eyes were closed, he was no longer conscious. Hero trod on something under foot and saw it was the cork that had been removed from the needle. He replaced it over the sharp point, then with his own breath still coming in heavy sobs, he heaved the body up off the floor onto the chair and quickly and efficiently trussed him there with the clothesline, and then hauled the chair to the back of the cabinet. He went and picked up the accordion and the tambourine from the floor onto which they had been swept during the struggle. He rattled the tambourine and gave it several resounding thumps. Then he rapped upon the table with his knuckles, beating out a tattoo of knocks. It was the signal to Sullivan to turn off the music. The man did so with a sigh of relief that he had not followed his impulse to interfere. Alexander Hero picked up the lazy-tongs, attached a damp, cold rag thereto, thrust it out from the curtains of the cabinet, extended it and passed it over the brow of Wiener, causing him to cry out, "Son-of-a-bitch!" in spite of himself.

Hero took up the accordion, played a few bars from "Mine Eyes Have Seen the Glory of the Coming of the Lord," and after that the seance went on as per schedule.

CHAPTER XX

Quod Erat Demonstrandum

"Lights!"

The call rang out sharply from within the cabinet. Sullivan threw the switch and brought back bright illumination to the men in the room who sat blinking their eyes which had become accustomed to darkness for almost an hour. It revealed the presence of three who had not been there at the beginning of the seance. Constable looked about him at these others with surprise, Ferguson with some consternation and even dismay.

Seated behind them were General Augstadt in civilian clothes; Brickman, the FBI man from Washington; and young Ferris, the fingerprint expert. According to plan they had been introduced silently into the room under cover of darkness.

Whatever Ferguson and Constable may have felt at this unexpected intrusion, they kept their thoughts to themselves for the moment and returned their attention to the cabinet as Peter Fairweather emerged from between the curtains, closing them again swiftly behind him, and stood there for a moment, almost like an actor taking a bow. Only Wiener noticed that he had a scratch on his chin and a discolouration under one eye that had not been there when he entered the cabinet and that set him to wondering.

Fairweather stepped to the table before the cabinet on which, before the seance, had rested the electric plate with the pot of melted wax and the pail of cold water. They were still there, but between them now reposed two objects, each covered with a white cloth. He touched the covering of one of these. Constable rose from his chair with excitement, and as the cloth was twitched away he leaped forward to the table and he stared down, his eyes popping from his head at what was revealed there. It was a wax hand, fingers outstretched in supplication, slightly curled, the fine lines visible on the palm, and on the tips of the fingers the ridges and whorls of fingerprints.

"By God!" Constable croaked hoarsely, and then repeated, "By God!"

He took up the wax glove on which there were still a few drops like dew from the cold water in which it had been immersed, turned it around, and inspected it carefully from every angle. Then going over to the case where the other hand rested upon its velvet base, he took it out, produced a small magnifying glass from a waistcoat pocket and examined the fingerprints. Replacing the first hand on its base and holding the new one, his face aglow, he returned to the table. He took Fairweather's fingers in a crushing grip and pumped them. He said, "By God, Fairweather! You've done it! You've got the power. You've brought her back to me. She's been here. It's the hand of my daughter."

"No, I have not! No one has been here." Peter Fairweather said it quietly and succinctly, and every word was like the tick of a time bomb, and all those in the room went steely quiet. Frank Ferguson turned pale.

The words at first did not penetrate, for having let go of Fairweather, Constable was engrossed with the wax cast and held it in the curve of his palm as though it indeed had been the flesh and blood of his child. And then, somehow, the negation registered.

He looked up sharply, "Eh? What's that you said?"

"I have not the power," Fairweather said. "I have not brought her back to you. She has not been here. This is not the hand of Mary Constable."

Constable's face became suffused with blood and a glare came into his eyes. "What the devil's got into you, Fairweather? What do you mean, saying that's not my daughter's hand?"

"Because," said Peter Fairweather, in the last speech he

would ever make in that name, "I made it myself. Will you take your seat again, Professor Constable? I have something to say to you."

For some reason, which even he did not understand, Constable shambled back and slumped in his seat, but he took the wax hand with him and nursed it in his lap.

"My name," Hero began, "is not Peter Fairweather and never has been. It was an identity assumed and for which I now offer my apologies. My real name is Alexander Hero and I am connected with the British Society for Psychical Research. My independent profession is investigator of so-called occult, psychic, and paranormal phenomena. In producing what you believe to be the hand of Mary Constable this evening, I am sorry to have to tell you that I have perpetrated a hoax upon you. That hand is not genuine, nor is the other in that case, which is the product of another swindle, a shameful, cruel, vicious, and evil one, which has been worked upon you for these past months."

"Hero! Have you been bereft of your senses? Have you gone out of your mind?" It was not Professor Constable who had violently exploded but Dr. Ferguson, standing up, white with anger and shaking his eyeglasses on the end of their black ribbon at Hero. "What do you think you're doing? Why have you summoned these others here, behind my back? You have no right! You gave me your undertaking that you would protect Constable."

Hero remained unmoved during this outburst and replied coldly, "When I came here I made it a condition that you would leave the entire matter in my hands, no matter who might be hurt, including Professor Constable. Do you remember?"

For a second Ferguson was flustered and said, "Yes, yes, of course," and then added quickly, "But you understood what was implied and the trust I put in you not to destroy my friend."

There was no one who felt more concern for the lone human being, thrusting his way from the cradle to the grave through the ever dangerous jungles of life than Hero, but this time he found himself arrayed on the other side, with those unhappy men whose fate it was to cope with the destinies of millions. Caught within this trap, he hesitated over his reply. There came then into his mind and ear the voice of his stepsister, Meg, at his shoulder, as she so often was when he was forced to reveal truth to angry or deluded clients, saying, "Go on Sandro! Never mind them. They asked for it. Let them have it."

He said, "Dr. Ferguson, you brought me over here to help you solve a problem—how the hand of Mary Constable was made, and to duplicate it if I could. I have done so. But you have engaged neither my opinions nor my course of action. One of these opinions is that you, Dr. Ferguson, have been coddling Professor Constable to the danger and detriment of your country and mine too. And you, gentlemen," and his glance took in the others there, "have done the same out of weakness. You didn't have the courage to face up to Professor Constable and compel him to play the game according to the rules. You were afraid that if you did he would run out on you."

Under his breath Wiener murmured, "Holy cats!"

"And so," Hero concluded, "he has been acting throughout all of this dangerous and testing time like a spoiled child and you have let him get away with it."

Professor Constable looked up from the wax glove with an expression of complete incredulity on his face and his gaze was directed at his friend, Dr. Ferguson. "I, a spoiled child?" he asked.

Dr. Ferguson blurted with almost comic haste, "It wasn't I who said it."

"But, by God, he's right." This outburst came from General Augstadt.

Professor Constable stuck out his chin in the direction of the burly General. "Football player," he said, his voice thick with cutting scorn, and Hero marvelled how, in this moment of crisis and deep confusion, what appeared on the surface was the old antagonism and contempt of the scholar for the athlete.

"And as for you," Constable continued, turning to Hero, "what did you say your right name was, young man?"

"Alexander Hero."

"Well, Fairweather or Hero, it doesn't make any difference to me. You've got the power. As for your opinions, I'm not interested in them. I have heard my daughter's voice speaking to me and felt her touch and I have seen her. Twice she has left me her hand as proof." He had been in a sense speaking to the room, taking them all in with what he was saying, but now as something struck him, he addressed himself directly to Hero. "Why, only this morning, in my own home, I heard her voice speaking to me and again tonight."

"You did not," Hero said and wondered whether Constable would spring at him in outrage.

Instead the scientist studied him coolly for a moment from the depth of his chair and asked, "Are you saying that I'm a liar?"

"You only thought you did," Hero suggested. "I asked all the questions and repeated all her answers. It was your imagination that supplied her voice."

"Nonsense," he cried. "You're wrong! What about the hand that was turned? You were bound and the case was locked. I unlocked it myself with my own key, in front of you."

"Every medium is adept at getting out of rope ties," Hero replied. "It's part of my job to be able to do the things that they can. As for the case, anything which locks can be unlocked, particularly a simple mechanism. Under cover of the Vivaldi I opened the case with a skeleton key in the dark, shifted the hand, locked it again, returned to my chair and replaced the ropes."

Constable's massive head jerked this way and that for a moment from the violence of the emotions Hero had now aroused. "What about the child who appeared here last week?" he shouted. "You heard her. You saw her yourself!"

"She was played by an ex-magician's assistant, contortionist, and sometime actress called Tina Cryder, introduced through a trap door. She was a tiny girl, able to confine herself in unusually small spaces. She was also a talented mimic."

"Produce her!" Constable commanded.

"I can't," Hero said, "she's dead."

The roar of harsh laughter, peal after peal, that burst from Constable's throat shocked everyone there and eventually even himself, as though he were laughing in a vacuum, and his triumphant guffaws finally died away to silence. When that silence had become thick and viscous, Hero broke it.

"But she has left us her palm print," he said.

Thrown off base again, Constable asked, "What? What? A palm print? What's that got to do with it?"

Hero indicated the hand in the glass case, over at the side of the room. "You will find the palm print of Tina Cryder on that hand there." Then, turning to young Ferris, the fingerprint expert, "Bill, will you show Professor Constable?"

Ferris reached for a brief case under his chair and produced some six-by-ten photographic enlargements of the crisscross lines of the palm of a small, feminine hand. He said, "If you will come over here, Professor Constable." He went to the case. Constable followed him. "I think you can compare them even without a glass," Ferris said, "the lines on the two palms are identical. See here, this very clear crossing which makes a 'w.' Here, the three 'x's' in a row. And here, the short, broken life line." The young man suddenly realised what he had said and looking up startled, muttered, "Oh, Jesus!"

"But the fingerprints!" Constable cried. "The fingerprints are my daughter's. I'll show you photographs. You can compare them yourself, if you're an expert."

"Yes, they are," Hero interposed. "The palm prints of Tina Cryder and the fingerprints of Mary Constable. One of the characteristic usages of misdirection in stage magic. Once the fingerprint identity has been established, no one thought to look further. Besides which, no palm prints of your daughter's hand existed, so there could have been no comparison. Even though an adult's palm is more defined than that of a child, neither you nor anyone else noticed because of the power of misdirection."

Constable's gaze was now fixed upon the hand in the case and a new light suddenly fired the glare in his eyes. "Impossible!"

he bellowed. "Utterly impossible! No human hand, living or dead, could have been withdrawn from that cast through that fine wrist opening without breaking the wax." He looked over in triumph at Hero. "Well, what have you got to say about that?"

"No human hand was," Hero said.

Constable was still too determined to protect his illusions, immediately to absorb the full impact of what Hero had said. He now went over to the investigator and pushed the second hand under his nose. "Palm prints, palm prints!" he shouted. "And whose palm prints might these be? Who came here tonight, if those are from someone you say is dead?"

Hero said, "If you will examine them you will see that they are different from those of the other hand, different, and those of a child. They belong to a girl by the name of Ellen Wiener. She is the daughter of Mr. Saul Wiener there, whom you know as Roth. Roth is a cover name for Mr. Wiener, who is the Regional Director of the Federal Bureau of Investigation for the five boroughs of New York and charged with security and counterespionage. His daughter is about ten years old."

Professor Constable glared from side to side and Hero for a moment was reminded of a bull in a corrida before the last desperate charge. "Your fiancée! What's her name—Ruth-something-or-other—when you went into the cabinet that first night, you said . . ."

Hero said, "I'm sorry. There never was such a person as Ruth Lesley. I never had a fiancée by that name who died, or any other name. But when I went into that cabinet the Bessmers had provided me with one—living and breathing—the same girl who played your daughter."

Professor Constable emitted a bellow of rage. "You bastards!" he shouted. "You dirty, filthy, stinking, lying bastards. What are you trying to do to me? I'll kill you for this."

The others in the room rustled and shifted uncomfortably and looked at one another as though to say, "Well, there it goes!" but Hero remained unmoved. He said, and he pitched his voice even lower to contrast with Constable's noisy outburst, "We are trying to show you a conspiracy, a most dangerous and deadly one of which you don't seem to be aware. And when I have finished, I will ask only one thing of you. I will put into your hands a transcript of the messages purporting to have been delivered to you by your daughter. They are in sequence from the very beginning and have been recorded by Mr. Charles Woodmanston, who hoped to publish them in the bulletin of the Society for Psychical Research. I will ask you to read them through in that order and judge for yourself."

Hero knew that this would not be necessary, even as he spoke, for the lightning intelligence of Constable was already at work reading them from memory, and as quickly the hurt in him and the loss of his child was reacting defensively. "But the fingerprints," he protested. "They are my daughter's. You have admitted it. It can't be done."

"It can be done."

"You can prove it?"

"Will you let me try? If I can offer you scientific proof, backed by testimony . . . ?"

Again Hero watched a word, loosed like an arrow, take its effect upon Constable. This time it was "scientific." He hoped it would prove irresistible, and it did, not only because it triggered all of Constable's work mechanisms but also because, unconsciously, it had aroused his curiosity. For nearly all of his creative life the scientist had been engaged in supplying proof of the seemingly impossible. He was unable to resist being present at another demonstration, if such there was to be. He went stumping back to his chair and sat down as though he were once more in a circle of professors attending a lecture. He did not need to say, "Well then, come on, man, prove it." His aggressive, thrust-out chin spoke louder than words. The other men in the room relaxed, and colour came back into their faces. They stopped looking at one another in panic.

"Up to this moment," Hero began, "there is no record of any kind, either in our archives in London or in the American ones, of a spirit hand, wax glove, or cast of any kind being produced by any medium in anything but total darkness. You will all agree that the hand which Professor Constable is holding was produced here tonight under identical seance conditions as the one turned out by the Bessmers; that is to say, in complete darkness. You heard the sounds of what you took to be a hand introduced into this bowl of melted wax and again the splashing when it was transferred to the cold water to solidify it. But you saw nothing. I will now reproduce yet another hand of Mary Constable, with her fingerprints, but in full illumination."

Nobody stirred.

Hero disappeared into the cabinet for an instant and returned bearing a tray containing a number of objects which had been handed up to him through the trap door. These included two pressure spray containers, a roll of adhesive tape, the complete cast of the hand of a young girl, showing the delicate wristbones as well as a silver coffeepot filled with water. There were also several rubber gloves and a number of photographic enlargements of the thumb and fingerprints of one hand.

Hero said, "Mr. Sullivan, will you bring in those three witnesses?"

Wiener's assistant left the room and returned in a moment with three strangers whom Constable and Ferguson had never seen before, one of whose clothes gave him away as a workman of some kind, dressed up for a visit, while there was an air of slight shabbiness about the other two. The first was a stooped, elderly man with glasses, the other somewhat younger and smarter. They stood uneasily at the side of the room with Sullivan and waited.

Hero commenced, "Professor Constable is quite right, it is impossible for a human hand to be withdrawn from within a thin wax glove without breaking it. He is also right to doubt that the fingerprints of the dead can be reactivated. Yet it seems to me that a more reasonable query would be why the souls or spirits of the dead, if such there be, should retain fingerprints at all. Also himself a breaker of barriers, he ought to have more appreciation of human ingenuity, particularly when the stakes played for consist of command of more than half of the civilised world. The making of the hand of Mary Constable called for long and careful preparations behind the scenes, which, like all slick, well-produced magic tricks, are never seen or even suspected by the final audience."

He picked up one of the spray containers and held it out for them all to see. "This," he said, "is a new dental compound only recently on the market, a plastic spray for making casts. It hardens instantly and then can be cut, drilled, or—engraved."

He indicated the second atomizer and said, "This contains liquid latex under pressure and is used for waterproofing, sealing joints, delicate insulations and other things of practical value.

"The living hand was that of the girl Tina Cryder. She was originally employed by the Bessmers to play various parts in their seances. Later she was persuaded to extend her activities. She was small and fine-boned. To prepare her for it, her fingertips were covered with this very fine adhesive tape and the skin of the rest of her fingers, palm, knuckles and wrist, oiled. The entire hand was then sprayed with Instantoplast."

Professor Constable's head came up aggressively, the expression on his face was as though he had already caught out Hero.

"The problem of getting her hand out of the cast was solved very simply," Hero continued. "They cut around it carefully on a median line, separating the two halves. The girl then withdrew her hand, and her part of the job was done. The halves were fitted together again, the seams sprayed and they were ready for the next step.

"We now have a thin, hollow, porcelain-hard, transparent cast of a hand, through which the lines of the palm prints could be seen, but the fingertips are blank, remember, because of the tape. An engraver named Polianski now went to work. He was an ex-convict who had done time for a counterfeiting."

Professor Constable said bitterly, "I suppose you won't be able to produce him either?"

"You are right," Hero agreed quietly. "He is also dead."

This time Professor Constable did not laugh.

"Simply tracing the palm lines through the transparency, the engraver transferred them to the outside of the cast. It is the peculiar quality of this Instantoplast that it takes tool work or engraving without crumbling, rather like copper plate. And thereafter, from photographs of Mary Constable's fingerprints, the engraver reproduced them onto the blanks of the fingertips, no problem for a man accustomed to imitate the intricate designs of a treasury note."

"No, no," cried Constable. "Not possible! How would they have got her fingerprints? The child was cremated!"

Hero said, "Yes, we know this. But you have forgotten that your entire family was fingerprinted as a precautionary measure."

"Of course, but the prints were kept in FBI files . . ."

"And in the files of the New York Police Department. In an organisation of some twenty thousand men, it is a reasonable assumption that one or two might be dishonest and for money have extracted the prints from the files, photographed and replaced them, or even some who have been politically corrupted might have volunteered to do the job."

Oddly enough, Professor Constable appeared to accept this.

"We are not yet ready to produce our spirit hand," Hero continued, "but soon. For the next step, this cast was sprayed with two coatings of liquid latex, the whole thing then placed in a small electric oven and dried carefully until the chemical components evaporated. It was then stripped from the cast inside out, with all the ridges, lines and whorls of the prints now on the outside of a perfect rubber glove."

Hero held up first a tin of the liquid latex, then a thin glove, and resumed: "They were now ready for the final step. A small, cylindrical wooden block with a plug at one end was carved and fitted into the wrist. The glove was then filled with lukewarm water, the plug closed, and a thin film of grease applied to the surface of the rubber. It was Mother Bessmer who controlled the final manipulation. The prepared article was, of course, handed up to her from below through a trap door by means of which her materialisations also made their entrances and exits. You remember that she was an adept at spiritualist hocus-pocus of every kind. Under cover of darkness she dipped the rubber glove, expanded with water at a slightly lower temperature than that of the wax, into the bowl until a skin had formed over it."

Hero paused and looked directly at Constable. "You are probably not aware of it, sir, but we can show you afterwards, that this entire room as well as the cabinet is bugged with infra-red light and that Mother Bessmer wore spectacles with special lenses which enabled her to see and move about freely. Here they are." He reached into his breast pocket and produced them.

Hero resumed. "When the coating was sufficiently formed, she withdrew the hand from the bowl of liquid wax and plunged it into the cold water, at the same time removing the plug at the end of the wrist and letting out the water, which then collapsed the rubber glove inside the cooling wax cast, which was, however, still sufficiently malleable for her to shape the curve of the fingers and give them a lifelike appearance. It was then put back into the cold water until it had hardened completely, after which the withdrawal of the empty rubber glove through the narrow wrist opening, without injuring or breaking the hand, was no problem. The glove was then concealed about her person, and she returned to the cabinet. The lights went up and on the table was the spirit hand of Mary Constable, fingerprints and all—that one there," and Hero looked towards the white hand on its black velvet cushion in the glass case.

The eyes of the men in the room were turned in that direction too. The expression on Constable's face was of pathetic bewilderment, struggling with disbelief.

Under his breath General Augstadt muttered, "T.D." It was the highest accolade that the General could bestow. "T.D." stood for "touchdown," the ultimate aim of the two football teams locked in battle in the favourite game of his youth.

Hero gave no time for any possible outburst from Constable but brought the glare back into his eyes, which only a moment before had reflected his misery, by picking up the white cast from the tray in one hand and the rubber glove in the other. "This is the cast we have made as I have described, and this is the prepared glove we have taken from it."

Hero then said, "Mr. Wiener and Mr. Sullivan were both present during the making of these, but we have further expert witnesses here." He turned to the three men standing over at the side of the room and said, "Carl Lobert," and the youngest of the three stepped forward, "you are an engraver, diemaker, and precision cutter of hard steel surfaces, working for the Acme Precision Tool Company of West Newark, New Jersey?"

"That's right."

"And you are prepared to testify, under oath if necessary, that this afternoon you worked upon this and another cast, cutting it so that the human hand could be removed, then rejoining it and eliminating the seam, as well as doing other engraving work upon it?"

"Yes."

"Mr. J. R. Richardson."

The elderly man stepped forward, "Yes, sir."

"Mr. Richardson, you are an expert technician and engraver working for the Federal Bureau of Engraving in Washington, D.C.?"

"Yes, sir. That's right."

"And you are also prepared to testify, under oath if necessary, that late this afternoon from photographs of fingerprints with which we supplied you, you engraved an exact duplicate of these prints, except reversed, onto this cast which I show you here?"

"Yes, I am."

"Tom Pellegrino."

The workman, uneasy in his Sunday clothes, nodded.

"Mr. Pellegrino, you are a foreman in the Rubber Accessories plant of the Goodyear Rubber Company at Akron, Ohio. Are you, too, prepared to testify that under your expert supervision this afternoon, this rubber glove which I show you here, was made from this cast?"

"Yes, sir. That's it."

"Thank you," said Hero. "And now, gentlemen . . ." Into the wrist of the glove he fitted a wooden cylinder, and, picking up the silver coffeepot, he poured in water through the opening and then plugged it with a stopper. As the hand expanded under the liquid, it took on a horribly lifelike quality. Professor Constable stared transfixed, but Frank Ferguson turned his head away. Hero now donned a second glove himself, picked up the hand and plunged it into the bowl of hot wax. Then, following in every detail his explanation, he produced the third hand of Mary Constable before their eyes and laid it dripping and shining on the table.

"Mountebank!" The very explosiveness of his shout seemed to bring Professor Constable out of his chair and across the room to the table, and with a great crash he brought his fist down upon the wax hand, shattering it. "Trickster! Charlatan! Liar! It isn't true. I won't believe it. It can't be done. The child is dead and ashes. She's not here to speak for herself and throw your lies and tricks into your teeth."

All the others were on their feet in alarm as the tortured man turned upon them with almost maniacal fury. "Goddam you!" he shouted. "You're all in it, to take her away from me. Goddam you and all your works!" He seemed to be unaware that he was still holding the second wax cast in his other hand.

White and shaking, Ferguson said, "Well, Hero, you've done it now. I took you for everything but a fool."

Hero nodded and looked for an instant in the direction of Sullivan, Wiener's assistant. The big man got the message and quietly touching the three witnesses led them from the room.

Hero then said, "You are right, Professor Constable. The child is no longer here, but you are."

The incongruity of the remark stopped Constable in his tracks and he turned his massive head and baleful glare once more upon the investigator. Before he could speak, Hero said quietly, "There is still something else I would like you to see."

He removed the cloth from the second object on the table and revealed a new wax cast, but this time of a large, powerful, masculine hand, showing the marks of hair upon the back and strongly defined unmistakable thumb and fingerprints.

Constable stared. "What is that?" he asked. "Whose is that supposed to be?"

"Yours," said Alexander Hero quietly. "And you are very much alive. The palm prints are Sullivan's, who is about your size, but the fingerprints, Professor Constable, are yours. Will you compare them?"

The fire in the scientist flared up once more in one deadly glare turned upon Hero, then curiously flickered out. He put down the cast he had been holding, picked up the man's hand, and stood looking at it in bewilderment. He turned it over so that the fingerprints were visible and held it close to his own. He stood like this for a long while, silently comparing them.

An exultant chuckle broke from General Augstadt, "I always said it was a lot of boloney, this religious stuff and all that crap about spirits and the hereafter. When you're dead, you're dead, and that proves it."

Hero looked up sharply. "What's that you said?"

Augstadt gave his reply a succinct pronunciation of every word for emphasis.

"I said, you proved that this life-after-death stuff is a lot of baloney."

The separation of Hero's words was just as succinct and abrupt. "I have done nothing of the sort," he said loudly and clearly, so that even Wiener looked at him in surprise.

"What?" cried Augstadt. "What the hell do you mean? You've just shown . . ."

"I repeat," Hero said, "I've done nothing of the kind. I have proved that the Bessmers as mediums were tricksters and fakers. And I have shown you how the hand was done. But I'll ask you, General Augstadt, and any others here who may be so minded, not to ascribe to me things that I have never said and never done."

Samuel Constable had stopped examining the hand and was now regarding Hero, a curious expression upon his face.

"Up to now," Hero said, "I consider there has not been one iota of convincing proof offered that there is life beyond the grave. But, may I remind you, that at the same time neither has any evidence been presented that there is not. Whether or not the spirit survives is a matter still for future discovery and until such is made, remains a subject of faith of the individual."

Quite calmly now Professor Constable asked, "Is this your opinion, young man?"

"Yes," replied Alexander Hero, "What else are we to believe —or cling to?" And then he added, "But of one thing I think we may be certain. If a breakthrough is ever attained it will not be by such methods as have been attempted up to now, or by the kind of people engaged in them. It will be something entirely new and different, perhaps not yet even dreamed of by man, who has only begun to reach behind the stars. Who knows, it might in the end even be a scientist who achieves it."

Professor Constable nodded his head in thoughtful agreement and then addressing Hero once more said, "I accept the evidence of this hand—my hand," and he set it down upon the table. Then, turning to the others in the room, he said with a grave unassailable dignity, "I will see you in the morning at the laboratory, gentlemen." As he walked out of the room he passed by, but did not so much as even glance at the hand of Mary Constable in its glass case.

"Holy, jumping Jesus K!" breathed Saul Wiener, letting down for all of them. "Brother, you shaved that one close! What were you betting on, the man?"

"No," Hero said, "the scientist. Didn't you notice? He still worships and bows down before the Great God Q.E.D."

Relief had brought colour back into the countenance of Dr. Ferguson and his accustomed urbanity as well, but with it too, so Hero felt, still a remainder of his earlier hostility and, in fact, some of this was present as well in the others, now that the show was over.

Ferguson came over to Hero, picked up one after the other the articles on the tray, including the wax gloves of father and daughter, and murmured, "How very simple. So clever of you, dear boy, to have seen it. I knew that my confidence would not be misplaced. I suppose you want to hurry back to London to your own work now. By all means don't fail to let me have your bill and any expenses, of course. I must be going now. If you have a moment before you leave, do call me. Perhaps we might be able to have lunch together." He left the room.

Augstadt said to Wiener, but quite loudly enough for Hero to catch it. "Hell, if we'd have grabbed that gang the way I wanted to, we could have found all this stuff ourselves, months ago. There's nothing to it."

Brickman, too, came over and fingered the exhibits, looked at Hero, started to say something, and then apparently thought better of it, for he closed his thin lips again.

Wiener suspected that his superior was not too happy over the whole business, even though the danger was over. Now that the trick was exposed, it seemed suddenly hardly worth all the risks they had run. He felt somehow impelled to challenge Hero again. He said, "Why did Constable reject the evidence of the copy of his daughter's hand that you made and accept that of his own?"

"Because," Hero replied, "the resistance of his mind wouldn't permit him to do otherwise. Remember, where the child was concerned he was on the rack."

"And supposing he had refused to accept your last exhibit as well, and walked out on Operation Foxglove? And why didn't you ever bring up the subject of the Communists or the murders?"

"Because that," Hero replied, "is your business. Mine was to demonstrate how the hand was made. However," and his significant pause here made them all turn and look at him, "if it hadn't worked, there was still another piece of evidence I had in reserve."

Brickman said, "I'd like to see what it is." He was hoping that it was something which would make him like Hero better, or have more respect for his curious profession.

"If you will come with me, I'll show you," Hero said. "I suggest three of you. Mr. Brickman, you, Saul, and General Augstadt."

Ferris took the hint. He said, "Sullivan and I will wait outside."

Hero drew open the curtains of the cabinet and pointed. "That," he said, for there was no longer any point to saying "him." The Russian's head had fallen back leaving the chin upturned, the flaring nostrils like two tunnels. His face was suffused, the muscles of his neck standing out like cords. There was no breathing. He was indubitably dead.

Saul Wiener and General Augstadt both said, "Jesus Christ!" almost simultaneously. But Brickman, ever cold, said nothing until after a cursory examination of the man, when he asked, "Who the devil is that? And how did he get there?"

"I think you will find," Hero said, "that this is the fellow who killed the Cryders and Polianski, and who twice tried to take care of me, the first time in my room when, fortunately, I was out, and the second time tonight, here in the cabinet. As to how he got here; they had some way of getting in and out of this house which we still have not found. I don't doubt that you will. He was their executioner. Fortunately, I had slipped my ties before he came in, otherwise you would now be looking at me propped up there."

Wiener stared at Hero and said, "What happened?"

Hero replied simply, "I'm afraid I killed him."

General Augstadt's eyes bugged; Brickman's bland expression remained unmoved, but Wiener could not keep the admiration from his voice. "Why, you cold-blooded bastard! And there was a time when I thought you were sissy."

Hero mused upon the dead man for a moment and then said, "Well, it wasn't entirely in cold blood. He had come to kill me. And on the other hand, it wasn't exactly fair play either. I could see and he couldn't. I had on Mother Bessmer's spectacles. You might call it self-defence, but I thought of it rather more as an execution, in payment for."

Brickman finally spoke. He said, "How?"

Hero lifted the limp right arm of the corpse and spread out the fingers not yet stiffened by the onset of *rigor mortis,* and showed the ring, the needle, and the cork. He said, "You'll probably want that looked at in the lab. But be careful how you handle it." He turned to Wiener. "My guess is that this piece of equipment was supplied to Tina Cryder, who was ordered to use it on me the next time I came into the cabinet to meet Ruth Lesley. She may or may not have known that it was lethal. She took a chance and wrote me the warning. If I obeyed it, she could report that I had changed my mind about entering the cabinet. If I didn't and went in—well . . . " He shrugged and then added, "The case would have been looking a lot different by now."

Wiener said, "They were probably watching the house. When they saw you come out with me they figured that she had disobeyed and never gave her a chance to explain."

Turning to the others, Hero said, "I thought you would prefer to have it kept quiet, which is why I have told only the three of you. You'll obviously want to get him out of here without being seen and dump him somewhere."

It was now Brickman's turn to look curiously at Hero. "Is that the way you fellows operate over there?" he asked.

Hero replied, "I wouldn't know. I shouldn't be surprised if people still disappeared now and then. They did during the war. It seems practical to me and the coroner's report on the Cryders could well be food-poisoning. Nobody will be around asking questions about this one here. I'd say he was one hundred per cent expendable."

General Augstadt said, "I still think we should have grabbed the Bessmers while we had the chance. Now they've blown."

Wiener looked at Hero. "What do you suppose put the wind up them?" he asked.

"Scared!" Hero said. "They're lucky they're not dead. They were frightened and managed to get out in time. They'd found your little black box for recording their visitors, but it was the

Russians they were probably afraid of. They'd been stupid, you know, and greedy when they allowed a stranger into the seance. That's what started to let the water out of the bathtub—putting Tina Cryder up to playing Ruth Lesley. They probably knew that the Russians had found out." For Augstadt's benefit he added, "You'll be able to pick them up, if you really care to. They're bound to surface somewhere, if they don't want to starve to death. They hinted they might want me to sponsor them in England."

Wiener said, "Yes, but in the meantime we've let the big ones get away—the ones who hired them and sent *him*," and he nodded towards the dead man.

Hero asked, "What good would they do you? By tomorrow they'll know that you will have got Constable out of their trap and will be on their way home. Incidentally, when they get there they're going to have considerable explaining to do. I suspect they'll probably be in even more hot water than if you laid them by the heels."

And then with sudden passion Hero cried, "I'm even for Tina Cryder. If she had lived, you'd have had to put her in gaol. I suppose she's better off dead." He wondered for a moment whether his nerves were going to crack. He saw that all three men were staring at him in open-mouthed amazement, and said, "Sorry!"

It was Brickman who had the last word. "I don't suppose we'll ever figure out the British," he said, "but it's just as well we're on the same side." Then he added, contemplating the corpse, "He's right. We'll dump the son-of-a-bitch."

There was only Saul Wiener at the airport to see Hero off the following late afternoon when he embarked to fly back to London. The FBI man had driven him out to Kennedy in his car, and all during the ride Hero was conscious that Wiener had something on his mind. Earlier he had written *Finis* to the case of the hand of Mary Constable by revealing that the scientist had resumed work on Operation Foxglove as though nothing had happened. But thereafter the conversation had only limped along.

When Hero had been checked through by BOAC and was ready to pass Immigration, they stood at the barrier for another few minutes of chat which, at the end, turned into an embarrassed silence.

Wiener swallowed and was obviously about to make an effort. Hero thought: *I wonder what it is he wants to say . . .*

The FBI man managed finally. "Look here, I know you British hate this sort of thing, but next year I've got some months' leave coming, and I promised my family and myself our first trip to Europe, kids and all. I wonder, if when we get to London, you would let us look you up. I'd like it, if you wouldn't mind. In the meantime I might drop you a line occasionally to let you know how things are going. In a cock-eyed sort of way, I've enjoyed working with you."

Hero suddenly found his heart overflowing. When he had said good-bye to Brickman, the latter had mentioned drily that there might be a quiet decoration for this, and he was not to be surprised if some day he was called to the American Embassy to collect it.

But this man Wiener, whom he had liked from the beginning, was offering him something different, his friendship. He realised that in many ways Americans were as shy in their approach to the British as vice versa.

"Do, please," Hero said. "I would like you to meet my mother and my stepsister, Meg, and I know they would like to meet you. Perhaps you would all come and stay with us at Heth Castle. By all means let me know when you'll be coming."

There was now no longer any embarrassment between them. Something of value had been proffered and accepted, and for a moment they relished this new relationship and smiled at one another with respect and frank liking in their eyes. Then they shook hands, and Hero marched through the gate that led out of the United States of America.

The wind was from the west and after take-off the aircraft flew towards Manhattan to gain its altitude before circling and heading out over the Atlantic.

Hero looked down once more upon the city. In one of those crowded-together downtown buildings, the body of a girl lay on a marble slab, a sheet draped over the exquisite figure, the blue fire of her eyes extinguished forever. It was thus that he had seen her for the last time, when he had accompanied the FBI man to the morgue to confirm the identification.

The aircraft climbed steeply; Hero's thoughts hovered over the dead girl. She had been venal, greedy, and treacherous. She had sold out her country. But she had been a warm, vibrant human being too, miserably weak; yet for a night she had loved him, holding nothing back. And in the end, it seemed certain, that by sparing his life she had paid with her own.

Manhattan was now spread out below them like the map that Hero had been studying during his stay, and he was able to pick out the campus and complex of buildings that was Columbia University, as well as the great, white marble square of the Public Library.

Was Constable working down there, angry or chagrined at having been taken in, or horrified by the narrowness of his escape from the conspiracy woven about him? Probably not. Men with the overweening egos of Constable's did not waste time reflecting upon their shortcomings.

Before his departure Hero had had a farewell luncheon with Dr. Ferguson. They had discussed Egypt, atonal music, the proper way to jug a hare, the stock market, British politics vis-à-vis American, the gigantic hoax known as abstract art, and the psychology of oriental people—everything but the hand of Mary Constable. Except, at the end of the meal, taking his leave of him, Dr. Ferguson had murmured vaguely, "Dear boy, it was so very good of you to have come over to help us out. I hope you will find this adequate." The "this" had been an envelope containing a cheque, which had turned out to be more than generous.

The jetliner approached its cruising altitude. The whole of the five boroughs of New York had become a panorama. Were the Bessmers somewhere down there hiding, in fear of their lives, or likewise dead and empurpled in some sleazy rooming house? Or had they taken alarm in time to flee not only the house on Ninety-first Street, but the city and perhaps the country as well, some day to set up their odious bag of tricks in another place to the detriment of the gullible?

He despised them for what they were, but he hated them for having led him to yet another disappointment in his long and earnest quest for some proof of a hereafter. Each new case that swam into his ken seemed in some way to offer hope of survival, each one seemed to end in disillusionment and tragedy, the mystery of the unknown still unpierced.

Yet, in his heart, Hero knew that he was not giving up. If there was no limit to human corruption, chicanery, and greed, neither was there any boundary to that endless space which man had named the universe. The enigma of its meaning was yet to be solved. Poised now between earth and sky, looking down upon the last of the great metropolis teeming with life, he was more than ever convinced of the insignificance of man in the face of the obscure, the still unintelligible, and the unknown. Millions of sincere people believed in and searched for a hereafter. One would have to keep on trying.

Staten Island and Brooklyn vanished from beneath the silver wing. Below was a grey and choppy-looking Atlantic Ocean. Alexander Hero remembered suddenly that he had had little sleep for more than forty-eight hours. Fatigue and melancholy were heavy upon him. He put his head back and closed his eyes.